FIVE PASSENGERS FROM LISBON

They were three days and two nights out from Lisbon, past the Azores and on the broad, dark Atlantic. The tiny Portuguese cargo ship the *Lerida* was about to go down, and its five passengers were preparing to abandon ship.

To them it seemed ironic that they could have survived five years of war in Europe only to perish in the cruel waters when safety seemed at hand.

But Luther and Daisy Belle Cates, Marcia Colfax, Mickey and Gilli do not perish. Adrift in a lifeboat with two seamen and an officer from the *Lerida*, they are picked up by the U.S. Hospital Ship *Magnolia*. But when they are hoisted aboard, the Portuguese mate is found to be dead. Murdered.

FIVE PASSENGERS FROM LISBON

M. G. Eberhart

First published by Collins
This edition 1989 by Chivers Press
published by arrangement with
the author

ISBN 0 86220 739 8

Foreword copyright © John Kennedy Melling, 1989

British Library Cataloguing in Publication Data

Eberhart, Mignon G. (Mignon Good), *1899–*
 Five passengers from Lisbon. – (Black
 dagger crime)
 I. Title
 813'.52 [F]

ISBN 0–86220–739–8

Printed and bound in Great Britain by
Redwood Burn Limited, Trowbridge, Wiltshire

FOREWORD

A CLOSED COMMUNITY has frequently proved an ideal setting for the murder mysteries of many of our leading crime writers—Agatha Christie's island, Ngaio Marsh's theatres, Hugh Pentecost's hotel. Fenced to keep strangers out and a usually diminishing circle in, these locations tighten the tension, reduce the suspects, and increase the surprises. So, a hospital ship in a fog on the high seas earns full marks for Mignon G. Eberhart, one of America's most respected crime writers, her awards including the Grand Master Edgar from the Mystery Writers of America in 1972.

Her first book came out in 1929, *The Patient in Room 18*, a classic featuring Nurse Sarah Keate and detective Lance O'Leary; it was filmed in 1938 with Ann Sheridan (the 'Oomph' girl) and Patrick Knowles. Despite having a nurse heroine in her first five successes, Miss Eberhart does not indulge in gruesome clinical descriptions, preferring at most a 'dark stain' at the murder. She has different sleuths in her books, and has been likened to Mary Roberts Rinehart, creator of the 'Had I But Known' school, who herself had a nurse heroine, Nurse Adams, known as Miss Pinkerton.

Miss Eberhart begins *Five Passengers from Lisbon* with the line: 'The three women sat miserably in the cramped stateroom and waited for orders to abandon ship.' They are preparing to leave the stricken Portuguese steamer *Lerida* as it sinks in mid-Atlantic, for a lifeboat, with two of their menfolk, ship's officer Castiogne, and two seamen. When they are saved by the U.S. Hospital Ship *Magnolia* they find Castiogne murdered. The brilliant lights of the ship, the realisation that Portugal was a neutral haven for espionage, the covert implications of Nazi and Resistance allegiances— all these go towards creating an atmosphere of claustrophobic breathlessness, a neurotic hysteria heightened by dim windowless corridors and decks blanketed in damp mists from which even friendly shadows emerge menacingly.

What reason have the three American women of contrasting background, the wealthy American husband and the testy French fiancé for wanting to leave Europe for South America, a destination now dramatically switched to the United States? Can the invalid U.S. Army Colonel be trusted as his enquiries fall foul of the ship's Captain? Two more deaths and puzzles of identity, lead to the climax when the heroine, in true 'Had I But Known' tradition, walks into the empty cabin to meet the killer.

Miss Eberhart's life, world travels and education have given her a broad view of life which is reflected in her fifty or more distinguished mystery stories. *Five Passengers from Lisbon* is one of her lesser-known, but excellently written, books. Its publication should bring in many new fans to add to her already enthusiastic following, all eager to read stories that end 'like this, for ever'.

JOHN KENNEDY MELLING

THE BLACK DAGGER CRIME SERIES

The Black Dagger Crime series is a result of a joint effort between Chivers Press and a sub-committee of the Crime Writers' Association, consisting of Marian Babson, Peter Chambers and chaired by John Kennedy Melling. It is designed to select outstanding examples of every type of detective story, so that enthusiasts will have the opportunity to read once more classics that have been scarce for years, while at the same time introducing them to a new generation who have not previously had the chance to enjoy them.

I

THE THREE WOMEN sat miserably in the cramped stateroom and waited for orders to abandon ship. The stateroom creaked and the ship creaked and strained and came down in the trough of a wave with a shaking, trembling series of shudders so strong that Marcia held her breath, listening, thinking: Now—now the ship will be torn apart ; this time it will go. Its rotten timbers cannot hold together ; its long, worn and rusted bolts must pull apart.

Miraculously they didn't ; at least so far as the three women in the stateroom could tell. Marcia knew that the others had shared her thought. Daisy Belle's thin, fine-drawn, over-civilised face wore a taut and listening look too ; and Gili's enormous green eyes slanted to one side, warily, like a cat which senses a danger creeping upon it.

They were three days and two nights out from Lisbon. They had passed the Azores, with all its windmills whirling. They were on the broad, dark Atlantic, and there was no help anywhere.

The ship gave a plunge and lurch ahead ; Gili's long yellow hair hung over her face as she looked down again at the coat she was wearing ; she was hunched together in the upper berth, her handsome legs drawn up to her chin. Marcia and Daisy Belle shared the lower berth, which was a trifle wider. The stateroom was very small and in frantic disorder ; the few bags and boxes they had managed to bring as far as Lisbon, and on board the little ship, were open with clothing strewn about ; they'd had to select quickly such small articles as they could take on the lifeboat with them, when and if they had to take to the boats. Nobody had taken much, naturally—passports, such money as they had . . . Daisy Belle had pinned a chamois bag full of jewels under her sweater and brassière, and now sat in slacks and a mink coat, her thin hair tied up in a woollen scarf, smoking a small cigar coolly and—always—listening. She had put brandy in the pocket of her mink coat, and some morphine and more cigars. Gili had given her own battered box one contemptuous look and taken nothing from it ; she, too, wore slacks, and a fur coat which Daisy Belle had given her—another mink coat. Only Daisy Belle Cates, thought Marcia a little wryly, could emerge from five years of warring Europe with two mink coats. And only Daisy Belle would have presented one, casually like that, to Gili.

"You may as well take it," she'd said ten minutes ago. "It'll go down with the ship."

Even at that moment Gili was delighted. She gave Daisy Belle one of her avid, darting looks, as if questioning the offer, and then snatched the coat and put it on, looking down at herself and stroking the fur greedily. " Suppose the ship doesn't go down. Suppose somebody picks us up. Will you want it back ? "

A queer expression flickered over Daisy Belle's face. " Then you can keep it," she said, her long thin fingers with their broken nails working at the enormous safety pin with which she was pinning the bag of jewels inside her brassière.

"Oh," said Gili, stroking the fur and twisting around to get a glimpse of herself in the small fuzzy mirror over the wash-basin, " good, then. Of course if we ever get out of this you'll have all the fur coats you want."

Daisy Belle's mouth tightened. " I doubt it."

Gili, exactly like a cat at an unexpectedly yielding garbage can, seemed almost to lick her full lips. But then you couldn't really blame her, thought Marcia wearily. In all probability Gili had actually scavenged for food, literally in garbage cans. Gili had not talked of her past during that short, now interrupted voyage ; she never made an allusion or said a word that could indicate even that she had a past. She might have sprung into being just as she appeared at the dock there at Lisbon—brightly blonde, luxuriantly curved, with a heavily handsome face and full round chin, and long, bright-green eyes. Her blonde hair had been dyed and was getting rapidly darker at the part ; her eyebrows and lashes were darkened. She had a certain strength that was rather attractive in a queer way, for it went with the frank predatoriness of some small, harried, and hunted animal. Nobody could enjoy food or warmth or clothing as Gili obviously did, who had not had to go without them.

But then Daisy Belle Cates, with all her money and her

internationally famous and social name, probably had had to scrounge for food, too, while France was occupied.

What happened when you were adrift on the Atlantic in a lifeboat ? Nothing about the *Lerida*, the tiny Portuguese cargo ship in which they had finally set out from Lisbon, led Marcia to think that the lifeboats would be either adequate or in good condition.

Marcia, like the other women, wore slacks and two sweaters and heavy seamen's shoes. Even at that time of year it was cold on the water at night. She felt bulky and stuffed with clothing ; if the lifeboat swamped she wouldn't have a chance with all that clothing. But there wasn't a chance to keep afloat, swimming, in a sea like that anyway.

If the lifeboat didn't turn over while they launched it, if it didn't capsize at the first wave, they might drift for days before they were seen and picked up.

And they might never be picked up.

Well, there was no use of thinking that. She got up quickly ; merely to move, to stop thinking, to do something. There was nothing to do, of course. She went to the mirror and tied her thick, red scarf round her neck. The ship lurched and she steadied herself against the wash-basin. It brought her very near her own reflection in the mirror, and she looked at it for a moment with a kind of objective interest. Her face, that she had lived with nearly twenty-five years ! It was very strange to think that the curious and deep association of body and spirit could snap so suddenly.

She was frightened. Well, why not ? All of them were frightened. She reached for lipstick automatically, pretending she wasn't afraid, and was not in the least fooled by her own pretence. How many times had she lipsticked the mouth she saw now in the mirror !

It was a good mouth, warm and sweetly curved. It was a good face ; as a matter of fact very tanned, so her blue eyes, with their heavy black lashes, looked intensely blue—as blue as the Mediterranean whose sun had provided the tan. Her hair was black, smoothly drawn to a chignon at the back of her neck. She wore a snug, black beret. She didn't look frightened ; she looked puzzled ; the black slender arches of her eyebrows drawn together.

Daisy Belle was watching her, understanding. Marcia

turned and caught her clear, hard gaze. Daisy Belle said:
"Seems queer, doesn't it? In another hour this face, this
hand . . ." She smoked, and said with a little shrug: "My
face isn't much to part with, but I've always been proud of
my legs."

Gili gave a faint scream. Daisy Belle added practically:
"All the same, you'd better get your coat on, Marcia. We're
not dead yet."

Marcia lurched to the bunk and put on her fur coat. She
caught a glimpse of the label: "Revillon Frères, London,
Paris, New York." How queer it was to see that label, pro-
claiming the incredible existence of another world incredibly
remote. She remembered when she'd bought that coat. It
was a crisp fall day in Paris, and she had met Mickey later
in the cocktail room of the George the Fifth. They'd gone for
a walk in the Bois de Boulogne, with the trees a hazy pinkish
bronze, and he'd bought her violets. The Maginot Line was
still standing, and outwardly Paris was unchanged. By the
time the next fall came round the Germans were in Paris,
and Mickey was in a concentration camp, and she was in the
cold little villa near Marseilles.

Mickey suddenly opened the door, and as he did so the
ship plunged down, down into the trough of a wave again,
and nobody spoke, nobody moved until that terrible shudder-
ing and groaning and straining ceased. Sluggishly, as if with
a great effort, the ship began to climb another wave. Mickey
said loudly and roughly above the tumult. "Are you
ready?"

She felt a sudden surge of pity for him, he looked so white.
It was so wrong, so very pitiable, that all his enormous,
stubborn struggle just for life should have come at last to this.
He had looked like that the day, almost a month ago now, that
he'd come to her in Marseilles, stumbling, white and hungry,
wearing a hunted look, as if the Nazis were still after him.
They weren't, of course, he'd escaped, and now the Americans
were in Marseilles and the war was over; but Mickey couldn't
comprehend it physically. He knew it in his mind, but his
tortured, starved, sensitive body still cringed. Even in Lisbon
he would not believe in his own safety. He still walked
close to buildings, in their shadow, listening nervously behind

him; he hated lighted places and people; he slunk along,
his blond head bent and his shoulders slumped and his eyes
darting quick, surreptitious glances this way and that. It
had made her heart ache to contrast this present war-scarred
Mickey with the Mickey she had once known—who walked
so confidently, head up, shoulders back, smiling and easy
upon a concert stage ; who bent so effortlessly and yet so full
of power over the keyboard. And his hands ! She couldn't
even now bear to think of his hands—those beautiful, strong,
square-fingered musician's hands, now so scarred and mangled.

She got up again, staggering as the ship staggered. Gili
slid down from the upper bunk and lurched towards Mickey
and seized his lapels in her strong hands. " Mickey, Mickey,"
she cried, " this is horrible. I don't want to leave the ship.
I'm afraid."

It was queer how alert, how receptive to small impressions
your mind could be in a moment of danger. Marcia thought
swiftly that Mickey had learned patience. He had been
patient, even kind, with Gili ever since she had joined their
small party. Luther and Daisy Belle Cates, herself and
Mickey, Gili—all trying to get away from Europe, joining
forces in Lisbon because they drifted together, because they
got passage together on this small, dirty cargo boat, which
was now going down.

Mickey said patiently, looking down at Gili : " We've got
to leave the ship. The Captain says she's going down. Come
on . . ."

Daisy Belle put out her cigar as carefully as if she intended
to return. " Where is Luther ? "

" He's on deck. Hurry."

" I hope he's wrapped himself up. He catches such
frightful colds. He's had pneumonia twice. And with his
heart . . . I hope he's wrapped himself up."

That was fantastic, too ; as fantastic as the thought that
she, Marcia Colfax, stood a very excellent chance of ceasing to
exist in another hour or so.

" Hurry," said Mickey. " They're waiting. . . ."

" I won't go," screamed Gili suddenly. " I won't go. . . ."

There were sounds from the passageway beyond Mickey.
Somebody ran past, shouting something in Portuguese.
Mickey dragged Gili's clutching hands away and shouted

above the tumult : " Come on—I tell you they're waiting...."

So this was what it was to abandon ship : something you never thought to find yourself doing. The passageways were no different ; just as narrow and dark and smelling as strongly of stale cooking as they'd been all along. Presently this very linoleum her feet were treading upon would be at the bottom of the Atlantic, there to rot for ever. These steps, this ladder —Marcia followed Mickey, and Gili followed her, and Daisy Belle, who must be feeling much the sense of unreality that Marcia felt, came last. They got on deck, and wind and spray and darkness flung themselves upon their faces so they leaned against the nearest bulkhead. Mickey shouted : " Keep together. . . ."

There was no sign of the ship's Captain. There was tumult, voices shouting all around them, but Marcia could distinguish no words. The lights were thin, diffused, so running, moving figures were blurs of blackness. She felt Mickey's hand and reached backwards vaguely for Daisy Belle ; but Luther came out of the chaos, his thin, bony face vaguely white. " Where's Daisy Belle ? " he shouted. Marcia tried to tell him she was near. There was a rattle and clatter as of chains, and something bumped hard against the ship. There was a loud shriek and scream of metal somewhere near. Daisy Belle's voice rose shrilly, telling Luther not to leave her. Then seamen were lifting Marcia through the furious darkness and chaos and clamour of storm and night and wind. She could feel their arms and swift motions and could barely see their faces. Suddenly she was in the lifeboat.

She moved over on the seat ; Daisy Belle was beside her. Others, dim shapes, with blurred white faces, were in the boat, too. Two of them, seamen apparently, were shouting at each other in Portuguese. She could not understand a word, and their voices were rough with terror and angry sounding. There was some difficulty in lowering the boat, for there were loud and peremptory shouts from above and from the boat. They were waiting, of course, for a good moment to lower. What could be a good moment in a storm like that !

Perhaps it wasn't such a bad storm ; perhaps it was merely the unseaworthiness of the little ship. Daisy Belle said grimly yet breathlessly : " I keep thinking of the *Titanic* Luther's father was on her, you know."

Luther himself, not far away, said hoarsely: "I hope to God they don't spill us all in the sea."

It was horrible to feel motion and to be able to see so little. How did they know what they were doing, those seamen up above and the others in the boat? "She's going down," shouted Luther suddenly in a high, shrill voice. "For God's sake hurry . . ."

The lights of the ship were tilted crazily; perhaps they themselves were tilted; the whole world revolved itself into a crazy pattern of noise, of light, of darkness, of tumult, of spray and of cold.

Daisy Belle said, panting: "Now if they can pull away quick . . . Luther, I'll take an oar."

Mickey was there. Quite suddenly he came, lurching, from the roar and tumult and crazy quilt of motion. "It's okay," he was shouting. "It's okay. . . . Now then. . ." But they dropped down, down, down, as if there was never any end of that drop. A wave broke; there was salty cold water everywhere; they were going to be capsized.

She reached backward into the wetness and darkness. Mickey wasn't there. She clutched the seat beneath her. Some force seemed to come up strongly under the little boat, pushing it upward, and there was air again in their faces. Luther Cates was swearing and Gili somewhere was screaming. And then Marcia knew the lifeboat was moving, pulling away from the ship, which already stood out a black bulk with lights above them. "We made it," said Daisy Belle harshly. They started then again, down the long, long, horrible glide into the trough of a wave.

The rest of the night was like that.

Nobody knew when or even if the ship went down. She was a small, crowded Portuguese cargo boat, with a few cabins which were at a premium, so many people wanted to get away from Europe out of Lisbon; and her destination had been Buenos Aires. Sometime in the maelstrom her few tilting, blinking lights simply disappeared and nobody noticed it. If other lifeboats were successfully lowered they did not know that either. Their only preoccupation was the darkness, the waves, the cold, the sea water; the long, sickening glides down, thinking that every second was to be that second which would pitch them into the sea, and then the equally long, and in a queer way equally sickening, thrust upward. All existence became a matter of clinging to the boat, of huddling together, of trying to row, of trying to bail out sea water. It was a completely instinctive and completely primitive struggle with wind and waves and cold—horribly wet cold, that stiffened hands and body, so it seemed the blood could not flow through so stiff and hard a substance, as if there could be no life in anybody's heart. At first, spasmodically, the women tried to help. Soon they could only cling to the boat, to each other, fight for air, for life.

This went on through the night.

Marcia did not know when she became aware of some of the others in the lifeboat. Alfred Castiogne was there and giving orders about rowing and bailing, he was one of the ship's officers. A sudden, more or less violent flirtation had sprung up between him and Gili on the ship; but probably he was there, not because of Gili, but because he was in charge of that lifeboat. He was behind Marcia then, at the rudder. She could hear his shouts now and then above the crash of the waves. There were herself and Mickey, Gili and Luther, and Daisy Belle Cates. There were two other seamen. It was a small boat, but it was not full. Once she wondered vaguely why more people from the *Lerida* had not accompanied them; but they were the only passengers, so she supposed that the others, the seamen and ship's officers, had either remained with the ship or taken other lifeboats. They started down another wave and Marcia stopped thinking.

Once there was a sort of lull, and Daisy Belle made them drink from her flask of brandy. Marcia's hands were so numb she could scarcely feel the flask. They passed it round from one awkward, fumbling hand to another. From time to time the men changed places, moved about. Marcia was aware only of the motion, not of the time and order of any of it. Alfred Castiogne and Luther seemed to be directing the efforts of the men to keep the boat from being swamped. Luther had had some experience with small boats. Alfred Castiogne was a big, dark ruffian of a man, strong as an ox. He took long turns rowing. Once Marcia caught the flash of his white teeth and smelt garlic as he crowded between her and Daisy Belle to crawl forward. Not that there was much use rowing, Marcia thought dimly; but she supposed it was better to try to attack the waves than to be resigned and swamped by them. That must be the theory.

Marcia never knew either when or how she began to feel that they might ride out the storm. Not that, by then, she cared. Nobody cared; they were too numb, too cold, too desperately tired. They were merely organisms, struggling in spite of themselves. Sometime, years and years and years after they had gone down into that black and heaving water, Marcia thought in some faraway recess of her mind, I can see Mickey's shoulders. How horribly tired he looks!

She could see him dimly. Other shapes were beginning to emerge dimly from the blackness. One of the two seamen, bending over an oar, made a short, thick outline; the other looked thin and wizened, and wore a stocking cap, which very much later began to take on a reddish tone. Daisy Belle had taken another turn at rowing, and then crawled back to a place near Marcia. Her nose and chin were sharp and grey and haggard, etched in dreary stone. Gili was huddled ahead of them, her head down in her arms. It was getting to be morning; there was a faint grey light showing at the rims of the world. The waves seemed to be abating in violence.

There were no signs of other lifeboats; although once a barrel floated past and they thought at first it was a man, and another time it was a man, on his face, dead when they reached him. Alfred Castiogne bent down to drag the floating, dark bulk a little out of the water, and to cast it back again. Marcia remembered the way his thick shoulders hunched over, and the moment while the boat drifted and Gili's whimper. But nobody said anything; it seemed so natural an event, so precisely and expectedly part of the pattern of the night.

Gradually the darkness was broken into by a sort of glow, away ahead, dimly red, like a distant fire, or like the late reflection of a crimson sunset. Only it was towards the east.

The glow and redness slowly grew.

All of them saw it and watched it—dully, at intervals, preoccupied first with that increasing and frightful struggle to keep alive another minute—through another wave.

It was Luther who first said it was a ship; and then they shifted about confusedly, all of them searching in the dim grey light for rockets. They found them in a small locker along with the inadequate supply of dry rations and brackish water, compass and knife and tarpaulin with which the lifeboat had been sparsely equipped. Mickey sent up the rockets. Long streaks of flame curled up above the lifeboat. Sometime about then Alfred Castiogne collapsed; he lay in the stern, and Luther and one of the seamen moved him. Luther again took an oar, while one of the seamen, the one with the thick, strong silhouette, huddled over in the dim light, and worked at Castiogne to revive him and did not succeed, for at length he gave up and tried to arrange the third mate fairly comfortably against a seat and went back savagely to rowing. The ship lay dead ahead, and had the strange rosy radiance now all about her, but it was not fire.

Marcia was past anything so human, so vital as hope. She watched as if from delirium, as if it didn't matter to her. She heard the men talk; she tried to help in a fumbling way to find the rockets; she saw the streaks of fire curve up at last over the distant ship—above the ship and above that strange rosy radiance, acknowledging their own signals.

Daisy Belle said in a far away hoarse voice that mumbled the words: "It's a hospital ship. See the Red Cross on the side."

Mickey was then just ahead of them. He jerked around towards Daisy Belle. His face looked queer, too, stony and drawn; his dark eyelashes coated with brine, his lips purple. His mouth was stiff from cold, too; his words were barely intelligible: "American—is she American?"

Marcia could have told them both yes. She knew the hospital ships; she'd seen them often at Marseilles. Words stirred faintly in her consciousness; but not strongly enough to induce numbed muscles and nerves to speech. As a matter of fact, when they were picked up thirty minutes later Marcia was only dimly aware of it. She knew when she was slung over a shoulder and carried up a swaying Jacob's ladder. She knew when they lifted her from a litter to a bunk, and warmth and returning circulation made her cry with pain.

The others were in various stages of shock from exposure and cold, except for Alfred Castiogne, who was dead.

He had not, however, died of exposure.

"This man," said the doctor who examined him, looking at the knife wound in his back, "was murdered."

II

MARCIA opened her eyes.

She was aware first of warmth and comfort, of soft blankets and clean, sweet-smelling sheets; she had been aware of that for some time really, and of the distant throb and vibration of the engines.

For an instant she looked at the small, cheerful cabin. There were double-decked bunks, accommodating four people; gay, chintz-covered chairs; a book shelf; a door leading to the passageway probably, and another, open, to a tiny bathroom; there were two round ports, and the light was on, so it must be again night. She was still on a ship, but it was so sharply different from the dirty little Portuguese ship, so clean and shining and warm, and with such an atmosphere of comfort, that she savoured it gratefully, not thinking. And then she saw a slipper, shabby, high-heeled, rimy from sea water, lying on the floor. It was Gili's slipper.

Sharply then she remembered everything and sat up. Every muscle ached as if she had been beaten, but she was alive and warm. The miracle had happened: she was still Marcia Colfax, breathing, thinking, still linked up with her own destiny.

The two bunks directly opposite had been slept in and were still not made up. A tray with empty dishes and a coffee pot stood on the table. Someone had placed a crimson bathrobe across the foot of her own bunk. She was wearing, she discovered, pale-grey flannel pyjamas which smelled of soap. She reached for the bathrobe, and every muscle throbbed, but the pain was just then welcome; it confirmed the miracle of simply being alive. She wrapped the crimson robe around her, and as she did so, the door into the passageway opened quietly and a nurse looked in, saw that she was awake, smiled, and came into the cabin. She was young and pleasant; she was in uniform, beige and white striped seersucker, which looked very crisp and clean, and she carried some clothes over her arm.

"Awake," she said. "I'm Lieutenant Stoddard. How do you feel? I've brought you some clothes."

"I feel wonderful," said Marcia. Her voice sounded hoarse and weak. "I can't believe it. It really is a miracle."

"Not at all," said Lieutenant Stoddard. "People are rescued every day." She put down the clothes, carefully depositing a pair of brown oxfords on the floor. "I'll just make sure you are all right," she said, and came to Marcia and put her fingers on her wrist. "Well, no double pneumonia here. I'd better take your temperature, though."

She shook the thermometer briskly.

"Where are the others? Is everybody all right? Is— Mickey . . . ?" She suddenly remembered that on the *Lerida* she had had to address Mickey as André in order to square with the papers he was using. But that didn't matter now. If they were on an American boat, headed for home, they could tell the truth; explain everything, and everything would be all right. The nurse put the thermometer in her mouth and said: "No double pneumonia anywhere, in fact. We got you just in time, I imagine."

She must have thought that Marcia's eyes were questioning for she went on pleasantly: "I expect you don't even know where you are. It's a hospital ship, the *Magnolia*. We are on our way home with wounded and sick soldiers. We picked you up just about dawn; you were unconscious, I think. We put you and Mrs. Cates and Miss—well, the other young lady—in this cabin. Neither of them seem to be suffering any ill effects, although, of course, you'll feel pretty washed up for a while."

"The others . . ." said Marcia around the thermometer.

The young lieutenant turned to close the port behind her. "Quite all right, I believe. We gave everybody treatment for shock. Mr. Cates was the worst off; he had to have digitalis and I don't know what all, but he's all right now except for a cold. Mr. Messac is up and about, too. He looks quite like right." She turned back, but her eyes avoided Marcia's. "We let you sleep as long as you could." She waited another moment of two, removed the thermometer, glanced at it and said: "Perfectly normal. Now, then, I'll get you something to eat."

She smiled again, gave a little nod, and went quickly away. Marcia, still savouring the warm comfort of the bunk and the tiny shining cabin, lay back luxuriously on the pillow. It was night again; she had slept probably almost around the clock. Mickey was all right, then; everybody, thought Marcia comfortably, was all right; and she slipped into a dreamy state which was not quite sleep but near it, so it seemed to her only a moment until the crisp, pleasant young nurse came back.

It was not, in fact, until she'd had food, hot soup and hot steak and hot coffee; until she'd had a hot bath, with the incredible luxury of all the soap she wanted, and was dressed —in a nurse's uniform, as a matter of fact, which luckily fitted —that she had any warning that everything was actually all wrong. But even then she did not know that Alfred Castiogne was dead. The nurse only said that the ship's Captain wanted to see her. " He asked me to bring you to him as soon as you were awake. Do you think you're quite up to it ? "

She had been thinking, naturally, of seeing Mickey. " The ship's Captain ? "

" Captain Svendsen." The nurse hesitated. " I think it is rather—important." Something in the nurse's manner and voice seemed to be evasive. Five years in warring Europe had given Marcia an awareness of the very breath of danger. She looked quickly at the nurse. " What is wrong ? What has happened ? "

Lieutenant Stoddard bit her lip. " I'd better take you to them. If you're quite sure . . ."

This time Mickey's assumed name came out naturally, without intention.

" Is it André ? André Messac ? Is anything wrong ? "

" Oh, no, no. Mr. Messac is quite all right. Really, Miss Colfax. It's only—they'd like to ask you some questions, I think."

Questions ? She considered it slowly; but naturally there would be questions: her name, her destination, matters of record.

The nurse continued: " I brought you a coat, too, Miss Colfax. I'm afraid yours is ruined with sea water. It's a nurse's coat. I guessed at size twelve." She held up the brown, trimly tailored coat with its gay scarlet lining, and slipped it round Marcia's shoulders. " How do the oxfords feel ? We had a time getting clothes for Mrs. Cates; she's so thin and yet tall, you know. And those beautiful fur coats . . ." The nurse shook her head and ushered Marcia into the narrow, long passage that ran the length of the cabin doors. It did not occur to Marcia that she kept on chattering, " We cleaned them as best we could, but sea water is so horrible. This way, Miss Colfax."

The passageway was painted grey and glittered with cleanliness. The air was fresh and warm, and there was an inviting, floating fragrance of coffee and the clean smell of antiseptics. She caught a glimpse of a slender, crisply uniformed figure of the nurse going into a cabin ahead of them ; doors were open here and there, giving glimpses of other cabins ; of a glittering little diet kitchen ; then they emerged into a transverse corridor, and open stairs, like very sound and substantial ladders with stout railings, going up and down. There were people—corps-men in white, two medical officers in uniform—talking to a transport corps officer ; she had a quick glimpse of a corridor leading to a sick ward with its rows of double bunks and lights, and several soldiers also in red bath-robes helping put up a screen for movies. Over and above everything was an indescribable sense of warmth and cleanliness, happiness and home. It struck Marcia with a poignancy that was like a comforting hand. An American ship ; a mercy ship, and she and Mickey were on it, safe and cared for and warm and going home. The nurse must have seen something of her feeling in her face, for she laughed a little, softly. " I know what you're thinking."

" It doesn't seem real. It's all so—so American. Clean and efficient-looking and plenty of everything. It's like being at home."

" I know. You should see some of our patients when they get their first meal aboard. Milk. Eggs. Steak. Some of the cast cases gain so much weight that we have to change their casts. Around this landing. That's right. I'll take you through the wards sometime. Up again."

They climbed more stairs. They were easier for Marcia to climb than the first ; her muscles were less stiff and sore ; sleep and a hot bath and food could work miracles, too. The whole ship seemed a miracle, with the radiance of its lighted Red Cross shining out over the sea. But a modern and a scientific as well as a merciful miracle. They reached another deck. Everywhere, above and below, she caught glimpses of men in uniform, nurses in uniform, going quickly and quietly

about their business. None of them so much as gave her a
glance. She had even then a sense of the organisation, the
detailed direction, and never-relaxing activity that went on
constantly, at every instant, all over the ship. Later, gradually,
a complete and awe-inspiring picture of that organisation was
to emerge—its scientific thoroughness, its personal devotion,
its vigilance and its immeasurable triumphs.

Lieutenant Stoddard, her bright bar shining on one collar
lapel and the nurse's badge, equally shining, on the other,
again caught something of Marcia's thoughts. " It's a floating
hospital," she said. " We have everything—laboratories,
X-ray rooms, three operating rooms . . . I'll show you that,
too."

Her face was shining almost as brightly as her lieutenant's
bars. Marcia said : " I envy you. To be able to serve like
this. . . ."

" I wouldn't trade these three years for anything in the
world," said Lieutenant Stoddard, simply and sincerely. She
took Marcia's arm lightly. " We go forward now. This
way. . . ."

Again they walked along a narrow, shining grey passageway, with the slight, accustomed motion of the ship seeming
to push itself a little stronger against their feet as they
approached the bow and the Captain's quarters. They stopped
before a door at the end of the passageway. It was closed.
Lieutenant Stoddard knocked, and it opened. The nurse
said : " This is Miss Colfax, sir," and a slim, young major said,
" Thank you, Lieutenant," and held the door wider for Marcia
to enter.

It was a small room, panelled, with built-in wooden cabinets
and shelves. There were deep red leather-covered chairs and
a sofa, a rack of pipes, a solid table built crosswise below the
square windows opposite, and laden with papers and books,
photographs and lamps. It had a look of home and comfort.
An open door at the left showed a bunk neatly made up with a
cheerful red plaid cover. There were three men in the room
and Mickey was one of them. He came to her at once.

" Marcia ! Are you all right ? They said it was better for
you to sleep. I've been worried about you," He took her hand
and smiled down at her. He was wearing an olive-drab army
uniform, but without insignia. He looked still rather white

and drawn, but was cleanly shaven and obviously rested, with his blond hair still damp apparently from the shower. "Something pretty bad has happened, Marcia. They want to . . ."

"If you don't mind, Mr. Messac," said someone rather sharply behind him. A man had risen from the chair beside the table ; he was in blue uniform, with the four gold stripes denoting his rank across his sleeve. He was stocky and very powerful looking, with very yellow hair, eyebrows that were white and heavy, a red, weathered face and narrow, intensely sharp blue eyes. He said : " I am Captain Svendsen, Miss Colfax. This is Major Williams." The young Major who had opened the door bowed briefly. Captain Svendsen indicated one of the red chairs with a thick, powerful pink hand and said : " Will you sit down ? "

Mickey said : " May I tell her, Captain ? "

But Captain Svendsen's hand remained firm until Marcia sat down. Then he replied shortly : " I will, Mr. Messac." He resumed his own seat, and said : " Miss Colfax, did you know the third officer on the *Lerida* ? "

" The third officer . . ." began Marcia, puzzled, looking to Mickey for enlightenment, and Mickey said quickly : " Castiogne. I told them, of course, that you had never seen him before we got on the Portuguese ship. . . ."

" Mr. Messac." The Captain's voice snapped out like a whiplash. He leaned forward. " I am master of this ship, Mr. Messac. The responsibility for this is altogether mine."

" You are making it unnecessarily hard for Miss Colfax," said Mickey.

" Mickey, what is it ? What is wrong ? "

" Castiogne . . ." began Mickey, and the Captain said : " That is all, Mr. Messac. I'll talk to Miss Colfax alone. Major . . ." He nodded towards the door. The slim young Major advanced imperturbably and opened it. Mickey said : " Oh, nonsense, I'm going to stay. Miss Colfax and I are to be married as soon as we get to America. I have a right to stay. . . ."

" You have no right that supersedes mine on my ship, Mr. Messac," said the Captain.

Mickey shrugged, started to speak, stopped, finally said : " I beg your pardon."

The Captain leaned back in his chair. His thick, white

eyebrows were drawn angrily together above his deep-set, shrewd eyes. "I've no objection to your remaining, Mr. Messac, if you'll be so good as to keep quiet. Answer my question, please, Miss Colfax. Did you know Alfred Castiogne?"

She glanced at Mickey, who was now staring at the rug, his hands linked behind his back as if to hide the deformity of tortured fingernails. She said: "He was in the lifeboat."

"Did you know him before you left Lisbon?"

"No. To my knowledge I had never seen him before."

Mickey made a movement of impatience and checked it. The Captain said: "You know, of course, exactly who was in the lifeboat?"

"Why, I—yes, of course. Myself and . . ." She started to say Mickey, and sensed something very still and waiting about Mickey's bent head, and quickly substituted "and André. Mrs. Cates and her husband. Gili—that is, Gili Duvrey. This man, Alfred Castiogne. I think two seamen, but I don't remember their faces and I don't know their names. That's all."

"Who of them knew Castiogne best?"

"We were all passengers, that is, except the seamen."

"Please answer my question."

"But none of us knew him!" Suddenly she remembered Gili's flirtation with the dark, garlicy third officer. Was that what he meant? But why? She said slowly: "I think Miss Duvrey saw something of him on the ship. We were only three days out when the storm struck. She couldn't have known him well. If you'll tell me, Captain Svendsen, why you are asking . . ."

The Captain leaned forward. "It is no secret, Miss Colfax. This third officer, this Alfred Castiogne, was murdered."

It had no reality. She repeated, "Murdered . . ." almost politely, as if she had not heard it rightly.

"He was stabbed," said the Captain slowly. "He died of hæmorrhage from a knife wound in his back. Obviously . . ." He frowned and said: "Obviously he was murdered in the lifeboat."

It was very quiet. No one moved. For a second or two it was as if no one breathed; as if the word itself had a paralysing effect. But that, thought Marcia strangely, finally, was the thing they had left behind. Murder and more murder. Violence, terror, and betrayal: bombs and guns and knives and torture. Her hands were digging into the red arms of her chair. The young Major over by the door moved suddenly, got out a package of cigarettes, glanced at the Captain and shoved it back into his pocket. Mickey was staring silently again at the carpet, his hands knotted behind him. Mickey, who had seen so much of the blood and horror of Nazism.

"But I don't understand . . ." A small blurred memory of the night returned to her. She cried: "He was rowing! He was directing everybody. And a dead man floated past and he—Alfred Castiogne—looked at him. I saw it. He lifted the body from the water."

"When was that?"

"I don't know." It was confused, horrible, all of it. She looked at Mickey for confirmation and Mickey was trying to tell her something. She could see it in the look he gave her; but what was it?

The Captain insisted. "When did that happen, Miss Colfax? Try to remember."

"I don't know. I can't possibly say. But Castiogne was alive then."

"You say you *saw* him lift the dead man from the water. It must have been light enough to see objects and movement. It must have been nearly dawn."

She nodded, still aware that Mickey was trying to communicate some message without words, without motion, with only that steady yet somehow warning look in his clear grey eyes. She replied to Captain Svendsen: "Why, yes. Yes, I suppose so. I can't remember much of it."

"When did Castiogne collapse, then? How much later?"

She tore her gaze from Mickey's urgent look and met the Captain's intent, shrewd eyes. "I don't know exactly. I believe that I noticed that he had collapsed about the time we sent up rockets."

The Captain turned to Mickey. "Is that as you remember it?"

Mickey shrugged. "It's as I told you. I remember thinking that he'd collapsed and somebody tried to revive him, one of the other seamen, I think. It was about the time we sighted your ship. But everything was very confused."

The Captain looked again at Marcia.

"Miss Colfax, let me put a frank and point-blank question. It will save time and trouble for everybody if you'll answer it frankly. Is there anything at all that you know or saw in that lifeboat which might have something to do with the murder of this man ? Take your time. Try to remember."

But there was nothing. She shook her head.

"Everything was terribly confused. Time didn't mean anything. People moved about ; we had to. But the only thing we thought of was the storm and the waves, and keeping the boat from being swamped. I cannot believe that he was murdered. . . ."

Captain Svendsen interrupted. "Miss Colfax, I want you to tell me everything you can remember of the lifeboat ; everything that happened. . . . Don't be in a hurry ; take your time. Start with abandoning the ship. Who put you in the lifeboat ? Who sat beside you ? Who in front of you ? What was said and done ? Who saw the *Magnolia* first ? Everything."

"I didn't know Castiogne was dead. I didn't see anything. . . ."

Captain Svendsen sighed ; he had a deadly patience ; it angered him to be obliged to draw upon it, but he never quibbled with necessity. He began : "Who sat nearest you ?"

His patience, though, had few results, beyond the small details Marcia remembered from the night. Replying to his questions, she told how they had left the *Lerida ;* how they had rowed and bailed and hung on to life ; the way they had huddled in the boat. She had sat for the most part beside Mrs. Cates ; but there had been moving about, change as the men changed places.

"After you sighted us ? "

She thought back as one tries to pierce the convolutions of a long and shifting dream. "Yes. We hunted for rockets. Everybody seemed to shift about and move about."

" Castiogne, too ? "

" I don't remember."

" But it was after that that he collapsed ? "

She corrected him : " It was after that that I saw he had collapsed. One of the seamen tried to help him."

" Which one ? "

" I don't know their names. He was short and thick."

"Go on."

Go on? Well, what had happened then. They had sent up rockets. They had rowed and watched the waves and rowed and looked when they could, when they dared, when there was no curling black waters rising between, for the red glow that was the *Magnolia*. Somebody—Mrs. Cates, she thought—had said it was a hospital ship. She remembered being carried upward aboard the *Magnolia* and the wild rocking of the lifeboat. That was all.

Again the sounds of the ship, the small sighs and creaks, the rush of distant water, the ticking of a clock on the long, solid table were the only sounds in the cabin. Mickey did not move; his eyes, as clear and grey as the sea, looked straight ahead. The young Major stood by the door, his face without expression, smoking.

The Captain watched her thoughtfully. Finally he leaned back in his chair. " Your name is Marcia Colfax. Right? You claim to be a United States citizen? "

" I am an American citizen. My passport . . ."

" I have here." He pulled open the deep drawer of the table beside him, and then, as if he did not after all require to refresh his memory, closed it again. " You came to Lisbon from where? "

" From Marseilles."

Captain Svendsen reached for a pipe which lay on an ashtray near him and began to fill it carefully, his great pink hand looking extraordinarily powerful. " How long had you been in Marseilles? "

" Since the first summer of the war." The Captain's thick, queerly bleached eyebrows seemed to wait further explanation. He pushed and packed the tobacco in his pipe. Impelled by that waiting, Marcia went on, again giving the bare facts. " I had gone from New York to France, to Paris, the summer the war began. I stayed on in Paris that winter. Then when the Germans occupied Paris I went to the South of France; to a villa outside Marseilles, as a matter of fact."

" You were there all that time? "

" Yes. Until about three weeks ago, when I went to Lisbon." He had filled the pipe now and was lighting it; he shot a shrewd glance at her over the small flame. " Where is your present home in the United States? "

She thought of home. It was a swift, flashing picture of the big old house with the wisteria and maples and sunshine across the hills beyond—a picture that had haunted her through those grim and troubled years. She thought of the pleasant, high apartment overlooking the park. She said: " Maryland and New York City."

" Why didn't you go directly to the United States ? Why did you set out for Buenos Aires ? "

" Because we could get passage to Buenos Aires ; it would have meant waiting to get directly to the United States."

" We ? " said Captain Svendsen. " You mean yourself and Mr. Messac ? "

Mickey said suddenly : " I've told you all this, Captain. We were going home to be married. . . ."

Without replying, the Captain turned toward the table, wrote quickly on a memorandum pad, tore off the paper, and held it towards Major Williams. " Thank you, Mr. Messac. I'll not require your presence further," said the Captain as the young Major took the paper, read the scribbled note briefly, and turned toward the door. " Oh, Major, take Mr. Messac to the officer's lounge, if you please. Or his own quarters, if he prefers it."

" Yes, sir." Major Williams paused, eyes on Mickey. Mickey, looking white again and strained, said: " But I'd like to stay, Captain. I'll not interfere. . . ."

" Please remain here, Miss Colfax." The Captain nodded abruptly toward Major Williams, who waited for Mickey. " Very well," said Mickey. He stopped beside Marcia. " Don't let them upset you, Marcia. Castiogne was nothing to you and me. I promise you, darling, as sure as my name is André Messac that all our trouble is in the past. For ever." He smiled, but his eyes were very clear and grey and intent. So she saw then what he'd been trying to tell her. She ought to have realised it when she first heard them address him as Mr. Messac.

He had been André Messac on the Portuguese ship ; he was still using that name, the name on his passport, and wished her to do so. There was no time to consider the reasons. She said quickly, to show him that she understood : " Yes, André, I'll see you when the Captain is finished."

Mickey nodded, giving an almost imperceptible wink.

Major Williams cleared his throat and Mickey turned to follow him. The door closed behind them both. Captain Svendsen leaned back in his chair again.

"I don't think you have quite understood the situation, Miss Colfax," he said. "There were only a handful of people in that lifeboat—you and André Messac, Gili Duvrey, two seamen, Mr. and Mrs. Luther Cates." He paused and added on the same level tone as if merely checking another fact: "One of you murdered that man. Which one was it?"

III

SHE HEARD everything he said; she did not think beyond the incomprehensible fact of murder.

It is one thing to state a truth; it is another thing for the mind to accept it as truth. Or perhaps the mind accepts where understanding rejects. It wasn't possible that during the horror of those hours in the lifeboat another horror had added itself quietly to the night, and that was murder. She rejected it and yet had to accept it as true.

After a moment Marcia said slowly: "If he was murdered in the lifeboat, if there is no other possible explanation for his death . . ."

The Captain looked ahead, showing a hard, strong profile. After a moment he said flatly:

"He was murdered."

"Well, then, I see, of course, that someone in the boat must have done it. But we were so preoccupied with a struggle for life, all of us, that it is hard for me to believe that anybody could have cared enough—to—to murder anybody." Suddenly murder itself, the fact of murder, became tangible, as if it had a stealthy and furtive and horrible being. Then and there, in that cabin, so she moved uncomfortably, suddenly chilled and cold; suddenly aware again of the slight motion and creaking of the ship.

But murder, if it had existed, was in the lifeboat, not the hospital ship. The seeds of that murder had been sewn on the Portuguese ship. She said suddenly: "The two seamen . . ."

"Did you see either of them kill Alfred Castiogne?"

"No, no . . ."

"Why, then, do you imply that one of them killed a man? It is a grave charge, Miss Colfax."

"I don't know anything of the murder, Captain. It is very difficult for me to believe it—that is, to understand how it could have happened."

The Captain rose abruptly, paced across the cabin and back again, and stopped before her, looking down. "That part of it seems fairly obvious," he said, his thick white eyebrows jutting out over his shrewd, sharp blue eyes. "Almost any one of the people in that boat could, I believe, have managed to stab Castiogne without being seen. You were all, as you say, confused, preoccupied, changing places when necessary, each aware mainly of his own danger and his own discomfort. If the murder occurred after you sighted the *Magnolia*, it is even easier to understand its being done without any of you seeing it, for you were all watching the *Magnolia*—nothing else. No, *how* it was done is easy; the question is *who* did it? Why did you mention the two seamen?"

"Because they knew him; they must have known him. There may have been some—oh, some grudge, some quarrel. The rest of us were passengers only."

"In other words, you are deliberately blaming both or one of these men?"

"No, I didn't say that."

"Listen, Miss Colfax, every one of the passengers in that lifeboat has suggested that solution. It is so unanimous a belief on the part of the five of you that one might be inclined to think that you actually knew of the murder and mutually agreed to blame the seamen."

"No, no, you are wrong. Don't you see, Captain Svendsen, how confusing it is, how terribly shocking and . . . ?"

He interrupted: "How long have you known the Cates couple?"

"I met them in Lisbon for the first time—that is, of course, I'd heard of them. I knew their name; everybody knows that, I suppose. They were always in the papers."

"Where in Lisbon did you meet?"

"At the hotel, while we were waiting to get some sort of passage."

"What about Gili Duvrey? How long have you known her?"

"She was at the hotel, too. I saw her, here and there, in the cocktail lounge or the lobby. Then, when we reached the ship, we—Gili and Mrs. Cates and I—shared a cabin."

"Do you know anything of her other than that?"

"No."

The Captain lighted his pipe again, with slow deliberate puffs, watching her closely with those bright, shrewd blue eyes. Again incredulity caught at Marcia. She tried to see Gili or Daisy Belle, or Luther, creeping forward in that lurching mad lifeboat, knife in hand, stabbing at the hunched figure of the third officer, but it was a picture which she simply could not summon up in her mind. All her instinct rejected it as completely and finally as if she had tried to fit herself into that fantastic picture. The Captain said suddenly: "Miss Colfax, look at that thumb."

She saw with a start that he was holding out his great fist towards her, the thumb upward, wide and powerful. "There are hundreds of lives under that thumb," he said, "all the time—lives in my care. I am responsible for the ship and every life upon her. I can marry people and bury people. And I can kill people, if need be."

He smoked for a moment and said simply: "I am the master of this ship. You and all those people from the lifeboat are now on this ship and under my care. I am particularly responsible because of the load I carry—sick and wounded men who have fought for America. For you, for me. It is my job now to see to them. I had to pick you up last night. I had to circle as I did, in case there were other lifeboats; I found none and continued my course. A short time after I picked you up the doctor who examined the body of Alfred Castiogne reported the murder to me. There are two things I can do: I can put you all under arrest and in confinement until we reach home. Or I can induce you to tell who murdered him. I don't propose to let a murderer run at large on my ship. Do you understand me?"

His honesty, his force of character, something enormously solid and strong in the very way he sat, a thick blue bulk in the chair, and looked at her with those deep-set, steady eyes, compelled respect and a kind of liking.

She said: "Yes, I think I do understand. But I . . ."

"You still cannot quite believe this man was murdered. Never mind that now. The point is the *Magnolia* is not a fast ship; it will be some time before we reach port. For the sake of my ship and of everybody concerned I want to settle this thing now. It is my duty." He said it so simply that it was a mere statement of fact and thus convincing. "Now then"—he tapped the pipe against the ash-tray, neatly and precisely—"why did you not return to America before now?"

That had nothing to do with the murder of the third officer of a little Portuguese cargo ship. And he was waiting for a reply. Why hadn't she returned to America sooner? Long ago when the war began?

Her thoughts went swiftly back over those war years that had seemed so long and ugly, so filled with terror and despair, so tenuous with hope that Mickey would escape and would come to her—as eventually he did. In fact, of course, it was a very brief story, and not unusual.

"I hoped that . . ." She caught herself; she must say André Messac, not Mickey Banet; she must remember that. She went on: "I hoped that André would return. He was taken to a concentration camp when the Germans occupied Paris." She paused. The man opposite was still tapping his pipe lightly, watching it. The small taps were like little periods, spacing and punctuating memories.

So many memories . . . Marcia's mind went swiftly back five years, to the great grey ship, the *Normandie*, pulling out away from the pier on one of her last trips. Her father, on the pier, waving and laughing. It was actually her last glimpse of him. Teresa, a school friend, and Teresa's aunt, their chaperon, beside her.

That day had launched the gay holiday voyage during which she had met Mickey.

There followed a packed and important—but very quickly passing—period of time. London and humid July weather and Mickey. Paris and August and Mickey. September and war, and Mickey telling her he loved her.

After that, naturally, she remained in France, and would not return to America with Teresa and her aunt in spite of their pleading, in spite of the war, in spite of the frantic cables from her father. She could remember saying good-bye to Teresa and the older woman in the wild turmoil of the Gare du Nord and her return to the small, very French hotel back of the Madeleine.

And then there was the first autumn of the war. She had walked with Mickey, lunched with Mickey, dined with Mickey ; listened to Mickey practise at the great piano in his apartment for hours on end, and listened to Mickey and his friends talk of the war. She herself had been lulled as Paris was lulled that winter with the Maginot drug ; but not Mickey and not a small select nucleus of his friends. All over Paris actually there were men who believed that they could see ahead ; already that winter the seeds of what was later to be a vast organisation for French resistance were sown.

She had not known actually, however, that Mickey was a part of that beginning movement. Up to then his only interest had been music ; he was on the beginning wave of what would certainly have been a great career ; already people were beginning to know his name ; he had played in London and in New York with brilliant press notices ; he was, in fact, returning from a series of American concert engagements. including an almost spectacular reception at Carnegie Hall when Marcia met him on the ship. He was then a slender, gay, contentedly engrossed young man, with his tanned face and light, sun-streaked hair and grey eyes, which, Marcia had always thought, were exactly the colour of the sea, as deep, as clear, as changeable ; he had no thought of politics, no thought of anything but music. And the war ended that.

It ended his career in the first place, because it brought all the bright world of the thirties crashing to an end. It ended his career later for a more specific reason.

In May the Germans entered Paris ; Mickey and three other men she had known were arrested.

Captain Svendsen was still tapping the pipe lightly and precisely upon the tray. It seemed strange that her memory could travel so many weary months while a man waited and tapped tobacco from his pipe. He said, lifting the pipe at last to frown into the bowl : " You were in Paris, then, when the war began ? And you went to Marseilles ? "

" I went to Marseilles later, that summer, after the Germans occupied Paris. I was with a friend—Madame Renal. She had a car and we drove to her villa. It was on a hill just outside Marseilles."

Again, as if a swift series of pictures flashed across some mental screen, she remembered that flight from Paris. They had all intended to go together ; at least that was what she thought when the plan was made. She and Mickey and Madame Renal—the kind, stout old Frenchwoman her father had cabled her to get in touch with ; somehow, somewhere in business probably, he had known Madame Renal and her husband. Madame Renal had a car, gasoline, and a villa near Marseilles ; she was old and ill, and she could not make the journey alone. Otherwise, Marcia would not have gone with her, for at last Mickey did not come. She would never forget, and she did not want to remember that day in Paris, the frantic, seething day of unutterable confusion while she tried to find Mickey, and in the end gave up and went with Madame Renal. They left Paris about nightfall. At five o'clock the next morning they were exactly three miles away, but by that time she could not have made her way back to the city. Mickey would find them ; he knew where they were going ; he knew the address—so Madame Renal assured her over and over again. Somewhere along the road they picked up three women, and old man and a cat. When they reached the villa, cold with its stony floors, Mickey was not there. A month later she learned that he had been arrested and sent to Germany.

The women drifted away ; the old man and the cat stayed on with her and Madame Renal. The thought of those long, cold, waiting years was too close and too full of tragedy to bear remembering.

She said to Captain Svendsen : " André finally escaped, just at the end of the war ; he knew where I'd be, of course, and came to me there as soon as he could."

The Captain began to refill his pipe. " Wouldn't it have been better to wait in Lisbon until you could get passage directly home ? If your people are there . . ."

It seemed to Marcia for an instant that the man sitting opposite her, watching her so closely over his pipe, was bent upon touching all the sore and poignant scars of the past years. She said : " My father died while I was in Marseilles ; the first summer after the Germans entered Paris. I learned of it months later through the Red Cross."

There was a slight pause; then the Captain said: "I'm sorry, Miss Colfax. Go on, please."

Go on? Oh, yes, why had they taken passage on the little Portuguese ship bound for Buenos Aires instead of home? But how could she tell him or describe to him her anxiety about Mickey, the urgency of her wish for him to leave Europe, with all its inevitable and tragic souvenirs of war? New surroundings, any new surroundings, a fresh start, a different place . . . These things Mickey had to have, for his soul's sake. His eyes were alight, his face had looked young and gay again, and full of hope and vitality for the first time when he had brought her, actually, another man's passports and the news of the possibility of a Lisbon sailing.

Practically, however, there was another reason, one she hadn't talked of to Mickey. She said slowly: "He had suffered greatly; I wanted him to be away from Europe as soon as possible. Also . . ." She hesitated; the passport situation would have to remain as it was, at least until she had talked to Mickey and they had decided together to tell the truth of it; but there was no harm in telling Mickey's profession. She went on, being careful again to say "André": "André, as he may have told you, was a musician, a pianist. Perhaps the Germans knew that; perhaps it was merely one of their unspeakable forms of torture. In any case, you've seen his hands; his fingernails and the ends of his fingers . . ."

Her throat grew rigid and hard, she stopped. The Captain nodded, his face hardened. "I saw them. I've seen several such."

"I wanted to get him to a plastic surgeon. I don't think he can ever play again; but there may be some hope. It seemed important to get him home, by any means that we could, as soon as possible."

"I see. Yes, I see that. There may be some hope. Miss Colfax; are you being quite frank with me?"

Mickey's passport was not Mickey's; she had not told him that. There had been, however, no other evasion. "Yes."

"And there is really nothing you can tell me of the murder of this man Castiogne?"

She wondered briefly if he had questioned her, urged her to talk in the hope that she might inadvertantly give him some

grain of information relating to Castiogne. She shook her head.
" Nothing."

" Very well then . . ."

Someone knocked, interrupting him, and Captain Svendsen said : " Yes ? Oh, Colonel Morgan. Will you come in ? "

A tall well-built man, a patient obviously, for he wore a long crimson dressing-gown, came into the room, followed by Major Williams, who closed the door again behind him. Captain Svendsen said : " Miss Colfax, this is Colonel Josh Morgan."

The tall man in the red dressing-gown turned to her quickly. She caught a flash of narrow and rather intent blue-grey eyes before he bowed, and then took the hand she held out toward him—took it, however, with his left hand, as his right arm was in a sling. He said, conventionally, except for that intent look in his browned face and in his level eyes : " How do you do, Miss Colfax ? "

Captain Svendsen said : " You haven't met before, I take it."

" Why—no." Colonel Morgan hesitated, looked at Marcia again directly, and said : " Or have we ? "

She had met, casually, many Americans in Paris before the war, and in Marseilles after the Americans came. But she would have remembered this man, she thought suddenly ; his black hair, the curve of his mouth ; his quick, direct look ; something strong and substantial and yet daring and youthful about him, that suggested imagination and inventiveness held in reserve, weighed and tested by a matter-of-fact good sense ; she would have remembered him for all that. But also there was some spark, some extra bit of electricity in the air between them ; it was curious, a small and unimportant fact, but a fact. She knew that she'd have remembered him. She said slowly ; " No, no, I'm sure we've not met," and Colonel Josh Morgan said : " No, of course not. I'd have remembered you," and smiled briefly.

It was merely a conventional, pleasant compliment, but it startled her a little, because it was so near her own thought. She met his eyes for an instant that suddenly seemed a long time ; as if she had met that deep and direct look, unguarded, with no barriers between many, many times. Which was nonsense ! She turned abruptly towards Captain Svendsen, who said: "Colonel Morgan was a newspaperman in civilian life. He spent considerable time in Paris before the war. I thought conceivably you might have met."

Marcia thought swiftly: he is trying to check my story, my identity. Why?

Josh Morgan said shortly: "Paris is a big place."

"Yes," said Captain Svendsen, heavily. "Yes. Still the American colony was not large. One often knows one's compatriots in any city. There were some other Americans on the lifeboat we picked up, Colonel."

"Oh, is Miss Colfax one of the *Lerida* survivors?" said Colonel Morgan.

Captain Svendsen nodded. "There were five passengers," he said exactly. "And two seamen, besides the man who was killed. They were"—Captain Svendsen's blue eyes watched Colonel Morgan sharply as he named them—"a Mr. and Mrs. Cates, Americans. I mean United States citizens. Gili Duvrey, French. Miss Colfax here. And André Messac—French also."

It seemed to Marcia that a flash of something like surprise came into Colonel Morgan's eyes. When he spoke, however, his voice was flat and impersonal. "*The* Cates?" he asked. "The Famous Cates? I think his name is Luther."

"Yes. Do you know them?"

Colonel Morgan reached for cigarettes, and with his free hand managed to extract one. "I knew of them. It's a famous name. Tons of money—patrons of the arts—fashionable, smart. Rather decent as I remember. But I never knew them."

"Well," the Captain sighed and rose. "I won't trouble you further just now, Miss Colfax. I hope you are comfortable. I see they've made a nurse of you. There was no civilian clothing for any of you; the Geneva Convention forbids us to carry civilians. But we couldn't leave you to float around in a lifeboat!"

There was a faint brief twinkle in those deep-set, far-seeing blue eyes. She said quickly: "I haven't thanked you, Captain Svendsen..."

He would have none of that. He made a brusque motion with the great hand that held the pipe. "Part of my job, part of my job. Fortunate we happened upon you and saw your rocket. Unfortunately, once we'd rescued you we cast the *Lerida* lifeboat adrift. That was before the doctor attending you discovered the fact about Castiogne. So "—he lifted his massive shoulders—" if there were any clues to his murder in the lifeboat they are gone now. Well, that's all now. Thank you. . . ."

Major Williams opened the door. Colonel Morgan made a sort of motion toward her, stopped, and said : " I hope we'll meet again, Miss Colfax."

" You're very likely to," said Captain Svendsen rather dryly. " The ship is not a large one."

Major Williams at the door, looking very young and thin and tall, and smiling down at her in a friendly way, said : " Do you feel all right ? Shall I take you to your cabin . . . ? "

" I'm quite all right, thank you, Major." She took up the nurse's coat, which had slid back upon the chair.

Colonel Josh Morgan turned to watch her leave. Captain Svendsen, very thoughtful-looking, returned to his pipe. The door closed behind her, and she walked along the narrow, shining, grey passage.

Murder, in that tossing, frantic lifeboat, with the crash of wind and waves all around them—while they sat huddled together ; while they watched. Only, of course, they hadn't watched, really. Anything could have happened during, say, one of those blinded, frantic forays of wind and waves and terror.

Yet it was still impossible, really, to comprehend it. Who would have wanted to murder Alfred Castiogne ? Who cared, just then, about anything in the world but the next wave, the next breath of air, the next pulse of life ?

She reached the central passageway with its flights of open, ladder-like stairways going up and down, and Mickey was waiting for her, lounging against a bulkhead, smoking and talking to Luther Cates and a young lieutenant with the golden, spoked wheel of the Army Transport Corps on his sleeve. Mickey sprang forward when she emerged.

" Okay, Marcia ? Let's get out on deck. Better put on that coat. It's still cold."

Luther Cates had followed him ; the young lieutenant gave them a brief look and disappeared into an office near at hand. Luther looked tired and old, as if the previous night had added years. His face was drawn and grey ; there were deep pouches under his pale-blue, rather bewildered eyes, but he was freshly shaved, and the thin grey hair over his temples was plastered down neatly. He, too, wore an Army uniform from which the insignia had been removed, and managed somehow to look, as he had done in black beret and shabby topcoat on the Portuguese ship, exactly as if he had stepped— although rather wearily—from the pages of *Esquire*. He took her hand in his own thin and boneless clasp. " How are you, my dear ? Better ? Daisy Belle said you were sleeping, so none of us called you. I suppose they've been questioning you about this man, Castiogne ? "

" Yes."

" They've questioned all of us. Daisy Belle was quite annoyed ; said the only thing she knew of him was that he smelled of garlic. Well, well, it's a queer thing, of course. I can't understand it myself. I don't remember anything at all that is suggestive : I had no idea he was dead. But obviously one of the two seamen did it. Nobody else would have had a motive."

" How is Daisy Belle ? "

" Oh, she's all right. She always says she has the constitution of a horse. More than I've got. . . ." He coughed a little, apologetically. " I think she's in the dining-saloon now. With —er—Miss Duvrey."

Mickey took her coat and slipped it over her shoulders. Luther added, smiling : " You make a very beautiful nurse, my dear. Daisy Belle is quite enchanted with her uniform. They seem to have taken up a collection for us in the way of clothing. I believe we are the only civilians aboard. And very lucky to be aboard, I'm sure."

He waved as they turned towards the deck.

The air was fresh and cold, suddenly, on her face. It was night and the sea was very black, but the ship was lighted everywhere. The Red Crosses painted on her sides and on her smokestack were brilliantly outlined with red lights ; portholes all along the decks were lighted ; floodlights shone down further to illuminate the enormous Red Crosses. Those painted, lighted symbols of mercy had been the ship's protection. The sound of a radio came from an open port nearby ; somewhere in the distance some men were singing.

The storm was over, although the sea was still so heavy the ship rolled a little. Marcia slipped her arm through Mickey's and they crossed the slippery deck and stopped to lean over the railing. The sky was cloudy, with scarcely a star showing, but the radiance of the lighted Red Crosses on the ship touched the black water so they seemed to move in a glittering track of red and gold light. Mickey, his shoulder pressing against hers, said suddenly: "What did the Captain say? What happened? Did you tell him that I am using André Messac's name?"

"No, no. But Mickey . . ."

"André, darling."

"That's it, Mickey. We've got to tell them your real name."

He sighed and took out a package of cigarettes. He had never got used to having cigarettes, plenty of cigarettes, all he wanted. He said now again, as he had said so many times in the past weeks: "Cigarettes! Think of it! Real cigarettes! Have one?"

She took it and bent to the small flame in his cupped hands. As she did so, she saw the mangled, twisted scar tissue of the fingers. She wanted to put her lips upon them; she mustn't do that and wound his pride, or let him know how terribly that sight wrenched at her heart. He said: "I wanted a chance to talk to you before the Captain did and simply couldn't make one. The first I knew of the murder was when they got me up there in the Captain's quarters and I couldn't get away to warn you not to tell them that I'm using a borrowed passport."

"But, Mickey, we've got to tell the truth."

"Tell them who I really am? Why? The passport is all right. They'll never question it. If that's what you are worried about . . ."

"No, no, it's not that! It's because—oh, there are so many reasons, Mickey. For one thing it's—well, it's the truth."

He smoked for an instant, his fine, sensitive profile clear in the rosy light. "You subscribed to my idea of using that passport when I suggested it," he said finally. "You agreed to it."

"Yes, but . . ." She could not say, but that was so we could leave quickly, so I could get you away from anything and everything that would remind you of all the horror that you must forget. She said, substituting: "Yes, it seemed convenient and much quicker than waiting. It didn't seem important so long as we were not going directly home. I thought that later at Buenos Aires, when we applied for passports home, we could simply tell the Consul exactly why and what happened. But now we are going directly home; we'll arrive at a home port. The only thing to do, I think, is to tell the truth and make an appeal to the State Department."

"They'll send me back to Europe."

Would they? She wished desperately that she knew more of law. Had they been not only mistaken in attempting something that at the time had seemed so natural and so right, but had they been criminally wrong as well, offending the law? She said slowly : " We were wrong to do it, Mickey. I shouldn't have let you. You weren't well, you weren't yourself. All that . . ."

"Listen, Marcia," said Mickey suddenly, "that's beside the point. You'd better know right now that I'm André Messac from now on. Everybody thinks that Michel Banet, the concert pianist, is dead. Well, then he's going to be dead."

"Mickey . . ."

"André. I am André Messac from now on. Marcia, for God's sake, pride is the only thing left to me. I *can't* let people know the truth ! If you tell them who I am, there'll be nothing but pity and curiosity and failure for me for the rest of my life. I've got to have my chance at a new life. Some sort of new life . . ." Mickey flung away his cigarette, a tiny red rocket, into the sea. "Pity and curiosity, a man stared at, pointed at, talked about. Michel Banet, they'll say ; he could have been the world's greatest pianist. Look at him now. And look," said Mickey, his voice rough, " at his hands."

He spread them out, pitilessly, as if they had a separate being, subjecting them to the light.

IV

SHE WANTED to cover them with her own hands. As she had had to do so many times, she smothered the impulse which would disclose pity. She had already in her heart recognised the necessity of preserving the pride which, he had said, was the only thing he had left out of that golden wealth of promise.

She started also to remind him, sensibly and as matter of factly as possible, that the important thing was to be alive, to emerge—living, breathing, able to talk and walk and even laugh again—from a horror which so many did not survive. But that, too, seemed without substance ; contemplating the misfortunes of others does not lighten one's own trouble, but, instead, adds to it.

The thing to do, then, was to fasten upon the subject at hand, think about that, talk about that. André Messac and a false passport, on which Mickey proposed to enter the United States, and perpetuate a false identity which he proposed to assume for the rest of his life. A shadow of all sorts of potential legal complications hovered at the edge of her mind ; but just then the main point at issue was a simple, clear question of honesty. In a curious way the project of using André Messac's papers had not seemed dishonest in Lisbon. It had seemed an expediency, a therapeutic measure which was so important just then to Mickey that the use of the passport was as uncomplicated by scruples, as direct and purposeful as the use, say, of an oxygen tank for a person with pneumonia. It had seemed lucky that the photograph on the passport was, Mickey had said, so bad and blurred that Mickey—or indeed almost any one could—use it. Once in Buenos Aires they would straighten the thing out, make a clean breast of it, wait until Mickey could enter the United States on the quota, if that was necessary. He was a French citizen ; she knew that. He had been educated not only in Paris but in New York, so English was like his mother tongue.

Concerned mainly with the desperate and sometimes despairing hope of restoring Mickey to himself, she had thought only of that. The way had opened which seemed right, and she had snatched at it gratefully and tucked the other and inevitable problem away to be faced when they reached it. And now they had reached it, suddenly, unexpectedly, and urgently.

It was the more urgent, naturally, because of the murder of Alfred Castiogne. No matter how briefly he had entered their lives, nor how little he had meant to them as a person, the mere fact of the murder occurring, as and when it had occurred, entangled them, brought the light of an investigation to bear upon every person in that lifeboat. All her instinct was for going to Captain Svendsen and telling him the whole truth.

But Mickey, she saw suddenly, had intended all along to do this very thing. Never would any one really know what had happened to Michael Banet; a new name, a new personality was to be his shield. Knowing Mickey as he had been before the war brought a crashing end to his bright world, and knowing him now, she could not fail to comprehend it. It was exactly like Mickey. He had returned to her probably only because his love for her was greater than his pride.

She said suddenly, out of the silence: "Who was André Messac?"

Mickey lighted another cigarette and squinted at the smoke clouds floating off into the night. "He was one of us," he said.

She waited again, instinctively avoiding direct questions. He would tell her what he could tell her, whatever he could bring out of tragic memory and into painful words. He said: "He was arrested at the same time that I was. He died—later. I never knew exactly how, or, as matter of fact, when. But I saw his mother in Paris; she still had his clothes and papers and all that. There had not been time when we were arrested that day to do anything, to get any of our personal possessions. There wasn't time for anything. I remember trying to get them to let me phone to you."

She had tried to telephone to him, too. She had known in her heart that there was disaster; she had tried to reach his apartment. The telephone had been taken over at government orders; the streets were choked with people and frenzied confusion. When she reached his apartment the concierge had fled and nobody could tell her anything.

She said, shifting the memory of that day: "That's in the past."

"Yes. Yes, of course. You keep telling me that. It's true of course, but—well, never mind. To make it short, she gave the passport to me, and I knew somebody who could fix it all up with visas and so forth. You learn things like that—but . . ." He paused and then said deliberately: "I never really let you see his passport, did I, Marcia? You see, it's his passport but it's my photograph. I had it put on in place of his. I—never intended to resume my own name. You may as well know that now."

It was, then, as she had so recently guessed. She waited for a moment, seeking words, seeking arguments and finding none that would avail against that long and stubborn scheme. "No," she said. "No . . ."

"I have thought it over. That is my decision, Marcia. You must help me. It means so much to me."

"But Mickey, it isn't practical. People will recognise you. You've appeared in concerts. . . ."

"People in an audience never remember the face of a pianist. Nonsense!"

"All your friends, all the people who knew you . . ."

"Marcia, you don't understand. I'll never play again. I knew only a very small, circumscribed group of people, mainly interested in music. Well, all that and those people are out of my life. I am André Messac now. A new identity, a new life . . ."

"You can't. . . ."

"And I depend on you, Marcia. I want a new life. I didn't want it really when I found you in Marseilles. I didn't want anything except to see you again. I'd thought of you, all those years of horror. There were times when I could keep alive only by thinking as hard as I could about you, holding some clear memory as if it were a symbol, a tangible thing. The thought of you actually, my darling, was as sustaining as—a piece of bread. That doesn't sound very fancy and high-flown, does it? But it's true."

Her throat had closed up tight again. There was fine cool spray against her face, but there were tears, too, remembering the time at the villa with its stone floors and walls, its emptiness, the longing for Mickey that every minute held. She said, her voice uneven: "For me, too, Mickey. I often wished that we had married that winter in Paris."

"I wished it, too. Yet at the time, with everything so confused, so uncertain, it seemed better not to. We were wrong, I expect. I was sorry, too. There was so much time to think of everything as it might have been. Well, as you say, that's in the past. Only I desperately want it to remain in the past, my darling. I want everything new for us. Everything on a clean slate. No clutter from the past, and no echoes of what I might have become."

"We ought to have gone to America that winter while we still could. I thought of that, so many, so many times I thought of that."

"How could I?" asked Mickey simply. "I'm a Frenchman. How could I have gone?"

It had been his argument then. She sighed and shivered a little, and pulled the thick khaki coat with its brave red lining tighter around her. And suddenly, for a queer, illogical second, she wished she could talk over the situation with the tall man in the red dressing-gown she had met in the Captain's cabin—Colonel Josh Morgan.

A man she didn't know and had never seen in her life before!

She was tired; that was the explanation. She felt the need to lean upon someone, and, until Mickey was better, she could not lean upon him. Contrarily, she must make herself strong and certain, so that Mickey now, while he needed it, could derive some strength from her.

Obviously, then, she could only agree to his plan, fall in with it for the time being. Until Mickey himself grew stronger —not physically, but within that core that men can only call a soul. Until he was certain again that life was good, desirable; until he had regained confidence and assurance and, mainly, his grip upon the reality, the sunshine and gaiety and dear, homely honesty of home. It might be slow in coming, but it would come.

She said, however, with odd feminine tenacity: "I think we should tell Captain Svendsen—no one else. I liked him. I believe he'd understand and—and help. . . ."

Mickey whirled around towards her. "No, Marcia! He'd have to tell. He has to do whatever his duty is. He couldn't conceal my real name; he'd have to report it. There's nothing else for him to do. You can't say anything to him that would induce him to swerve an inch from his job. I saw him; I talked to him ; that's the kind of man he is. If you tell him who I am, Marcia, everybody will know it." He stopped and searched her eyes almost incredulously. " Does my only chance for a new life mean so little to you ? "

" Oh, no, no, Mickey. I love you. . . ." She put her hands upon his then, but his hands were cold. His eyes were those of a stranger for an instant, so she seemed to be reaching out towards someone who was not there.

That, too, must be the effect of fatigue and nerve strain. And Mickey said unexpectedly : " Do you really love me ? "

He didn't really mean that. She must have patience, infinite patience ; and again she thought, strength for both of them just now. If the night past had frayed her own nerves and physical endurance, what must it have done to Mickey ? She put her arm through his own. " Mickey— Mickey, you know that I love you."

" Well, then, call me André, not Mickey. You will, won't you, Marcia ? "

" Yes, until we can straighten it out."

" What do you mean by that ? "

It had been the wrong thing to say. She felt again that she was being stubborn and feminine. She was right and yet wrong ; it was almost as if they were quarrelling.

" Mickey, I'd never do anything you asked me not to do. We mustn't talk like this. It is wonderfully simply that we are standing here together, alive and beside each other. Last night . . ."

" Yes, last night ! I have been thinking about this man Castiogne. It is hard to believe that he was murdered in the lifeboat. I can see how it could have happened without any of us being aware of it. But what I can't understand is why. We were all on the point of being drowned at any instant. Even if somebody wanted to kill him, it seems pointless. Every one of us stood such a good chance of being dead at any time during the night. Luther Cates thinks the same thing. Naturally, it was one of the seamen, crazed, perhaps, by fear. Until he confesses, I suppose it will be more or less unpleasant for all of us."

He broke off as someone came out on deck behind them.

" There you are," said Daisy Belle Cates. Marcia turned ; Daisy Belle and Gili came towards them, both in nurse's

uniforms and coats like the coat Marcia was wearing. Gili
stopped beside Mickey. Her golden hair was twisted to a heavy
knot on top of her head; her face was without make-up,
except for her full mouth, which was deeply crimson with
lipstick she had managed to borrow. She said: " What about
the murder, André ? What are they going to do ? Do they
suspect any of us ? Do they think we did it ? "

Daisy Belle said: " Could I have a cigarette, Monsieur
Messac ? Thank you." Mickey—André, Marcia reminded
herself. André offered Daisy Belle the package in his hand and
lighted the cigarette for her. She took a long puff and said :
" Thank heaven for that. I hope never to see another cigar
in all my life, let alone smoke one."

Gili's long green eyes slanted once towards the older woman
and then came back to Mickey. " Who do you think killed
him ? "

Mickey said: " I don't know."

Daisy Belle took another long, relishing breath, and tilted
back her reddish-grey head and that fine-drawn profile to
expel the smoke, slowly savouring it. She said then: " Obviously it was one of the seamen. None of us knew or cared
anything about the man. The only thing I know of him is
that he was very handsome in a sort of peasant way, and
apparently lived on garlic."

Gili started to speak, sucked in her full red lips and stopped.

Mickey said: " I understand the seamen have been
questioned. One of them will talk to save his own skin."

" It's an ironic thing," said Daisy Belle suddenly. " Life
and death in that horrible lifeboat ; pitching up and down in
the waves and darkness ; expecting death for all of us at any
moment. Never suspecting that actually he was already dead.
You saw something of him on the *Lerida*, Gili. What do you
think of it ? "

" I know nothing of it ! " cried Gili vehemently, her eyes
flashing towards Daisy Belle. " Nothing at all. Oh, I talked to
him a little on the ship. I never saw him before. Never once.
But he "—she shrugged—" he was a man. He talked ; I
listened. He was nothing to me—nothing." She paused again,
appeared to consider her words, and then turned to Mickey,
linking her arm through his, and looking up confidingly and
appealingly into his face. " You see, don't you, André ? It

was—well, call it a tiny bit of a flirtation ; that's all. He was nothing to me. You understand ? "

It was, thought Marcia, an instinctive gesture on Gili's part to enlist Mickey's sympathy and aid. Probably in the world she had known she had never been able to put her faith in women's friendship. It was men who ruled everything, and men could be cajoled, men could be enlisted on her side, men could protect her. She leaned one cheek towards Mickey's shoulder and moved it softly against him like a cat rubbing its head, purring and begging for something.

Well, that wasn't fair. Naturally she didn't like Gili's approach to Mickey ; naturally she didn't like that arm linked through Mickey's, that golden head brushing his shoulder so softly, so gently. And it was silly, because Gili performed the little gesture as instinctively as she ate.

All the same, Marcia wished Mickey would move away from Gili, decisively. Which was silly too ; it meant nothing to him. Besides, Mickey was an attractive man ; certainly Marcia did not intend to go through life having twinges of something very like jealousy every time another woman so much as looked at him. Mickey said : " Did he tell you anything about himself, Gili ? "

" Nothing at all," she cried again. " Nothing. I tried to remember. I tried to tell the Captain. But there really wasn't anything. He "—a ghost of a complacent smile came into Gili's face—" he admired me, you know. He talked—oh, nonsense, mostly. But then, really, I only walked the deck a bit with him, leaned over the railing. Half the time I didn't listen at all. He was nothing to me. And now . . ." Suddenly the complacency of a woman admired left her face and her voice. She gave a shrug that this time was more like a shiver and said in a low voice : " I wish I'd never seen him. It's horrible. Death and murder and . . . I don't like dead men," said Gili.

There was a small, queer silence, with only the rush of the ship through the water and the murmur of the radio in the distance. Then Daisy Belle said dryly : " I don't think any one does, Gili. Especially if they've been murdered."

And Mickey said suddenly : " I'm going to talk to the Captain again."

" I'll go inside, too." Gili hunched up her shoulders. " I'm cold. The sea frightens me. I was sure last night that we'd all be drowned. I'm going inside, where it's warm and lighted." She turned with Mickey, still clinging to his arm. Mickey said : " See you here when I've finished, Marcia."

They vanished into the lit passageway behind them. And after a moment Daisy Belle said, dryly again : " A man's woman."

" She can't help it."

Daisy Belle smoked for a moment, considering. " No. Actually she can't. She was born that way. And I suppose she's had to live that way. By the favours of a man's world. But," said Daisy Belle, " I think she'll manage. And there was more to that little affair with Castiogne than she pretends ! " She laughed shortly, smoked, and added : " Not that I think she murdered him. It's merely instinct for her to cling to some man. The way she's "—she blew out smoke again, slowly, narrowing her eyes—" the way she's clinging to André. But André, if I may say so, is eminently clingable."

Marcia laughed. Suddenly, Daisy Belle's crispness and directness, the very sound of her flat dry voice seemed to dispel an annoying little cloud. How much did Daisy Belle know about her and about Mickey ? How much had those sophisticated, knowledgeable eyes seen and stored away ? She said, on an impulse : " You've never asked a question, Daisy Belle."

The older woman glanced at her rather sharply. " About you and André ? Why should I ? "

" Well, but—there we were, dumped down at that grisly little hotel in Lisbon. Travelling together . . ."

Daisy Belle laughed shortly. " My dear child, I've seen something of the world. You are obviously what you are—a decentish American girl who's been having rather a rough time of it somehow. André is obviously what he is, too—a man who has had his own share of "—Daisy Belle paused and caught her breath and said—" of war and horror. Well, then ; there you are, both obviously and comprehensively anxious to get away from Europe ; to get home ; to straighten out your lives ; to resume the kind of life that you and thousands of other men and women ought to have had. There you are— and I like you. What else is there to know ? Don't be a fool.

I wasn't born yesterday. And if it comes to that, what do you know of me and Luther ? "

" Everybody knows about you ! "

Daisy Belle's fine profile looked a little grim suddenly against the night. " What do they know ? " she said after a moment.

" Why, who you are, all that. You are sort of fabulous, you know."

Again Daisy Belle did not speak for a moment. Then she said : " You mean—it is rumoured that Luther and Daisy Belle Cates, well-known members of the so-called international set, are about to buy a house, or sell a house, or back a horse, or get a divorce, or—or any damned bit of nonsense anybody can think up ? That sort of thing ? "

" Well, yes. Only it doesn't seem to fit now that I've known you."

Daisy Belle laughed shortly. " You can't imagine me being one of the ten best-dressed women, can you ? Well, as a matter of fact, I wasn't. I only had big dressmaker's bills. It was all a question of money ; Luther had so much, and so had I. You don't choose your way of living, Marcia ; it chooses you. Not that any of that matters now. The point is, how did we get here ? At this moment," said Daisy Belle, her eyes narrow and thoughtful, as if she saw a picture somewhere in the blackness beyond that rosy area of light surrounding them, " at this special instant in history. Well, we were in Paris when the Germans came. We went to the Riviera. After awhile the Germans came there, too. They were everywhere. . . ." Her elegant, straight shoulders made a little movement of distaste. " Luther was very ill for a long time. We stayed with a—a friend ; in a château in the hills back of Nice. Eventually the war was over and we decided to go to Buenos Aires. So here we are."

She stopped. It struck Marcia that there was something tentative in her deliberate pause, something expectant.

Marcia said : " It will be good to be at home."

" Will it ? " said Daisy Belle. " Will it ? I'm sure I hope so. Well . . ." She had smoked the cigarette down to the last small end of it ; she tossed it abruptly into the sea. " I'm going to find Luther. I do think that this Castiogne person took a very inconvenient time to get himself murdered. Of course Gili could have done it, but I don't think she did. For one thing she was too scared. But one of the seamen will eventually confess and that will be the end of that." She patted Marcia's shoulder once, hard, and walked briskly away.

Marcia started to follow her, remembered that Mickey would expect to find her somewhere on deck, and, after waiting a few moments, leaning against the railing, she turned and strolled along the well-lit white lane of the deck, forward. Watching, as she strolled, the curling white tops of the waves, and the red and gold glitter of the reflected lights from the ship, listening to the murmur and rush of the ship ploughing her sturdy way through the water, and the lulling sound of the sea, the feeling of security, of being on an American ship, which was the same as being on American soil, seemed to give her a feeling of recovery of herself. As if the girl she had been, the Marcia Colfax who had set gaily forth on the *Normandie* so long ago, had disappeared, gone away, been asleep, somewhere; as if another girl had taken her place, a woman rather, who had had to summon the strength to combat terror, and hopelessness and sorrow and cold and sometimes hunger. And now that woman had gone again, and Marcia Colfax herself had returned. It was, indeed, as if the night just past had been a climax, a final curtain to a play in which she had played a hard and exhausting rôle.

But now it was done, the curtain down for ever.

She reached the bow and could look down on the fo'c'sle, its capstans and ventilators looming ghostly in the light with sharp black shadows. The deck, roped off in sections in the daytime to provide specified deck spaces for patients and nurses and doctors and ship's personnel, was now clear, so she could walk entirely around the ship. She rounded the bow and emerged on the port side, and another long strip of clean white deck, brightly lighted, stretched ahead of her. About midway along it she paused to lean against the railing and watch the red and gold glitter of light reflected from the shiny black waves. The air was fresh and cool on her face; she pulled her coat around her throat. Even the coat, thick and comfortable and warm, was like the blessing of her own land. By the very act of dressing in the nurse's uniform and chucking away the shabby, worn clothes she had had on the Portuguese boat, she had stepped back into her own identity, back to the Marcia Colfax who was really herself.

That, of course, was fanciful; and she wouldn't think of things that were now in the past.

She wouldn't, in fact, think of the previous night.

But she did, of course. The furiously pitching lifeboat, the cold, the despair, and a man who had been murdered in that tiny boat, while all of them were facing a death that had seemed certain.

But Daisy Belle and Mickey must have been right in believing that one of the seamen had done it—crazed, as Mickey said, by fear, or holding so deep a grudge that it superseded and held sway above the fear of death itself. A deep grudge, indeed, thought Marcia with a kind of horror. Yet she had seen human emotions on a strange and horrible rampage. She knew, every one knew now, that such things could happen.

Daisy Belle, with her cool knowledge of the world, was right. Mickey was right. One of the seamen would confess.

The wind was lessening but the sea was definitely heavier.

On the bridge, Captain Svendsen in a heavy coat, with his cap pulled down and shading those shrewd, deep-set eyes, peered into the darkness for awhile, and then went in to study the barometer and the weather reports. Unless he was greatly mistaken, the wind would soon drop off altogether and they would run into fog, and Captain Svendsen hated fog. He never left the bridge in a storm or in fog; he had food sent to him. If it was a bad storm or a long stretch of fog, he lived mainly on coffee and cigarettes, while his ruddy face took on a greyish tinge and large grey pockets came around his eyes. He sighed now, wearily; fog it would be, no question of it. And hundreds of lives in his care.

And this complication of a murdered third officer of a tiny Portuguese cargo boat was an added care. He could put all the people from the lifeboat under guard, of course; one of them must have murdered the fellow. But there was, of course, that annoying question of time and opportunity and rigor mortis. None of the *Magnolia's* staff or personnel could have done it; yet in sheer justice he must have another talk with the medical commanding officer.

He wished momentarily that he had not seen the rockets of distress and the lifeboat; and then, because he was a decent and honest man, and, besides, had the etiquette of the sea engraved not only on his heart but in his bones, he hurriedly retracted that thought. He'd have to do the best he could, and just at the moment the fog was the main thing, and the sick and wounded soldiers he must get home as fast, as comfortably, as safely as it could humanly be done. Alfred Castiogne would have to wait.

Otherwise everything about the ship was in its usual orderly groove. The engine-rooms were lighted and busy, the sick wards settling down for the night. The radio had been turned off and lights at the various portholes were dimmed as the nurses went about, seeing that their rows of patients were comfortable, checking the orders given by the doctors for each ward, reading the charts, following out every detail of the careful and unrelaxing routine. The ship had grown very quiet.

Marcia, however, still leaning against the railing, was so engrossed in her own thoughts that she did not hear the rapid footsteps of a man coming along the deck aft until he had almost reached her. Then she whirled, thinking it was Mickey.

It was not Mickey; it was, instead, Colonel Morgan. He wore a long Army overcoat and a cap pulled low over his face, so she did not recognise him until he stopped for a second under a light near the companionway. Then he seemed to recognise her and came on towards her. " Miss Colfax ? I thought that was you."

He had been walking rapidly; his voice, indeed, seemed breathless and uneven. He paused beside her at the railing, and fumbled in a pocket with his uninjured hand and drew out a package of cigarettes.

" I think I'll have another smoke before turning in," he said more evenly. " Will you join me ? I'd like to talk to you for a moment if you don't mind."

V

HE WAS wearing a uniform with Air Corps insignia. His coat was flung loosely around his shoulders. His face was shaded somewhat by his cap, but she caught the brief smile he gave her as he held out cigarettes.

"As a matter of fact"—he shifted the cigarettes, opened a lighter expertly with his left hand, and held the flame for her cigarette—" as a matter of fact, I'm not supposed to be here. I'm a patient, you know. And at this hour every patient is tucked away and accounted for. But they give me a little extra leeway because I drew a two-bunk cabin and the other bunk is empty. Or rather, my eagles drew it; the rank, not the man. Besides, the ship is not as heavily loaded this trip as she has been up to now. And then I'm what is called ambulatory. That is, I can walk around and don't require a nurse's care. One of the doctors sees me every day." He slid the lighter into his pocket; his coat swung like a cape over his broad shoulders. He looked down at her, and then leaned against the railing again and said : - " Looks as if we're running into fog after the storm. A good thing it wasn't last night. Your rockets might never have been seen."

It was curious how familiar he seemed to her, yet she was sure she had not known him. It was rather as if she had always known that she would know him sometime. And that, of course, was absurd. Nevertheless, she found herself leaning against the railing, too, companionably holding the cigarette he had lighted for her in her hand. He added quickly, as if he regretted introducing a topic which must inevitably hold horror for her; "But that's luckily in the past. I assumed from what Captain Svendsen said that you lived in Paris for some time."

Had Captain Svendsen set him to question her, spy out any secrets she had? If so, he'd find nothing. She said : " Yes, that's true. I was there when the war began."

He smoked for a long moment, staring out towards the black sea and sky, somewhere in the dark distance where they met. Finally, he said ; " I was in Paris then. But, of course, as Captain Svendsen said, it's a big city ! There were several million other people in Paris that fall, too. Still, the little American colony was pretty close. You often knew about other people from home. Especially . . ." He put his cigarette to his lips and the glow lightened his face " . . . especially after the war actually began. Who were some of the people you knew best—Americans, I mean ? "

" Why, I . . ." She hesitated ; yet probably it was actually quite in order, and quite American ; the old business of finding mutual friends. In any case it didn't matter. She replied literally : " Not many, really. The war began so soon and most of the Americans went home as soon as possible. The friends with whom I was travelling went home almost at once. Of course there were some other people . . ." Smoking slowly, she dredged names and faces out of her memory, casual acquaintances all of them, but all forgotten in the intervening time. He listened to each name rather intently, so again the thought crossed her mind that Captain Svendsen might have asked him to question her with a view to proving her own identity.

If so, however, he was not doing it very expertly or very objectively, really. It was more as if he had some obscure yet personal motive of his own.

Yet that was not likely ; it was, in fact, extremely unlikely. She dismissed it abruptly. And when she'd finished the little unimportant roll call he said merely : " The good old business of it's a small world doesn't seem to fit in in this case, does it ? Of course I recognised the Cates name. Any school child would know that ! " He laughed shortly and put his cigarette to his lips. " André Messac is not a common name."

Mickey must have returned to the deck by now. She glanced over Josh Morgan's shoulder, but the deck was empty and white. She replied : " It is not an uncommon name."

" No ? Well "—he smoked for a moment and added: " Was he around Paris that first winter ? "

" Yes. But then the Germans came."

He seemed to wait for a moment, as if for her to add to that. When she didn't, he said finally : " It's queer, really, to accept the fact that the war in Europe is over. I can't, yet. I know it with my own mind, but I feel . . ." Again he paused, looking out into the darkness beyond the rim of light close to the ship, and then said, in a different, harder voice : " I feel as if there are still things to do."

She glanced at him ; his mouth looked stern and hard ; the one hand that lay on the railing had doubled up suddenly into a fist. " I don't know what you mean. The war in Europe *is* over."

" Yes, yes, of course. You realise that Captain Svendsen asked me to come to his quarters in order to discover whether or not I knew you."

" Yes—that is, I supposed so. Because of the murder."

Colonel Morgan's shoulders lifted in a quick easy shrug. " He probably hoped to check your account of yourself. I know about the murder—it isn't supposed to be known, of course—but that's due to my eagles too. Later I—well, I got to thinking we *had* met somewhere."

" I don't think so."

" No . . . No, I must be wrong."

It was an odd little interview. Mickey would be waiting. She'd better return to the other side of the deck to the place where he had left her and would expect to find her again. She moved away from the railing, and without a word Colonel Morgan fell into pace beside her. And, smoking, began to chat about the ship. The food . . . " Steak," he said, " and milk that you'd swear was not twenty minutes from a cow. And eggs." The doctors, the nurses. " They've been in combat most of them. Under fire off the invasion beachheads. Taking men direct from battle, loading them, operating all day and all night, all three operating-rooms going, working at top speed. You'd think, to hear any of them talk, that the patients are the only heroes. Fact is, there's not a nurse nor a doctor on this ship who's not, quite simply and honestly, a hero."

He laughed a little as if to cover the depth of feeling in his words, and shrugged his shoulders to adjust his coat. They reached the bow, and the deck seemed to rise to meet them at every step. And as they turned, with the sea air strong in their faces, an unexpected small thing happened. The ship thrust into a wave with a sudden heavy motion. Marcia made an unsteady step, wavered, reached for a bulkhead which was too far to touch, and Colonel Morgan caught her in his free arm. Caught her closely to him and held her for an instant or two there in the darkness, while the ship seemed to hold herself steady, riding the wave. His hard, warm cheek brushed her own; his arm was tight and strong, so he seemed to be, just for that fraction of time, the only safe and unmovable thing in the night. Then he laughed a little again and said, but rather unevenly: "Okay?"

"Quite—thanks." Her own voice was uneven too. She pulled herself away, although his arm held her but lightly then, until she was steady and balanced. He said: "It's always tough going around the bow. Better hang on to my arm."

She slid her arm through his; she felt a little confused, which was silly. Neither of them spoke. It was darker as they rounded the bow, and, as so often in the night at sea, there was the strong sense of being alone and very small in an immensity of darkness. They emerged on to the other side of the deck and Mickey was not there. They reached the door into the main lobby, and Colonel Morgan said rather abruptly: "I'd better get back to my quarters before I'm sent back. Coming in?"

"Not just yet. I'm waiting for André."

Something flickered in his face under the bright floodlights; yet actually there was no definable change in expression. "Well, I'll see you again, I hope. It's swell to talk to an American girl again. Good-night, Miss Colfax." He smiled, touched his cap in a little friendly salute, and disappeared into the lighted passageway of the ship.

She'd wait a few moments more for Mickey and then go down to the cabin.

The ship was quiet and asleep by then. The fog was perceptible now, grey wraiths floated at the edge of the area of light surrounding the ship and reflected a wavering red and gold haze. The *Magnolia* ploughed sturdily ahead through the fog and the heavy waves, carrying her load of men, intent upon her errand of mercy.

Still Mickey did not come.

Gradually the chill night air and the fog crept through the heavy coat Marcia was wearing. She turned her back to the railing, watching the lighted doorway for Mickey. Thinking once how strange it was to find herself there, on that lighted ship, so full and packed and safe inside, its decks so white and empty, a floating, rosily lighted little hospital going its steady way through the sea and the night.

What a long path had led her to that particular point in time and to that particular place!

How had Josh Morgan happened to reach that same place and that same point in time? Obviously he'd been in active service; probably wounded, which accounted for his presence there and for the right arm in a sling. He did rather well, however, with his left arm!

Not that it mattered; she thought of the moment on the moving, slippery deck when he'd caught her, with, again, an absurd and childish feeling of confusion. Not that that mattered either! She moved away from the railing. She'd give Mickey three more minutes, then she'd go down to the cabin. She walked slowly along, this time aft.

She passed another, smaller doorway, and, as a matter of fact out of the bright lane of lights. She strolled into the thick bank of shadow below a rank of lifeboats.

It was unexpectedly dark just there; her eyes were adjusted to lights. But she saw then, a deeper shadow huddled against the bulkhead near her and stopped abruptly.

The outline became clearer. It was a man sagging down upon the deck. His head was bare, his hand outflung limply. She was on her knees beside him, and it was Mickey.

" Mickey, Mickey! . . ."

He didn't answer; his head sagged limply as she moved him. " Mickey! " she cried despairingly. And remembered Alfred Castiogne, who was murdered in the lifeboat the night before with a knife in his back.

But Mickey could not be dead. His heart was beating—unless it was the faint, constant vibration of the ship. She thought there was a faint pulse at his wrist. " Mickey . . ." she whispered again, and thought, I must get help. I must hurry . . . She lowered his head gently to the deck again, turned into the nearest doorway into the ship, and was instantly lost.

Passageways stretched forward and aft across; there were lights everywhere and closed doors everywhere. She turned to the right and hurried along a grey-painted passageway. Which way were the wards? There would be nurses there and corpsmen. She came on a bisecting passage, and turned again and found herself among offices and laboratories. She turned back. She mustn't scream; there were sick patients asleep but she must get help somehow. She hurried back, took another turn and then was completely lost.

A strange ship is as confusing as a strange city. If she had not been in the portion of the ship reserved for storerooms she would have immediately found people: nurses, corpsmen, and doctors on night duty, alert for every sound and every movement. Just there for the moment there was no one.

But nothing could really have hurt Mickey; he had slipped and fallen. He had somehow struck his head against the stairs or against the bulkhead.

That was it. He wasn't dead; he might not even be injured. She was hysterical and terrified because Alfred Castiogne, who had nothing to do with Mickey or with her, had been murdered. No one could have struck Mickey. No one could have crept along that deck on stealthy, furtive feet. No one could have waited in the black, small rim of shadow. Murder had been in the little lifeboat—not here.

She pushed open a door and was on deck, but this time again she was on the port side. The deck stretched forward, white and lighted; aft, around the stern, it lost itself in shadow. She'd go back around the deck, back to the starboard side of the ship and Mickey. It seemed a quicker and more direct way than through the ship. She ran along the lighted strip of deck and entered the heavy, sudden shadow around the stern.

It was so sudden and dark a shadow that she groped for the bulkhead to guide her. Fog creeping closer upon the ship was cold and misty on her face. The width of the ship still divided her from Mickey, and the fog was like a curtain further obscuring the shadowy curve of the deck ahead. Behind was a rosy brightness, reflected all around against the wraiths of fog. Here it was only dark and empty, with the rush of the ship through the dark water below sounding very loud.

And very near there was a curious regularity about the whisper and rush of the waves—like someone breathing heavily.

She stopped.

But murder had been in the little lifeboat! Not here . . .

Then, with indescribable suddenness and finality, the black

water seemed to roar and crash upon her ears, engulfing her, dragging her down across the slippery deck into its own blackness and chaos.

Her fighting, blind hands brushed the middle railing, caught at it, missed, caught hard into space again, and then there was nothing but darkness and fog.

It was, indeed, at about that time that the *Magnolia* actually entered the thick bank of fog lying ahead, and Captain Svendsen took the telephone and gave an order to slow down the engines.

VI

GRADUALLY the throb of the engines emerged from darkness and the rush of water and began to beat against Marcia's ears. Light cut through the darkness, too, and beat upon her eyes. Someone was holding her; she was taking great gulps of air that stung her throat and burned her lungs, and her heart was louder than the engines. The light seemed suddenly so bright upon her eyelids that she couldn't lift them; it was dazzling, dizzying, whirling around. Someone was rubbing her hands inadequately somehow, inexpertly, saying something she could not understand. She opened her eyes and the light was not half as bright as it had seemed.

A man held her and bent over her. He was in uniform; the coat hung like a cape over his shoulders, so it fell around her, too. His cap shaded his eyes, but she knew the face and she knew the voice. Only she couldn't just then say to whom the face and voice belonged or how she knew.

She felt, however, an enormous sense of safety, as if she had been awakened from the chill horror of a nightmare and brought back to the reality of a normal world. It was so extraordinarily comforting, that sense of security, that she closed her eyes again, sinking into it as if it, too, had warm, safe arms. He held her against him and said: " Do you hear me ? Marcia . . ."

A faint question touched her. It seemed odd somehow that his voice should speak to her just like that, call her — Marcia. He said more urgently: " Can you walk ? I'll help you. Try to walk . . ."

The strength of the supporting arm was, too, extraordinarily comforting. Of course she would walk. She was on her feet, leaning against this man she knew so well and yet somehow could not name. Lights were in her face; she opened her eyes again.

The light was diffused, coming from misty halos touched with a strange rosy haze. The deck stretched ahead of them and lost itself in the foggy halos of light. All around the ship fog lay in thick curtains and reflected the radiance of the Red Crosses on her sides and on her smokestack, so it touched everything with a soft glow like firelight. It touched the face of the man beside her, holding her close against him, urging her along that narrow, glistening strip of deck. She looked up at the strongly curved mouth and broad chin. The shadow cast by the visor of his cap fell over his eyes. She said in a husky voice that seemed to hurt: "Colonel Morgan. That's who it is. . . ."

"In this way," he said, and held open a door, and suddenly they had left the deck with its queerly rosy fog and were in a warm, dry, brightly lighted passage. And she remembered the nightmare.

Only it hadn't been a nightmare.

"I caught the railing. I caught the railing and missed, and caught again and someone . . ."

"Don't talk. I'll get a doctor. It's only a little farther . . ." He looked different in these lights, which were undimmed by fog; his face was set and hard and very white around the mouth.

They were at a door which was open; she was still half dazed by the warmth, by the lights, by the nighmare. A man in officer's uniform got up quickly and inquiringly from a desk chair and came towards them. Colonel Morgan said rapidly: "There's been an accident. . . ." And another memory of the nightmare came to her. "*Mickey!* . . ." she cried. "He's hurt! He's on deck! . . ."

She was on a small white couch; the man in uniform was leaning over her. Colonel Morgan had disappeared. Everything glistened around her. It was a dispensary, with a clear, bright light over everything.

"These slippery decks," said the Doctor. "Here, let me look at you. Anything broken?"

She tried to tell him. " He is out there. I tried to get help. Someone was there. . . ."

He was busy at a table across the room ; he came back towards her with a glass of water and something in his hand. " Take this."

" You don't understand. . . ."

" Take this." He held her head up so she could swallow the little pill. He pulled a blanket over her. " Now then, just don't move for a minute. I'll send a nurse in to you. Don't worry. . . ."

Then he, too, had disappeared, closing the door firmly behind him.

But her mind was clearer ; by snatches the whole nightmare was revealed, and it was not a nightmare ; it was a murderous attack upon her.

As it had been upon Mickey.

But why ?

What had they brought from that sinister, harried little lifeboat on to this ship ?

She sat up, and was pushing away the blanket, dizzy still, confused, when the door opened again and a nurse came in to the room.

More time than she had realised must have passed while Marcia groped backwards into the blackness of the nightmare. The nurse knew everything ; someone must have had time to tell her, to explain. She came to Marcia and said quickly : " Everything is all right. Your—your friend slipped on the deck and was hurt, but not seriously. Major Strong—that's the doctor who was here—took him to the other dispensary to dress his wound. He struck his head against the bulkhead, but it is nothing serious. Do you understand ? "

" Someone was there. . . ."

" Major Strong said you were not to talk and not to worry. I'm to stay here with you. Are you warm ? "

" There, by the lifeboats, in the shadow, I heard something move. I felt it. . . ."

" You're not to talk." The young nurse smiled. Her face was young and pretty her eyes were firm. She pulled up the blanket again. " I'm going to sit here by you. Don't talk."

" Who was it ? " whispered Marcia, searching the nurse's face for knowledge. But the nurse shook her head ; her face was unreadable. And suddenly drowsiness and calm seemed to enter the shining room, with the nurse in her crisp uniform and cap, sitting on the foot of the cot within reach of Marcia's hand. She seemed to Marcia everything that was normal and staunch and American. Her very presence denied the nightmare that had reached out of the fog, there on the black curve of the deck.

Murder had been in the lifeboat; not here, thought Marcia drowsily, not here. Her eyes closed heavily against the light.

Actually, of course, she had not yet recovered from the horror and strain of the previous night. Actually, she was still unutterably weary, with nerves strained and taut. She slept suddenly, like a child, secure again in the presence of the nurse and in the things the nurse had said. Mickey really was all right.

Only it hadn't been an accident.

The nurse must have moved quietly to turn off the ceiling light. When Marcia suddenly awoke there was a small, green-shaded desk-light on the table at the opposite side of the room. She was drowsy from the pill the doctor had given her; she had a confused sense of much time having passed. The nurse was beside her saying, quietly: "Miss Colfax— Miss Colfax . . ."

She sat up, blinking. There were other people in the room. Captain Svendsen was removing an oilskin that glistened with moisture; Josh Morgan was there, too, still in uniform; and another man, also in Army uniform—a tall thin man, forty or so, with a thin face and very intelligent, quick, brown eyes, who looked at her sharply and came over to the cot to put his hand on her wrist. He wore a lieutenant colonel's insignia and the medical badges. She had not seen him before, but there was an air of authority about him which was instantly recognisable. He said: "Miss Colfax, I am Colonel Wells. I'm sorry I haven't had a chance to see you before. I've been busy." His fingers were delicate and sure on her wrist. His eyes were extraordinarily perceptive and swift. He said: "Pulse seems to be steady enough."

The nurse said: "She's been sleeping, sir." She glanced down at Marcia. "Colonel Wells is our medical commanding officer, Miss Colfax."

Captain Svendsen, his thick white eyebrows glistening with

fog, sighed and sat down. Josh Morgan leaned against an examining table. Colonel Wells said quietly : " Miss Colfax, Captain Svendsen wishes you to tell us what happened to you." He looked at the Captain. " I think she's able to talk, Captain. She's had a bit of a shock, I imagine, but that's all."

She glanced at Josh Morgan, who was looking at her soberly, his eyes very intent, yet somehow encouraging.

Captain Svendsen ran his hand over his thick yellow hair impatiently. " I've got to get back to the bridge. Now, then, Miss Colfax, what happened ? Colonel Morgan says he found you on the deck, and then found Messac, knocked unconscious. Messac says he slipped and hit his head on the bulk-head. But Colonel Morgan said that you claimed somebody tried to put you overboard. Now, then, what exactly do you mean ? "

She could still feel the movement of a presence in the shadow near her. She could still hear the rushing of the black water in the wake of the ship far below.

Colonel Wells, watching her keenly, said : " Take it easy, Miss Colfax."

Obviously there was scepticism, which was quite natural. So she must keep her voice even, tell them briefly and quietly what had happened.

She tried to do so. She had found André—she remembered to say André—unconscious on deck ; she had gone for help and become confused ; she had come out on the port side of the deck, opposite the way she had entered ; had decided to go back to André ; had hurried along the deck, intending to go around it ; and just as she entered the shadow around the stern had been—her voice faltered there, and she was aware of a tense and strained silence on the part of the others—had been caught and forced towards the railing.

Perhaps the break in her voice, as much as her determined self-control, shook their scepticism. There was a short silence while Captain Svendsen frowned at her. The nurse made herself a very quiet but very alert piece of background, the medical commanding officer studied the toes of his shining brown shoes, and Josh Morgan got out cigarettes. Captain Svendsen shook his head at Josh Morgan's offer of cigarettes, and said heavily : " Do you mean somebody attacked you ? Who was it ? "

"I don't know. I couldn't see anything. It happened so suddenly."

"But that would be a deliberate attempt to murder you."

Put like that, in the slow, hard voice of the Captain, it was not conceivable; it could not have happened. Yet it was not conceivable either that murder had struck in that small, plunging lifeboat, before their eyes which yet did not perceive that quick and furtive presence. She met Captain Svendsen's cold blue eyes without speaking.

He said: "Who on the ship wants to murder you?"

That, too, came up against a wall of incomprehension. Attempted murder implies a deep and frightful intimacy.

"No one," she said. "No one."

The big blond master of the ship seemed to brood for a moment. Colonel Wells continued to study his boots, and Josh Morgan lighted a cigarette with considerable care and deliberation.

Captain Svendsen said: "See here, Miss Colfax, you may not understand the discipline of our ship. I needn't explain to you the details of the routine; but I cannot believe that any of the ship's staff or personnel, or any of our patients, could have tried to murder you."

"Someone was there. . . ."

"If you please, hear me out. This is a hospital ship; details are important to the care of the men we are bringing home. We have been operating in war zones and we are still operating under the discipline required by that fact; we have not relaxed it in a single instance. So, while obviously it is not possible to check on the whereabouts of every person at every minute, yet in this case we can do so at least for a number of people with a fair amount of accuracy. When Major Strong reported this to Colonel Wells and Colonel Wells naturally informed me, I had the deck searched, and I had a quick check made of the ship's personnel and wards. As I say, it is impossible to make a complete check of every person on board a ship. But the fact remains that it is extremely unlikely that any one of the *Magnolia* should attack you. You do understand this?"

"Yes. Yes, but . . ."

"In view of the fact that you had a very painful and exhausting experience in the lifeboat, and also that the man,

Alfred Castiogne, was murdered, don't you think it possible that you are only nervous and frightened? Perhaps you slipped, perhaps you struck something there on deck. I don't doubt your good faith, but I think it possible that your nerves deceived you. Don't you?"

She shook her head, but before she could speak he went on: "You admit that you were frightened when you found Mr. Messac. Don't you think it possible that in the darkness and fog and in your confusion you actually imagined this attack upon you?"

"No," said Marcia. She thought of the black water so near and so loud it seemed already to beat in her ears and choke her throat. "*No!* There was somebody, Captain. It was—horrible."

Again there was a small, tense silence. Then Captain Svendsen turned to Josh Morgan. "You say you didn't see anybody near her when you found her?"

Josh Morgan took a long breath of smoke. "No. Of course, it was very dark there. At least it seemed very dark coming out of the lighted portion of the deck. My eyes didn't adjust themselves to the darkness right away. But I only saw Miss Colfax; or rather, I only saw that somebody was there on the deck. I ran to her and picked her up. I thought she'd slipped and hurt herself. The deck is very slippery with the fog."

"You came from which side of the deck?"

"The port side. I thought I'd have a last cigarette before going to bed."

The medical commanding officer gave him a brief, cool glance. "Of course, you're not supposed to be on deck at this hour, Colonel."

"I know that, Colonel."

For an odd, fleeting instant their punctiliousness seemed too polite and too formal. Then Marcia caught the fractional grin they exchanged. Ranking officers probably conceded certain privileges to each other. Captain Svendsen rubbed his forehead impatiently again. He said: "If anybody had been there, Colonel Morgan, could he have heard you coming along the deck from that direction?"

"I suppose so, sir. Or he could have seen me. I was silhouetted, I imagine, against the lighted portion of the deck. The fog made everything rather hazy."

"But you didn't actually hear or see anybody escape?"

"No, Captain. It's as I said : I only thought somebody had slipped and been hurt. Then I realised it was Miss Colfax and helped her inside. Major Strong took care of her and I went to find Messac. Major Strong joined me and we got Messac to his cabin."

"In all that time did you see anybody else on deck?"

"Nobody."

Captain Svendsen turned back to Marcia, his blue eyes very bright and blue in his broad, weathered face. "If anybody attacked you, Miss Colfax, it seems to me that almost certainly it was one of the people who were in the lifeboat with you. As I say, on a ship it is simply not possible to check on the exact whereabouts at all times of everybody on the ship. Nevertheless, I cannot believe that any of the medical staff, any of the nurses, any of the ship's complement, any patient could be involved in this. The trouble began when we brought the *Lerida* passengers aboard. I am convinced that one of them is responsible for it. You insist someone actually tried to murder you. So which one of the *Lerida* passengers was it?"

The light in the room seemed suddenly unbearable and too green. The cabinets and walls and instruments glittered too brightly. Marcia's thoughts touched them all—Gili, Daisy Belle, Luther Cates, Mickey, two unknown seamen. None of them could conceivably have wished to murder her.

Yet murder had been done in the wildly pitching lifeboat, in the darkness and confusion, during that battle for life. Again she thought, as the Captain obviously thought, that they had brought murder with them, an unseen and dreadful companion upon that ship.

But murder cannot exist alone, as an intangible, untetherable presence ; it must have physical form.

She said slowly ; "None of them could have done it. None of them . . ."

"Castiogne was murdered," said the Captain, watching her.

"But there is no motive for anybody to wish to murder me. There is no one . . ."

"Yet you say it happened."

"Yes, it happened." She felt drained of strength, as if even her thoughts could not function reasonably and clearly. Josh

Morgan put out his cigarette with a sudden gesture. He said:
" By the way, Colonel, I suppose you took a look at Miss
Colfax. If she was struck . . ."

Colonel Wells looked up quickly. " An excellent suggestion," he said, and got up and came to Marcia. " If you don't
mind," he said kindly and tipped her head back, turning her
so the light from the green-shaded lamp fell strongly upon
her. Again she was aware of the tensity of the silence in the
shining little room and of the far-away vibration of engines.
The motion of the ship was slower and yet heavy. Josh Morgan
had taken a quick step or two nearer and was looking too,
carefully, down into her face. Colonel Wells touched her chin
and temples lightly. " Does that hurt ? Did you strike your
head here—here . . ."

She could remember only that swift knowledge of motion
somewhere near her, and then a crash and roar as if of water,
and blackness. " I don't know. I don't know. . . . No, it
doesn't hurt."

His sensitive, professional hands explored deftly, pushing
back her hair, tilting her head again so he could observe her
throat. The nurse's coat that had been loaned her lay across
the end of the cot, its scarlet lining bold and gay. The doctor
pushed the crisp collar of the nurse's uniform back from her
throat and looked for a long moment. Finally he said : " It's
hard to tell. Were you wearing a coat ? "

" Yes."

" Does this hurt—or this . . . ? " Again his deft fingers
moved delicately over her.

" No—no . . ."

" The sedative would have dulled any pain. The coat
would have protected the flesh."

Captain Svendsen said rather gruffly : " Well . . ." Josh
Morgan turned abruptly away. Colonel Wells, a queer,
thoughtful look in his thin face, gently replaced the uniform
and turned to Captain Svendsen. She could not see his face.
He said : " I think Miss Colfax might take another sedative.
Will you see to it, Lieutenant ? " He glanced at the nurse, who
nodded, her face still and unreadable as the wall. " And the
nurse will see her to her cabin. I'll just go along with you to
the bridge, if you don't mind, Captain. I know you're anxious
to get back. . . ."

Josh Morgan said rather suddenly: " I'll turn in, too, I think, sir. Do you mind if I stroll along with Miss Colfax and the Lieutenant ? " Captain Svendsen got heavily to his feet and picked up his oilskins. " We'll have some coffee sent up," he said. " I've got to stay on the bridge the rest of the night. I've not run into a fog like this since the summer of 1936. After you, Colonel. . . ."

But the Colonel carefully waited for the Captain to precede him out of the dispensary. This was his department, his courteous and formal manner seemed to say. The ship's administration was the Captain's. The young nurse said pleasantly : " Here's another pill, Miss Colfax. You might take it now. I'll get some water."

Colonel Wells glanced back from the doorway. " Good night, Miss Colfax. Try to sleep. If you need anything, Lieutenant Hale will be glad to help you."

He disappeared behind the Captain. The nurse—Lieutenant Hale—turned on a tap across the room. Josh Morgan waited without speaking as the nurse came back, and held the glass and another small white pill towards Marcia. She took both automatically.

" Thank you." She handed the glass back to the nurse. There were no mirrors in the room. She said to Josh Morgan : " There are marks on my throat."

Josh Morgan glanced at the nurse, who quickly said : " Now, now, Miss Colfax, don't try to talk. We want you to get some rest."

Marcia got up unsteadily, as the ship rolled, so Josh, who was nearest, put out his good arm to support her. She said, looking up into his face : " Tell me . . ."

Lieutenant Hale, her uniform rustling crisply, bent to pick up the red-lined coat, and went to the door and turned the latch on the lock. Josh Morgan said : " What do you know about that affair last night ? "

" That . . ."

" The murder of Alfred Castiogne."

" I know nothing of it. . . ."

" You see, if you do know something, something that might be evidence against the murderer, somebody might try pretty damned hard to push you into the sea."

Again the deep vibration of engines, chugging slowly along

through the fog and heavy, hidden seas, seemed to fill the small room. Lieutenant Hale, her face disapproving yet intent, tried the latch to be sure the lock was turned. Josh Morgan was so close that she could see the bright dark pupils of his eyes, the few scattered grey hairs in the vigorous black over his temples. He said slowly : " You could have hurt yourself, accidentally, so as to make a red mark there. Or hands could have . . ."

Lieutenant Hale said rather sharply : " I beg your pardon, Colonel. My orders are to see Miss Colfax to her cabin."

" You are quite right, I'm sure, Lieutenant. We'll go at once. Would you be kind enough to pick up my cap ? I'll help Miss Colfax."

His brown cap with its leather strap lay on the examining table. The nurse took it up, waited for them to go into the hall, straightened the blanket over the cot, turned out the light and followed them, closing the door and trying to be sure she had locked it.

All that took a few seconds. They were perhaps ten paces ahead of her along the narrow, lighted passageway when she emerged. Josh Morgan, holding Marcia steadily with his left arm, said in a low voice, which the nurse could not possibly have heard : " There's a queer contagion about murder. Perhaps it is terror of being discovered ; perhaps it's—something else. The man last night was murdered. You were in the lifeboat when he was killed. Captain Svendsen and Colonel Wells are very able men. They'll do things their own way. We'll know about it *after* they've acted. That's the Army and that's sea discipline. But if somebody tried to kill you to-night . . ." He stopped, and they could hear the click of the latch behind them as the nurse tried it. Her footsteps came along behind them. Josh Morgan said : " Don't take any chances. If anybody tried to kill you to-night he'll try again."

Nothing that had happened since the storm began seemed real ; perhaps nothing that had happened since the war began seemed real. Yet all of it had happened. If the murderous attack upon her in the darkness and fog was connected with the tiny, sinister lifeboat from the *Lerida* and its occupants, then what about Mickey ?

She knew that, with her, it was not an accident ; someone

had actually been there. Josh Morgan had come barely in time to save her, as perhaps she had approached barely in time to save Mickey. For it could not have been an accident with Mickey either. The ugly resemblance was too close—darkness, fog, a slippery deck. A sudden murderous attack, so sudden and so stealthy that for Mickey there was not even the split second of warning that she had had.

She said: " I have to see André. Now . . ."

The nurse was coming nearer. All around them lay the hushed ship; they neared a bisecting passage. Josh said in a low tone; " Messac was given a stateroom on the next deck above and forward, on the port side—three doors this side of the officers' lounge."

VII

He left them both at the door of the cabin. Marcia herself would not have been able to find it; the narrow grey passage looked to Marcia exactly like every other. The nurse, however, knew the ship probably as she knew the palm of her hand. She led them along intersecting passages, through doors, across an entrance to a ward, into another passage and another, stopped before one of the closed doors that lined it, and opened the door briskly. The interior of the cabin was dark.

Josh Morgan said briefly: " Sleep well," took his cap from the nurse and went away.

The nurse put the coat over Marcia's arm. " Are you sure you're all right, Miss Colfax? Or shall I stay? "

" No, no. Thank you. You've been very good. I'm keeping you from other things."

" I'm on night watch. So I'll go along and get my supper before I go back to my ward. Two other nurses are on duty there and two corpsmen. We take turns in going down for supper. If you're sure there's nothing I can do for you . . ."

" No, thank you."

The nurse smiled briefly, turned away, and Marcia entered the cabin.

She closed the door. She'd wait until the nurse was out of sight and then find her way to Mickey's cabin.

Where were the lights? The other nurse, Lieutenant Stoddard, had said that Gili and Daisy Belle Cates shared the cabin with her. It occurred to her that they must be already in their bunks in the tiny room and already asleep, for neither of them spoke to her.

It would be better simply to wait for a few minutes until she was quite sure the nurse had gone, and then slip out again without turning on the light and rousing Gili or Daisy Belle or both. She wondered what time it was. Something about the ship, the hushed atmosphere, the quiet empty stretches of corridors and closed door, had given her a sense of lateness. The nurse had spoken of supper. That would be, she supposed, about midnight, as in a hospital.

There was no sound except the distant throb of engines and the rush of water beyond some open port. She waited, her hand on the round knob of the door, listening, because in the darkness one does listen, and counting. In two minutes, when she had counted twice sixty seconds, it would be safe to leave the cabin without being observed by the nurse.

She had reached thirty when an odd thing happened. She had heard no sound except the mingled sounds of a ship at night.

Certainly she heard no footsteps in the corridor outside, but the handle of the door turned under her fingers.

It turned very quietly and very steadily. Unconsciously her own hand tightened, resisting that pressure. For an instant there was a queer small combat, silent and quiet, one pressure against the other. Then, as suddenly and as silently as it had begun, that stealthy, steady pressure stopped.

She knew then the hand outside relinquished its hold, for the handle gave to her own. Her heart was pounding so heavily that she could hear nothing else.

If anybody tried to kill you to-night, he'll try again. Josh Morgan had said that only a few minutes ago.

But she was safe here, inside the ship with all its lights, with all the nurses and corpsmen and doctors awake and going about their tasks. With Daisy Bell and Gili in the cabin, so she could call them.

Were they in the cabin?

Her fingers still gripped the handle of the door as if frozen. She scrabbled along the wall with her other hand and touched

a switch, and the cabin sprang into light and nobody was
there.

The bunks were made up, flat and neat. Night clothes
borrowed from the wards, men's pyjamas and men's crimson
bathrobes, lay across each bunk above the neatly folded
blankets.

Where was Gili, then ? Where was Daisy Belle Cates ?
And who had turned that handle so silently and so stealthily,
and then, aware of her own resisting hand, had stopped ?

If it had been Gili or Daisy Belle she'd have insisted,
knocked, called out. Either of the other two women had a
right to enter the cabin openly.

She must look into the corridor quickly. Already seconds
had passed.

Again something Josh Morgan had said caught at her for
an instant. " There's a queer contagion about murder ; perhaps it's terror of being discovered, perhaps something else."

But there was nothing she knew ; nothing that could make
her a danger or a threat to any one. Yet she had not imagined
the attack upon her in the shadow on deck. And she had
not imagined that slow, furtive pressure on the handle of the
door. Suppose someone knew that Gili and Daisy Belle were
not there ; suppose someone knew that she was alone in that
tiny empty cabin.

She realised that thoughts like that alone were dangerous.
You could think anything—yes, and fear anything, if you let
yourself be conquered by such thoughts and such fears. She
took a long breath and opened the door.

The passage was lighted and narrow and perfectly empty.
No one moved anywhere along it ; no one stepped furtively
out of sight into some doorway ; there was no sly flicker of
motion anywhere.

There were doors all along the passage. She had an impression, although she was not then sure, that the cabin was in
a section of the ship reserved for women patients, military
or Red Cross workers, and that it adjoined or was in the same
section with the nurses' quarters. In any event the doors were
closed and no one was there.

She would go to Mickey.

She dropped the coat on a chair, and then, leaving the
lights on, closed the door quietly behind her and started

along the passage to the right in the direction of the main, square corridor and the nearest stairs. Up on deck, Josh Morgan had said, on the port side, the third door this side the officers' lounge.

The ship seemed very large after the tiny Portuguese ship, and again, very bewildering with its multiplicity of doors and passages. Any ship is at first confusing; but while passenger ships conform to a certain pattern, a hospital ship has its own pattern, and to Marcia that pattern was new and strange. She knew that she was now in the forward portion of the ship, and that, when she had entered the ship to find help for Mickey, she had been aft. There were officers here, too, but this forward passage seemed to be a lively and frequented portion of the ship. She came out into the lobby, and there were bulletin boards, a divan, a door opening upon a lounge, heavy doors at each side leading to the deck. The offices here were not quite deserted, even at night. From somewhere along a lighted corridor branching likewise from the main corridor, but back along the port side, came the subdued sound of some machine, a typewriter or a teletype, working away in the night.

It was a heartening small sound, indicating the presence of other people.

The *Magnolia* appeared to be a converted passenger liner. A closed wide desk opposite Marcia was like the desk of the purser; the cabins were exact duplicates of small staterooms; probably most of them had been torn out to make wards; the large saloons and lounges would have been easily adaptable as wards. It was now literally a floating hospital.

All hospitals at night have a certain atmosphere, a hush and stillness, indefinable yet almost tangible. It touched her now, so she thought, climbing the stairs, what feet have climbed these stairs, what hands have slid over this railing, what hopes and fears and tangled human destinies have lived for the space of a voyage within these solid bulkheads? Only a hospital ship was different in that the patients were soldiers, men who had gone to war in order to give people like her and Mickey a chance to live in peace and freedom.

She reached the top of the stairs. The port side, Josh Morgan had said, and forward.

She turned, moving very quietly as one does in a hospital at night. There was a faint, clean hospital smell of antiseptics and medicine and soap. Through a distant opening she caught another glimpse of a night-lighted ward. Two corpsmen in white were standing in the light of a doorway near at hand drinking coffee. Beyond them a nurse put a capped head from a ward office and glanced at her questioningly. She had on a field jacket, and the chart the small envelope contained in her hand. Marcia turned again, crossed to the left, found a narrow, lighted passage there, and went along it.

There were again rows of closed doors, and at the very end of the passage an open doorway and a lighted room beyond showing red lounge chairs and a table stacked with magazines. This, then, must be the officers' lounge, so Mickey's cabin was very near. She walked on lightly, but Josh Morgan apparently heard her footsteps. He appeared in the doorway of the officers' lounge, put down a cigarette quickly and came towards her. He'd changed to pyjamas and the crimson bathrobe in which she had first seen him; one sleeve of the bathrobe hung empty. " I was waiting for you," he said. " Messac's room is here." He knocked at one of the narrow grey doors.

There was a feeling of sudden stillness in the cabin. He knocked again, more firmly. There was the sound of quick movement and Mickey opened the door. He was still in the uniform that had been loaned him; there was a white gauze dressing across his temple.

" Marcia ! " He gave a surprised glance at Josh Morgan and said : " Come in . . . " and stood aside so they could enter. Gili was sitting on the bunk opposite, perfectly composed, her long, beautiful legs crossed, her slanting green eyes bright and curious.

" I expect you don't remember me," said Josh Morgan to Mickey. " You were in a pretty dazed condition. The doctor and I helped you to the dispensary."

" Oh, of course, Colonel Morgan. The doctor told me." Mickey closed the door. " Gili—Miss Duvrey, Colonel Morgan."

Gili's eyes were suddenly very luminous and warm. She tossed back a lock of her long golden hair and smiled slowly and leaned forward to put her hand in Colonel Morgan's. He said rather briskly : " How do you do," and let go her hand. "Did Major Strong fix you up, Messac ? " he inquired of Mickey. "He was just starting to work on you when I left."

Mickey's scarred fingers touched the dressing on his face. "Oh, yes, I'm okay. I've only got a thumping headache. Stupid of me ! I was looking for you, Marcia. I got back to the deck where I'd left you. The Captain was busy and I couldn't bother him just then, so I wasn't gone very long, really. You weren't there and . . . Do sit down. Here's a chair."

"There's room here. Sit by me, Colonel Morgan," said Gili. She put her large white hand invitingly on the bunk beside her.

"Thanks," Josh Morgan sat down, leaning forward, below the upper bunk. Marcia took the chair Mickey had pulled out. She said : " I had walked around to the port side. I met Colonel Morgan and talked awhile. Then I came back and you weren't there. After a few minutes I walked aft and found you."

" I don't see how I could give myself such a knockout blow. I certainly wasn't tight," said Mickey with a shrug. "It's as if somebody hit me."

The ceiling light cast a white illumination directly down upon them, so every face and every detail was very clear and sharp. Gili seemed to have moved imperceptibly nearer Josh Morgan. Her shoulder almost touched his. She was sitting crouched forward a little, too, to miss the upper bunk, but relaxed, and graceful with her long legs stretched out, and one hand spread out on the bunk backward so as to support her. She had loosened her hair from its heavy knot, and it fell now over her shoulders, bright gold at the ends and darker along the part. Her eyes were not made up as usual, but were brilliant and green and her mouth crimson. The severe neatness of the nurse's uniform that she was wearing seemed foreign to her, as if she were dressed for a masquerade. She was at ease, yet, as always with Gili, there was a suggestion of latent power, of muscles able to spring at an instant's notice, as with a slumberous cat. She was watching now and listening—and shifted just then, gracefully and deliberately and a little nearer Josh Morgan.

The officer under that strong, downward light looked rather

white and ill. His mouth was tight, with a curious look of
tension, and his grey-blue eyes rather narrow and dark. He
shifted his own position, only perceptibly, appearing to move
in order to give his arm, supported by its sling, more comfort.
The move was, however, a little away from Gili. Marcia
thought quite sharply and unexpectedly, sometime I'm going
to slap Gili—which was an absurd thing to think ; a fleeting,
childish bit of irritation, altogether silly. Josh Morgan eased
his arm again, his shoulders looking very wide and solid under
that crimson bathrobe, his hair very black, and curling
upwards a little over his ears. He said to Mickey : " *Did*
anybody hit you ? "

Mickey's face, too, was too brightly illumined. It showed
the sharp lines those years had brought, the hollows around
his grey eyes. He went to sit on the edge of the opposite bunk
and said, slowly : " I don't know. I was walking along the
deck . . . I just suddenly knew I was falling, that I'd hit
my head, that everything was black and confused and—that's
all."

" Didn't you see anybody ? "

Mickey shook his head. " I tell you there was nothing." He
brooded for a moment and said : " I fainted once or twice.
Maybe more. I mean while I was in prison." His words and
voice were matter-of-fact and even. His hands, as if they had
a secret, frightened life of their own, went out of sight,
behind him, holding to the mattress. " Everybody did, from
various reasons. That's in the past. But that's the way it
seemed to me there on deck to-night. I simply blacked out.
But it was with a kind of crash. I suppose that's when I hit
my head against the bulkhead. That is, understand me, I'm
not sick. I'm perfectly well. But it was like that."

Gili said : " Don't, André. Don't think of those horrible
things. They are gone." Her voice was warm and full of life
and strength, and yet was casual, as if she had bestowed a pat
to a wounded dog.

Marcia linked her own hands on her knee and said steadily :
" André, there was someone on the deck."

Josh Morgan cut in : " Miss Colfax had a rather bad
experience, Messac. She came inside to get help and then
decided to return to you, and on her way around the deck
she either crashed into something there in the darkness or

there was someone on deck who seems to have tried to—well, to push her overboard."

Gili sat up and gave a queer, small scream and clapped her hand over her mouth. Mickey jumped up and stared down at Marcia. " What happened ? Who was it ? Marcia, tell me . . ." He put his hand hard on her shoulder. His face was white and drawn.

Josh Morgan said quickly : " Oh, she's all right. The doctor looked her over. But it was rather a shock. The point is, Messac, if somebody tried to kill her, it was somebody from the lifeboat. At least . . ." He paused while Mickey's white face blazed down at her and his hand dug into her shoulder, and Gili sat there with her hand tight over her mouth and her eyes wide and dark as a cat's shining over it. Then Josh Morgan said : " At least nobody else on the ship could have done it. Nobody else on the ship would have a motive. Or so the Captain says."

Gili slid out of the bunk in one, long, sinuous movement. Her face was glistening queerly, and so white that it had a greenish tinge around the shadows of mouth and nose. Her eyes were blank and bright. She cried jerkily : " It is the murder. None of us is safe ! None of . . . He was killed. Alfred. He was big and strong, and—then he was killed. Just like that. In a moment—under our eyes, he was killed. We are not safe. We . . ." Her eyes darted around and around the cabin, her head moved to and fro like a panther's seeking a way out of its cage. A horrible kind of claustrophobia seemed to possess her. She cried, still gasping and hoarse : " I know who killed him. I know why . . ."

Josh Morgan rose suddenly, and André said : " Gili, what are you saying ? What do you know ? "

"What do I . . . ? " Gilli's searching, bright eyes reached him and stopped, and she caught her full lower lip in strong white teeth and held it so hard there was a tiny smudge of blood suddenly upon it. Josh Morgan said : " Go on. Who killed him ? "

Gili, still staring, let go her lip slowly. " That—that American woman did it. The Cates woman. She—she was afraid of him. She was a friend of the Nazis. Alfred knew it. She's rich. He'd have got money from her. She killed him."

VIII

THE LITTLE CABIN was perfectly silent, so again the ship made itself manifest and throbbed and pulsed around them. Humans might talk, might move and speak of murder, but the *Magnolia* had to go sturdily on her way, nosing along through the fog, meeting the heavy, rolling sea.

Josh Morgan stirred suddenly. "You'd better explain that, Miss Duvrey. What do you mean?"

Gili whirled around towards him. She shot one bright, cornered look at Marcia. Her strong hands doubled up as if they were claws, as if she might have to defend herself. She tightened her full lips stubbornly, shot another glance at Josh Morgan, and said: "I won't talk. I didn't mean to talk. You can see for yourself it is dangerous. Murder . . ."

Josh Morgan said coolly: "Oh, come now, Miss Duvrey. You'll have to explain all this to the Captain. You may as well tell us."

This time those lambent eyes flashed green and frightened fire. "Do you mean you'll tell him?"

Josh Morgan shrugged. "You just can't make statements like that and let it go. You'll have to take it back or explain what you mean. Why did you say that the Cates' were friends of the Nazis? How do you know?"

"Because"—she eyed him sulkily now—"because they were. And he knew it. Alfred Castiogne."

"How did he know?"

Mickey's hand released Marcia's shoulders. He gave her a kind of weary sigh and went back to sit on the edge of the bunk. "Don't talk nonsense, Gili," he said. "Don't invent. Don't embroider."

Gili spoke English with such ease and fluency that you felt she must have lived in continental hotels all her life. Yet once in a while Marcia had already discovered some colloquialism, some idiom or metaphor baffled her. She turned a puzzled look towards Mickey. "Embroider?"

"Tell the truth," said Josh Morgan.

Her green, lustrous eyes slid towards him. "Oh, well, but naturally, I'll tell you exactly how I know." She stopped, bit

her lip again, but this time in a perplexed way, as if arranging
certain events in her own mind and choosing her words. Then
she shot another veiled glance at Josh Morgan and said : " I
was with him—with Alfred, I mean. We heard them talking.
It was on the other ship." She bit her lip again and looked
at the floor. " It was at night."

The light was bright and too clear directly above her, so
the lines on her face were deeply etched, and she seemed older,
and her skin shone with faint, sudden dampness. Marcia
knew that Mickey's hands again had gone behind him. It
was a mannerism, one of many sad and dreadful souvenirs
that were like scars and that gradually she must heal. Gili
said : " If you must know, we were sitting in a lifeboat !
They didn't know that we were there ; they thought themselves alone."

Mickey said impatiently : " You've told nobody about this
before now. . . ."

Her green eyes flashed his way.

" But I . . ." she began, and Mickey said less sharply :
" This is a very serious accusation. You don't realise how
serious. If I were you I'd keep it to myself."

" *But* . . ." she began again, explosively, and then checked
herself. " Perhaps you are right," she said unexpectedly.
" Yes, I'm sure—but it can do no harm. I mean if they *are*
Nazis . . ."

" They ? " said Josh Morgan.

" The Cates two. The husband and wife. They were
talking."

Her voice sounded reluctant. Josh Morgan said abruptly :
" Having told us this much, you'll have to go on. What
exactly did they say ? "

She shot him a sullen look. " They—oh, they talked."

" What about ? " His voice was easy, his eyes inexorable.

Gili looked at her hands. " They—well, they said at last
they were on a ship. One said to Buenos Aires. The other
said yes, and they might better stay there for ever than return
to America—they meant the United States."

As she talked, staring down at her hands, either her seeming
reluctance to tell the little story diminished or her inventiveness speeded up. She went on more rapidly and with a
certain defiance : " Then she said, but there was nothing else

for her to do. She said what was money, what was anything. Then he said quite clearly, you understand, there was no mistake about it—he said, but we actually were collaborationists; we were friends of the Nazis; nobody will ever forget it. We can never go home. And after a long time she said in a quiet voice, it didn't sound like her, it sounded as if she had "—Gili fumbled for words—" if as she had a plan, as if she wanted to persuade him, she said, oh, so softly, ' No one need ever know ! ' "

She stopped and examined one thick fingernail closely.

There was another silence. Mickey's face was a mask, white and stiff. His eyes lifted to Gili's face as clear and deep as the sea. Josh Morgan seeming very tall and big and solid in the crimson bathrobe, said suddenly : " Did they say anything else ? "

" No ; no ; I think they saw us."

" Why ? What did they do ? "

" Well, Alfred made some motion, some movement. He understood English, you see. He heard the word Nazi. They were standing by the railing. They were very still for a moment, and then they seemed to whisper and they walked away. But I think they knew it was Alfred. So I think they killed him. For fear of—of . . ." she hesitated, fumbling for a word.

" Blackmail ? " said Josh Morgan.

" Blackmail. Yes, yes. Money from her to keep silence."

" Did he ask them for money ? "

Gili's face clouded. " I don't know that. I think he meant to."

" Why do you think that ? "

She shrugged. " Oh, I think so."

" Did he say he intended to try to blackmail them ? "

" N-no. But he said they were very, very rich. And he said to himself, you know, as if he were thinking aloud, something about money ; he used the word money. He said they'd never miss it. Then he thought of me, I suppose, and laughed and talked of something else. But that is what happened. She killed him. The husband wouldn't have the courage to do it. He is a mouse, that man. She has the strength ; she could have killed him. I think they knew I was there. I . . ." She hesitated, and then said very rapidly :

"So I was afraid just now. So I was frightened when you said someone tried to push you into the sea." She turned to Marcia, flinging out her hands, speaking still very rapidly and somehow all at once, theatrically, so her words took on a falseness they had not previously had. " So you see, I screamed. I was terrified. I am afraid. Of the Cates woman. She killed him. She did it when she saw that this was an American ship. She knew that it was going to the United States. They are people of importance and of money. If their friends know they were Nazis, if it is in the papers, if any one tells—well, they are kaput—finished. All their lives. Do you see ? "

It was, of course, true.

It did not square with anything Marcia had perceived or felt instinctively about Daisy Belle Cates, or about Luther. Yet it did square suddenly with certain other small facts. Daisy Belle had given the extra coat to Gili, and when Gili had said, but then, you'll have all the coats you want, or something of the kind, Daisy Belle had replied with a queer, bleak look in her face that she doubted it. Yet they had had money, a great deal of money. Theirs was one of the famous moneyed families, and had been for several generations. Did she doubt whether or not they would be premitted to claim that money ?

There was the care Daisy Belle took of her jewels ; not, somehow, as if she liked them as ornaments, but rather as if they might represent—well, food and clothing and shelter, the necessities of life. She had not struck Marcia as a woman who would actually care for jewels as jewels. It was a small, faint impression, but now it took on a certain validity. And there was Daisy Belle's solicitude about Luther. She loved him obviously, and cared for him ; but there was something else, something dimly felt that suggested trouble and anxiety.

But mainly there was the fact that they had worked so hard to get passage on the ship to Buenos Aires. With their money and connections, with their prominence as American citizens, it would have been reasonable to expect them simply to stay on in Lisbon until their passage direct home and in comfort could have been arranged. Marcia realised suddenly that there had always been to her something incongruous, something a little questionable and mysterious about their presence on that ship bound for Buenos Aires.

All those things bore out Gili's accusation in a way that had a certain ugly authority. Yet, to offset that, there was Marcia's belief in Daisy Belle.

Neither of the men listening, of course, could have that belief. Mickey's experience had been such as to lead him to suspect everybody. To doubt everybody; to question every motive—every impulse, every word. It would be a long time before Mickey could possibly recover any sort of faith in such simple things as goodness and honesty.

But he believed her. He had come to her; he had made her, he told her, a symbol and a talisman. Marcia turned to him : " Daisy Belle is honest. She couldn't have been a Nazi, ever."

Mickey got up, his white face taut and lined. Gili said with quick anger : " I heard it. That is what I heard. You don't believe me," flashed Gili.

" Oh, yes," said Mickey. " We believe you. But "—he moved restively—" accusation, threats, all that—if only there were a little peace somewhere."

" The man was murdered, Messac," said Josh Morgan. " Someone attacked Miss Colfax; someone may have attacked you."

Mickey rubbed his face wearily. " I don't think any one attacked me. I think I slipped. And as for the Cates couple. I—well, I think Gili's mistaken. She doesn't understand English really well; she may have got things confused. . . ."

" I didn't," said Gili furiously. " I'm telling the truth. . . ."

Mickey said quickly and peaceably : " I didn't say you were lying. I only meant it's better not to do anything hastily."

Gili subsided with another sulky flash of her green eyes.

Josh Morgan said : " If whoever murdered Castiogne thinks that you saw it, Messac, or have evidence against him, he might attack you or Miss Colfax, for the same reason. Don't you think we should tell Captain Svendsen Miss Duvrey's story ? "

" No," cried Gili, rising abruptly and changing her mind again. " No, I won't. I'm afraid to. You made me tell you: but I won't tell the Captain. I won't tell anybody. I'll deny it if you do."

And Marcia said suddenly : " No, please don't. Please wait. We can't do anything to-night anyway."

Josh Morgan said: "What about the two seamen? Who are they? Where are they? There were two seamen in the lifeboat; isn't that right?"

"Oh, yes." Mickey looked at the Air Force colonel sombrely. "There were two seamen. Their names are Para and Urdinola. The Captain questioned them first. I don't know what he did with them."

Gili knew. She said with a sullen look that they were quartered with the seamen of the *Magnolia*.

"Still at liberty, then," said Josh Morgan.

"Yes," said Mickey, "I suppose so. I asked Captain Svendsen about them. It seemed to me that one of them must have killed Castiogne. He said he did not have proof of motive or means."

"He's trying to be fair," said Josh Morgan. "He was a common seaman himself once, he told me. He came up the hard way. He's not going to railroad them for murder until he's pretty damned sure."

"It was the Cates woman," said Gili sullenly. "It was the Cates woman. She's as strong as a man. She did it."

Josh Morgan started towards the door. "We'd better all go to bed," he said coolly. "It's very late. As to the Cates couple—I don't know. There may be some mistake. Let's wait."

"I agree," said Mickey. "We'll keep it to ourselves and no harm done."

"And be murdered in our beds," flashed Gili. She did not, however, actually look frightened now. Her skin had lost that sudden look of dampness, her eyes their flat, bright look of fright. She seemed, indeed, rather pleased and complacent. It was a singular small change, yet perceptible, so it puzzled Marcia. She could not, however, try to solve it, if there were any real solution beyond Gili's childish and yet nevertheless cunning and devious instincts. She rose, and Mickey rose, too, and put his arm lightly around her. "I feel sure you are right about Luther and Daisy Belle," he said. "Besides, anything you say is right with me."

Gili gave a short, hard little sound, very much like a snort, and flounced out of the cabin. Josh Morgan said: "Good night, Messac. By the way, doesn't Cates share this cabin with you?"

"Yes," said Mickey. "I don't know where he is. I suppose he'll be along soon."

Josh said slowly: "It's odd, rather, that he is not here. I mean—the decks were searched. He wasn't in the officers' lounge when I was there just now."

"Oh, he's somewhere around," said Mickey. "We've all got a Cates bee in our bonnets."

"Maybe," said Josh. "But there aren't really many places to go on a ship."

Mickey shrugged. "There are hundreds of places! He'll be along any minute. And I'm not afraid of him, if that's what you mean. I can't exactly see him rising out of his bunk to murder me."

That, of course, thought Marcia suddenly, was the trouble. Perhaps it was always impossible to say to one's self, and believe it: this face I know is that of a murderer, these eyes have seen and approved a frightful thing; this hand has entered a dread conspiracy.

Mickey bent his blond head over Marcia's hand and kissed it, and then smiled at her, wearily but comfortingly. "Things will come out all right," he said. "You've been telling me that. Good night, darling."

Josh Morgan, at the door, said rather dryly: "I'll just stroll down to your cabin with you, Miss Colfax. I'm going that way."

He wasn't, of course. His stateroom was almost certainly in quite another section of the ship. But he had found her, as Mickey had not found her, there on the black and foggy deck. He was at least partially convinced, as Mickey was not, that someone had been there, that someone had meant to murder her. "If anybody tried to kill you to-night, he'll try it again."

She said good night to Mickey, and, because there was nothing else to do, really, went along with Josh Morgan's tall, crimson-clad figure.

She heard Mickey's door close. Gili had gone on ahead. The skirt of her curiously incongruous uniform flounced swiftly around the end of the passage. Already, probably, she knew the ship from stem to stern. Why had she been in Mickey's cabin?

Obviously to talk to him. As obviously as when Josh Morgan, an attractive and somehow very masculine man had

entered, Gili had instantly, instinctively, made room for him
at her side, leaned near him. Again it was childish and simple,
and, in its way, cunning. How long, though, had she been
there ? Had Mickey or someone else told her what had
happened in that dark band of shadow on deck ?

And where, actually, was Luther ? And Daisy Belle ?

They reached the central passage, and a bell sounded,
clearly yet very far away, somehow, as if striking against the
curtain of fog. Josh Morgan said : " One o'clock. It seemed
later. . . ."

Again the capped head of a nurse peeked at them from the
lighted ward office. A corpsman in white passed them on the
stairs. He was whistling softly between his teeth and gave
them a curious glance, and then, appearing to recognise the
Colonel, stood aside respectfully to let them pass.

When they reached the deck below, Gili had disappeared.
The typewriter was still ticking busily away in some office
along the farther corridor.

Josh Morgan said, low : " Who shares your cabin ? The
luscious blonde ? Any one else ? "

" Mrs. Cates."

" Oh ! " They crossed the main passage and entered the
narrow one. This time she counted and recognised her own
door. He paused just before they reached it. " Look here,"
he said, and put his hand lightly on her arm, his eyes very
direct and intent. " You're going to be okay, you know. Only
remember what I said. If anything, anything at all, seems to
you wrong or out of place or—oh, the least bit odd—run. Run
and yell like hell." The flicker of a grin touched his mouth.
His eyes remained, however, very grave and intent. " Will
you ? There are always people around."

" Yes. But there'll be the three of us. And it was a seaman.
It must be one of the seamen."

He understood her, of course. He had suggested it himself,
but he replied obliquely : " Captain Svendsen knows what
he's about. He's an able man. By the way, you and Messac
are to be married. Is that right ? " He hesitated and added
quickly : " I hope you don't mind my asking. I only thought
. . . " He stopped and did not say what he thought.

Marcia said, rather stiffly, with an odd sense of crossing
some boundary of making a decision that, certainly, was

already made and had been made for a very long time: "Yes. We . . . That's why we were going home."

The line of his jaw stood out squarely and firmly. "By way of Buenos Aires?"

Again she said: "Yes. We could get passage; otherwise we'd have had to wait."

"Of course," he said after a moment. "I see. Well, here we are." They reached the door to the cabin. He said good night, pleasantly and impersonally, and turned rather quickly away.

She wished for an illogical and unreasonable moment, that he had stayed. Then she opened the door.

The cabin was still lighted. Daisy Belle Cates, in grey pyjamas, lay in the upper bunk, smoking thoughtfully. Her thin, red-grey hair was done up in little tight wads of curls and tied with a piece of white gauze dressing. Any other woman would have looked ugly and grotesque; Daisy Belle even then had an irresistible air of elegance and dignity. Gili was in a corner, undressing furiously, flinging off her clothes, her face sulky and angry.

Both women looked at her—Gili sullenly, Daisy Belle coolly and pleasantly, yet with a sort of observation. (Daisy Belle a Nazi! With her proud, old American name, her niceness, her civilised, forgiving decency. Impossible!) Daisy Belle said: "Oh, there you are. I was beginning to worry. I turned in ages ago, right after I talked to you. Did my hair and went straight to sleep." She yawned. "I don't think I'll ever quite catch up with sleep."

Gili gave her a hidden, venomous look from behind a swinging lock of bright yellow hair.

Marcia thought, with a kind of sick stab, but you weren't here, Daisy Belle; you weren't here and you weren't asleep and you're lying. Why?

She could not just then question her. It was Gili who, hurling out the words jerkily, told Daisy Belle what had happened.

But in the telling, Gili, either intentionally or unintentionally, gave an account of her own actions during the two or three hours just past.

"I was in the nurses' lounge," she said. "I was there all evening. That is"—she bent to strip off a stocking—"for an hour or so. Then I strolled around to André's cabin. He wasn't there and I waited. I didn't know anything about it until he came with his head bandaged. It was terrible." She shivered and stripped off the other stocking, and Daisy Belle, sitting up, her face shocked, cried : " *Marcia!* I can't believe it ! Are you sure it really *was* somebody ? I mean—well, not just nerves and imagination ? "

She said, yes, she was sure. Marcia turned to hang up her coat beside Daisy Belle's, hanging in the shallow closet, and Daisy Belle's coat was damp and dark around the shoulders, as if wet with fog.

Yet they had searched the decks ; they had found no one.

They did not talk much after that. Daisy Belle, her fine face troubled, lighted another cigarette and smoked it with quick nervous puffs.

Gili crawled into pyjamas, muttering about their discomfort, and then into the bunk opposite Marcia. Marcia undressed quickly, too, and turned out the lights. In the silence of the cabin, again, the ship herself came to life, sighing, throbbing, steadily forging ahead, as if she knew the precious cargo she carried.

Marcia, staring into darkness that presently became faintly less dark, so she could see the greyish round outlines of the open ports, thought again of the sinister, unwelcome, and unwanted cargo that they had added to the ship.

Suppose it had been Daisy Belle ? Suppose it was Gili herself ?

Queer to be sleeping in that small, tidy cabin with, possibly, a murderess.

Again the feeling of incredulity overwhelmed her, and this time gave her what she knew might be a false security, but, nevertheless, was for the moment security.

But why had Daisy Belle offered a gratuitous, flat lie ?

It seemed to Marcia that weeks had passed since the storm had begun, as if she had been on the *Magnolia* for a long time, and as if she had known that deep throb and steady rush of water intimately and familiarly.

Just before she went to sleep, a memory of the night, a small thing, unnoticed at the time, came floating out into her consciousness. When Josh Morgan had found her, there in the fog, he had called her Marcia. " Do you hear me ? " he had asked, and held her ... "Do you hear me, Marcia?"

It was as if he had known her, somewhere, for a long time. It was as if the sense of security in his arms was an old and familiar one, too.

But that, she thought suddenly and sharply, was like disloyalty to Mickey. She loved Mickey; she was to marry Mickey, not Josh Morgan. And not that there was anything at all that required even a denial!

She turned on her side and suddenly fell into a deep sleep. The fog was thicker now. It lay all round the *Magnolia*. It was an impenetrable yet yielding wall, surrounding her, setting her off from the rest of the world. Quietly the night life of the ship went on. Somewhere a man turned in his bunk and dreamed of home; another lay awake planning and mapping a war-free life; another, in pain, moved restlessly and a nurse observed it and came to lean over the bunk and rub his back.

Up in the chart-room Captain Svendsen drank more hot coffee from the thermos beside him, and peered ahead through the window and could see nothing. Beams of light were struck back upon themselves by that thick, black veil. Staring into the fog, he decided to take decisive steps in the morning about the boatload of survivors he'd picked up from the Portuguese vessel. He wasn't sure just what had happened that night on deck; it was his first business to get his ship and his patients safely through that fog and home. But if the passengers from the storm-wrecked *Lerida* were going to make trouble, he'd stop it if he had to put them all in irons.

He'd better question the two seamen again: he'd better question them all again. In view of what Colonel Wells had told him, he'd have to question practically everybody on the ship.

It was all troublesome; it was all exasperating. Besides, there was that business of the passports. His stern mouth tightened.

Then he thought of the body of Alfred Castiogne as he had seen it, with the ugly, gaping knife wound in the back. It was so vivid a picture that it almost seemed to float there, against the fog ahead. Captain Svendsen was not afraid of anything; but he didn't like that picture against the thick, wet night.

IX

THE FOG entered the ship.

It was kept out of the sick wards—lights and warmth and activity kept it at bay. That morning was, so far as the sick wards were concerned, exactly like any other. The nurses in their neat beige-and-white-striped uniforms—slacks instead of skirts to facilitate the constant running up and down stairways and perching on the edges of the upper bunks to care for patients there as well as those in the lower tier of bunks—went briskly and quickly about their prescribed routine. Breakfast trays, which hooked neatly on to the sides of the bunks; charts, baths, the doctors' rounds; warmth and jokes and inexhaustible good spirits on the part of the patients. Which was not surprising at all; which was natural and real, because these men were soldiers.

But the rest of the ship was at the mercy of the fog.

It crept into the main passageways, it darkened the day, it permeated everything. The decks were grey and slick with moisture. The *Magnolia* proceeded slowly and very carefully, nursed along through a grey wall which ever yielded and yet ever enclosed. That morning the foghorn began to sound at long intervals. They were not on a heavy shipping lane. The Transportation Corps officer knew the exact location of every ship within miles of them. But a fog like that was a hazard, just the same; visibility was cut down to feet; the raucous blast of the foghorn seemed the only thing able to penetrate that thick grey wall, and even it was flung back in diffused multiple echoes upon the ship.

The sound of it woke Marcia.

It was late. Daisy Belle and Gili had already apparently dressed quietly and left the cabin. The ports were grey with fog, and all the metal latches and bolts had a faintly misted look, as if some invisible presence had breathed upon them.

Marcia's long, heavy sleep, the daylight look of the cabin, the secure feeling of being on an American ship, all of it was like a mantle of common sense protecting her from things that were not sensible, that were outrageously out of place. By the time she'd had a hot shower with all the fragrant soap she wanted, and had dressed in clothes that were faintly damp from fog but incredibly fresh and new and attractive in contrast to the nondescript odds and ends of clothing that she'd taken aboard the *Lerida*, she was ready to deny everything. If Castiogne were murdered, one of the seamen had done it, and by then, perhaps, had confessed. Daisy Belle Cates was no more of a Nazi than she was a man-eating tigress. The hand that had silently turned that now faintly blurred doorknob had been merely a hand, somebody mistaking that cabin for another. Gili had been in Mickey's cabin simply because she was Gili and she'd wanted to talk to Mickey and had done so. Why not? Everything that day would be straightened out and restored to the normal order of events.

She was even ready to accept Mickey's accident as an accident, and nothing more. And if the attack upon her had been what it seemed, then it was obviously one of the seamen, afraid for some unfathomable reason that she had seen him kill Alfred Castiogne.

One of the nurses had placed a little horde of toilet articles beside Marcia's bunk—a comb, toothbrush and powder, lipstick. She combed her dark hair back to a smooth roll, low on her neck; she put on lipstick. There was a small, feminine satisfaction in the fact that it was a gay soft red; her blue eyes seemed more deeply blue. She caught up the nurse's coat again, and the lining almost matched her red, half-smiling lips. Everything was going to be all right.

She went down to breakfast, passing wards and through passages and stopping at the door of what proved to be the nurse's lounge—a large, comfortable room, with deeply cushioned chairs and sofas, a piano and card tables, and a gay mural of the skyline of New York painted on the walls. A nurse, sitting under an electric hair-dryer and reading, looked up pleasantly and directed her to the nurses' mess, one deck down.

This, too, was a large, low-ceilinged pleasant room—white walls, white ceiling, and red chairs. The nurses ate at two long tables at one end, the officers at two round tables at the other end, so a mess-boy told her. And then he brought her orange juice and pancakes with butter and all the milk and coffee she wanted.

She was finishing when Major Williams, the young officer who had been present when the Captain first interviewed her, came into the room, saw her, and came forward. The Captain, he said, would like to see her again. But she must finish her breakfast, he added politely, and he hoped she had had a good rest and was no worse for her experience in the lifeboat.

The sense of well being, of being restored, somehow, to the right world (her world, the little sensible and normal world that Marcia Colfax had known before the war), still held good. She smiled at the young Major and finished her coffee and went with him. They walked through passages that were now beginning to seem familiar, past wards, with their atmosphere of comfort and home, past the equally busy and active transportation offices, and eventually to the Captain's quarters.

He was waiting for them and he looked tired. His ruddy face had a greyish tinge ; there were deep pockets around his eyes. A thermos bottle of coffee stood on the table before him. He turned at their entrance. " Oh, there you are, Miss Colfax. Come in. Bring in the two men, Major."

" Yes, sir."

The young Major vanished again. Captain Svendsen turned back to his desk and busied himself with some papers. After a moment, he said, over his shoulder : " Sit down, Miss Colfax."

The arms of the red chair felt slightly moist. The fog was everywhere, even here. The foghorn sounded again, long and slow and hoarse. When it died away, Major Williams returned, ushering in two men.

They were small, dark, active-looking. They were wearing obviously borrowed clothes gathered up from the *Magnolia* seamen. They looked about them with suspicious eyes under heavy black eyebrows. One was thin and wizened, like an elderly monkey ; the other very short, thick and sturdy. It was he, she thought, remembering the lifeboat, who had tried to revive Castiogne. Their swarthy faces were faintly familiar to her, but only that. She stared and they stared. Major Williams said cheerfully : " Here they are, sir," and Captain

Svendsen shifted his solid big body about and looked at the two men and looked at her.

"These men were in the *Lerida* lifeboat. Their names are "—he glanced at a paper on his desk—" Manuel Para and José Urdiola. Now then "—he turned to her, his shrewd, deep-set eyes were very direct and urgent—" was it either of these two men last night ? "

The two men shifted uneasily. Their dark eyes were angry, suspicious, and altogether impenetrable. She felt a curious embarrassment under that dark suspicious scrutiny, but she looked at them, thinking back, trying to dredge up some distinguishing mark, some sound, some clue. There was none. She only vaguely remembered their faces, here and there about the *Lerida*. She remembered them merely as black figures bending over oars, shifting about, huddled in the lifeboat.

She shook her head. " I can't tell. There was nothing I can remember. But someone . . ."

The Captain cut into her speech. " You told me that one of them tried apparently to revive Castiogne." He glanced at the short, sturdy-looking man, and said shortly : " Para, step forward."

He did so quickly. " Yes, sir."

" Was it this one, Miss Colfax ? "

" I think so. I could not see his face."

Para burst out in fluent and vehement English : " But, sir, I told you. I tried to revive him, yes. I did not know he was dead. I thought exhaustion, yes. A collapse. I told you. I did not know he was dead. I told you . . ."

" That's enough," said the Captain curtly. He nodded at Major Williams and said : " Take them away."

Para looking worried and angry, followed the other, who had said nothing. Major Williams closed the door smartly after them. The Captain said directly : " What do you know of the Cates couple ? "

She stiffened. Had someone already told him Gili's story ? She replied warily : " I met them in Lisbon while we were waiting for a passage."

" What do you know of them before they reached Lisbon ? "

Suddenly and disconcertingly she remembered Daisy Belle's

words : " We stayed with a—a friend ; in a château in the
hills back of Nice ! " What friend ? *And why had Daisy
Belle lied* so needlessly, apparently so pointlessly, the night
before ?

The Captain's eyes were too observant. For an instant she
felt that he could read her thoughts. She said quickly and
firmly : " They were caught in France and remained there.
He was ill. I think they lived somewhere along the Riviera."

He leaned forward, resting his elbows on the table, his
blue eyes very piercing and determined, and also queerly
impatient. " Look here, Miss Colfax. I've no time for evasions.
I'd better tell you some things that you may not know. For
one thing, Alfred Castiogne was murdered. You don't seem
to be able to realise it. His body is in the morgue now. We
never have a burial at sea. We've never, in fact "—pride came
into his voice for an instant—" we've never had a death at
sea. We've a proud record. But the point now is, this Portuguese third officer *was murdered*. There is no question in my
mind as to whether or not one of you in the lifeboat murdered
him. But . . ." He hesitated ; a sort of reluctance touched
his straight, hard mouth. " But I have to be fair. Colonel
Wells is the medical officer in command. He examined the
body, and he went to considerable trouble to investigate all
the circumstances and facts available. And, to make it short,
considering, he says, a question of rigor mortis and the length
of time the man was dead when he was discovered, there is
no proof that he was killed in the lifeboat."

" You mean someone else could have killed him ! Someone,
here on this ship . . ." She half rose to her feet.

" Wait ! I didn't say that," snapped the Captain. " Nobody
on my ship did it. I know my ship. My men are, as you know,
of the Merchant Marine. I took on some new men last trip,
but I investigated them thoroughly. I don't believe that
Castiogne was murdered on the *Magnolia*. I believe, and so
does Colonel Wells, that he was murdered in the lifeboat.
But "—the Captain sighed, and said rather wearily—" we've
got to be fair. So far as I can discover, this man, Castiogne,
was assumed to have collapsed. Manuel Para, as he admits,
tried to revive him. As you heard, he claims not to have known
that he was dead, which is perfectly comprehensible, but does
not prove anything. Castiogne could have been dead then,

already murdered, or he could have been in a state of collapse and murdered later. Two *Magnolia* seamen—whom I have questioned, I assure you, to my own satisfaction—carried Castiogne up the Jacob's ladder and put him down for a moment or two on the floor along the companionway. There was some excitement and haste about getting you all aboard; the sea was running rather heavy. They were bringing litters for those of you who could not walk. There were, in short, several minutes during which nobody actually had his eyes on the man Castiogne. Naturally there was a certain amount of going and coming, hurrying, trying to save you all," said the Captain, looking for a moment rather as if he wished he had not undertaken saving any of them.

"But then somebody—anybody on the ship . . ."

"No, Miss Colfax, not anybody on the ship. Nobody in the wards, none of the patients could have done it. And I do not believe," he was suddenly sarcastic, "that any of the nurses would be very likely to creep up to the man and stick a knife in him. Or any of the doctors. For one thing, I've seen all of them under fire; what they've done is save lives —hundreds of them—through their own personal bravery. You can keep the nurses and doctors and the patients out of your calculations. And, so far as I'm concerned, I don't believe any of my ship's personnel had anything to do with this. But the fact is"—he paused again and said in a sort of angry, but honest concession—"the fact is, there is a period of time on the *Magnolia* during which he *could* have been killed. He wasn't killed then," he said stubbornly. "I'm sure of it. But he *could* have been. So . . ." He shrugged. He was angry and stubborn, exasperated but honest. "So there you are. The simple fact is that he could have been killed in the lifeboat, or during the half-hour or so while he was on the *Magnolia* before the corpsmen seeing to him discovered that he had a stab wound. It hadn't bled much: flesh had closed over it, so the hæmorrhage was inside."

He glanced at the watch on his thick red wrist, and said: "I'm only telling you all this, Miss Colfax, because it's the truth. Because I want you and everybody else on the lifeboat to help, not hinder, my necessary investigation."

He shoved back his chair with a quick motion and got to his feet. He was reaching for his oilskins. "I'm going back to the bridge," he said. " I'm risking my ticket to leave it for a moment in a fog like this. Think it over, Miss Colfax. Try to remember . . ."

He held the door open for her courteously, and then walked faster than she along the passage, so she followed the rustling oil-skinned figure with its shock of blond hair. He disappeared around some curve.

Thinking again of Daisy Belle Cates, it seemed to her suddenly childish and unfair to give her no chance to defend herself against the nagging little question in Marcia's own mind. There could be a dozen reasons for Daisy Belle's absence from the cabin the previous night, a dozen reasons for the damp coat, a dozen reasons for a merely careless misstatement—all of them innocent.

She came to a main lobby. Daisy Belle was not about, neither was she in the cabin on B deck. She wanted to talk to Mickey, too; probably he would be on deck. She put the nurse's coat around her shoulders and climbed the stairs again to the lobby of the deck which, on the *Magnolia*, corresponded to, and in practice was, the boat deck. Still she saw none of the *Lerida* survivors. She went out on deck, and instantly, it seemed to her, she entered a remote and secret world. The fog was everywhere, the ship seemed to lie quite still in it, unmoving, except for that deep faraway pulsation. The railing was beaded with moisture. She could scarcely see beyond it. But Gili was standing at the railing. She, too, wore a nurse's thick warm coat. Her golden head was bare and looked rather lank and wet. She turned quickly and saw Marcia.

" Oh," she said. A flash of expectancy in her face changed to quite frank and open disappointment. " Oh, it's you."

Marcia said: "Have you seen André? Or Mrs. Cates?"

" No." Gili's voice was sullen. She waited a moment and shivered a little and glanced swiftly behind her, along the deck both ways, her green eyes darting here and there. She said : " I don't like the fog. I feel all the time as if somebody is near me, somebody I can't see or hear or . . . I don't like it."

Marcia, suddenly, didn't like it either. She said, however, lightly : " Why don't you go inside then ? "

Gili did not reply. Instead she tugged at a pocket and got

out a cigarette case and clicked it open. She offered it to Marcia. " Cigarette ? "

" Thank you, I . . ." Marcia stopped.

The case was Mickey's. She knew it and remembered it well—the thin, plain gold, the design around the edge. She stared at it and saw, besides the case, tables in restaurants with rose-shaded lamps, tables in the sun, along the walks, below the bronze-leafed trees of the Bois—she could almost hear the squawking taxis and smell liqueurs and coffee.

She said stiffly : " Where did you get that ? "

Gili was looking at her. Her face was secret, her eyes uneasy. She licked her mouth and said : " Oh, that. The case. I—I borrowed it. It belongs to Mickey."

Fog was so close it seemed to drift between them. For an instant, Marcia thought, how odd—she knows his real name. Mickey.

Then Gili's green eyes changed, and Marcia could see that change. Uneasiness was suddenly shot with brilliance, with triumph.

Gili gave a kind of shrug. She bit her full red lip and looked away. Marcia said, in a voice she did not recognise as her own, it was so stern, so queer and hard : " Where did you know him ? How long ? "

Gili bit her lip again. She shot a sidewise green glance at Marcia. She said : " All right. We may as well understand each other, you and I. I knew it would have to be sometime. It may as well be now. Mickey belongs to me. He only came back to you for your money. We wanted to leave Europe, you see, and we have no money." She smiled. " He knew he could get enough for both of us from you."

X

SOMEONE CAME rapidly along the deck behind Marcia. She heard the quick, hard tread, and she saw the flash of relief in Gili's face as she looked beyond Marcia over her shoulder. " Why, Colonel Morgan," cried Gili. Her voice was eager, her face alight. Her eyes avoided Marcia. " How nice," cried Gili, and Josh Morgan stopped beside them.

" Hallo," he said, looking at Marcia, then looking at Gili. His coat was faintly beaded with fog; the metal on his cap looked frosted. He seemed very big and substantial, looming up in the grey mist. Gili said quickly with a nervous sort of giggle: " I'm going inside. The fog is too cold. See you later. . . ." She hunched her coat up around her neck and slid away hurriedly across the wet strip of deck and inside the ship.

" Now what's all that for ? " said Josh Morgan. He looked from the door which had closed so quickly, with such a suggestion of slyness and haste, back to Marcia. " She's scuttling away like a scared cat. What's she done ?

Marcia moved, so she avoided his eyes, so she looked into the fog, so he could not see her face. Actually she was conscious only of a deep inner stillness, as if everything about her had stopped.

It wasn't true; it couldn't be true!

Yet hadn't an unwilling awareness caught and stored up certain small things—a look in Gili's eyes, the way her head moved against Mickey's shoulder, a knowledgeableness, somehow, between them? Only that morning she had thought of Gili's presence in Mickey's cabin—so assured, so at ease—and then she had reassured herself, almost without intending to do it. She had answered a question without admitting that it was a question.

But Gili was lying. She had to be lying. Mickey loved her, Marcia.

The man beside her said rather gently : " Come and walk with me, will you ? Have you had lunch ? It's past time, you know. . . ."

"I had a late breakfast," she replied automatically. She could not look at him. The railing was wet and cold under her hands, but it seemed just then the only fixed and certain point in life. If she held the railing tightly enough, long enough . . . Josh Morgan put his hand over her own. "Look at me. What's that woman done to you?"

She stared down at his hand. It was big and warm and well shaped, with a small seal ring on the little finger.

Then she thought of Mickey's hands—fine and square, with their pitiful scarred fingertips—fingertips that had once been so strong and fine—the fingers of a musician. Gili had lied.

Josh Morgan took her own hands from the railing and tucked one of them under his arm. "I've got to have a walk. Come along." She could feel the texture of his sleeve, the hard warmth of flesh and muscle below it. His overcoat, swinging loose because of the sling on his other arm, swung a little over her, too. The fog was cold and moist against her cheeks and lips. She moved along beside him, as if he had wound her up and set her in motion. They reached a sheltered spot beside a projecting bulkhead. It was not far, as a matter of fact, from where she had found Mickey in the darkness of the previous night.

Josh Morgan was watching her closely. He said: "Stay here, will you? I'll be back."

Close to the ship the water was visible; she watched the black waves with curling white caps rush away from the ship and then dissolve into grey. Josh Morgan returned, and he had a steamer chair, which he set up in the protected angle of the bulkhead. "Come on," he said, "sit here."

She said stiffly: "I've got to talk to Mickey."

"All right, all right. Anything you like. I'll get him for you. Only just for a minute or two, stay here. Are you warm?"

She was in the chair. He leaned over to tuck her coat around her chin. For a moment it was like any other ocean voyage—a steamer chair, the rush of water, the fresh, wet sea air.

He sat down on the foot of her chair and lighted a cigarette. "Don't talk if you don't want to. I'll do the talking. How about my life story? Let me see. Well, I was born in

California, I went to school in Massachusetts, studied law at
Columbia, and got a job writing for a newspaper. Then I went
to Paris and got another job. . . . You're not listening to me.
Well, it isn't very interesting, really. Listen, Marcia, that
woman's a little wharf rat. Don't let her hurt you like that.
I can't "—he tossed his cigarette over the railing into the fog;
he leaned over suddenly, quite near—" I can't bear it," he
said. He put his arm around her, holding her close, as one
might gather up a child. Only then he kissed her, turning her
face with his hard cheek, feeling for her lips. His mouth
moved away a little, but still so she could feel its warmth and
tenderness, and he kissed her again. There was only, in all
the world, the rush and murmur of the fog-shrouded waves
and the man who held her, close against him, his mouth upon
her own.

After a long time, time for the world to be remade, time
for a ship to go on and on upon its journey, he lifted his
face.

The long deep blast of the foghorn sounded, breaking in
waves around them, prolonging the moment, holding them
both suspended in time and space, searching each other's
eyes.

The last echoes dwindled in the fog. He said slowly: "I
didn't know I was going to do that. I didn't mean . . ." He
broke off abruptly and said: "That's not true. I did mean it.
I meant it since I saw you there in the Captain's cabin. I
meant it since . . ." Again he stopped; this time he released
her so she lay back against the chair. He got out another
cigarette, turned it in his fingers and went on: "So you see,
I can't let any one hurt you like that. Besides, I don't think
he's worth it."

Her breath was uneven; all the stillness inside her had
been driven away. She was suddenly and poignantly aware
of the smallest details—the wet cold air, the crimson fold on
her knee where her coat had fallen back, the throbbing of
the ship's engines, the distant clear sound of a ship's bell, the
level blue-grey eyes of the man sitting on the foot of her chair,
his tanned face, the way his black eyebrows curved. The little
half-smile on his mouth that had so lately touched her own.

But it was all wrong, confused. This was a man she did
not know. It was Mickey she loved.

He said again: "Believe me, he's not worth it. I mean Mickey, André"—he paused and added quite slowly, quite deliberately—"or whoever he really is."

She had said Mickey. She remembered it clearly. "Did I call him Mickey? It's a—a nickname. . . ."

"I see." He looked at the cigarette in his hand and said: "Do you want me to find him now?"

Now? she thought. Face Mickey now, ask him about Gili, hear what he might say? She took a long breath. "Yes, please."

"Shall I tell him to come here?"

"Yes."

He looked at her again, his eyes intent and dark. "You're sure?"

He waited a moment, as if to give her a chance to change her mind, then briskly he got up. "All right. I'll not be long." he said briefly, and walked rapidly away along the deck.

She watched his tall figure, the coat swinging, striding along the deck into the fog. He turned abruptly at some door and went inside without looking back.

The fog after he'd gone, seemed to come closer.

It was extremely quiet there on the deserted deck. She thought the decks were forbidden to patients that day owing to the fog. The white planks were slippery and wet, the brass and metal glistened with moisture.

She wondered where Josh Morgan would find Mickey and what she would say, and why she had let Josh Morgan undertake such an errand. When she heard footsteps coming slowly along the deck, she looked up quickly, thinking it was Mickey.

It was, however, Luther Cates strolling along towards her, his hands in the pockets of an Army overcoat which was much too large for him, and a black beret he had got from somewhere pulled rather drearily over his forehead. He looked tired and ill, with heavy pouches under his faded blue eyes and a purplish tinge to his lips, but smiled when he saw that she was looking at him and hastened his pace to stop beside her.

"Hallo," he said. "Not down at lunch?"

Again she said she did not want lunch. He sighed and leaned against the bulkhead, looking, somehow, extraordinarily concave because of his thinness and the loose bulk of the coat. "I hear there was some excitement last night," he said. "I got back to our cabin just after you'd gone. Found André all bandaged up." He looked at her sharply and anxiously. "Are you all right?"

"Yes..."

"I can't imagine..." He broke off to cough, and then got out cigarettes and offered them to her. His hands were thin and unsteady as they held a match for her. He lighted his own cigarette and went on: "Daisy Belle told me all about it, too, this morning. Marcia; you couldn't have just imagined that attack on you, could you?"

She shook her head, and watching her, he said, apologetically: "No, no, I'm sure you couldn't have. But it seems so inexplicable, somehow. I don't understand why anybody would want to attack you. Do you have any possible explanation for it?"

Again she shook her head, and again rather apologetically he answered for her. "No, I'm sure you can't have. But it"—he rubbed his eyes wearily—" it makes no sense. Who was it? Who was it that knocked out André, and why? Of course, he says he's not sure whether anybody hit him or not. But it seems reasonable to think that somebody did. I suppose he might know more than he's admitting...."

There was a question in his hesitation. Marcia said quickly: "He doesn't know what happened. He thinks he may have slipped. I'm sure if he knew anything about it he'd tell the Captain."

"Well," said Luther, rubbing his eyes again, "I think so, too. The Captain naturally thinks it was somebody from the *Lerida*, if it was anybody. I mean," he amended it quickly, "I believe you; I know you. He seems a little sceptical. However, he had me up this morning to question me. I think I convinced him that I hadn't gone around all night bopping my friends." He laughed and then coughed again, and Marcia, unwillingly, yet irresistibly driven by some impulse she would not have wished to name, said: "How did you convince him?"

"By being in the engine-room with his first officer all the time the ruckus was taking place, apparently," said Luther, with another thin chuckle. "Daisy Belle prowled the ship, she says, looking for me. She was furious; bless her. She thought I ought to have been in bed. But it was warm down

there, and worth the climb up again. But then I'm all right if
I take things slowly. I'm crazy about engines," said Luther
simply. " Always have been. I might have done something
about it if I hadn't had so much money. Oh, well," he sighed,
" you can't live life twice. I suppose I'd go along exactly the
same way if I had it to do over again. Only next time I'd
pick a better heart and a better pair of lungs. Not," he added
hurriedly, " that I've anything to complain about. Well, well,
I'll just go along and get a bit of exercise before Daisy Belle
catches me and sends me inside." His tone warmed, as it
always did, when he spoke of Daisy Belle. He gave another
thin chuckle, which again turned into a cough, and straightened
up. " See you . . ." he said, and started back along the deck
again. Marcia gratefully watched him go. So Daisy Belle had
prowled the ship looking for him.

It explained the dampness on her coat. It gave her an
alibi which, to Marcia at least, was a very real and complete
alibi, for Daisy Belle cared for Luther as if he were a child.
She was loving, stern, and indefatigable. And in speaking to
Marcia, obviously she had simply never thought of mentioning
so usual and probably so brief an errand.

Marcia's own short return to the cabin on B deck had
happened to coincide with Daisy Belle's search for Luther.
That was all. It might not have satisfied the Captain ; it did
satisfy Marcia.

She would put everything else out of her mind, including
Gili's story. Gili was unpredictable, Gili was emotional, Gili
could twist this way or that, like a cat, without the slightest
warning. She would put everything Gili had said out of her
mind.

Even what she had said of Mickey.

Again she thought of that, incredulously, yet lingering, in
spite of herself, to explore every word and look. Yet Gili's
words were merely words, certainly without basis of any sort
of fact. Everything about it was absurd and confused and—
and all wrong.

At least something, somewhere, was wrong. Something
outside emotion ; something within another province, as if a
small segment of a familiar picture had been turned askew,
placed inaccurately, so all at once the whole picture was rather
puzzling and strange.

She tried to seek out that obscurely wrong piece, pin it
down, decide exactly how it was wrong, but she could not.
It was too nebulous a glimpse, too tenuous an impression.
Her thought swerved back to the important thing—herself
and Mickey and Gili.

The fog seemed thicker and darker ; even the sky seemed
to press down blackly, smothering the ship, and the foghorn
sounded again, roaring all around, isolating the ship in sound
as she was already isolated in fog. Mickey did not come back.
Josh did not come back. Considerable time actually must
have passed. And suddenly Marcia didn't like the empty,
cold deck, and the fog, and the deep waves of sound crashing
upon her ears. Inside the busy ship were lights and warmth
and people ; she rose and then saw that someone was standing
on the deck, leaning against the railing—a patient, obviously,
for he was wearing a long red bathrobe.

Apparently he had only then come out on deck. She'd have
to pass him to re-enter the ship by the same door from which
she had come. She looked along the deck in the other direction,
orienting herself.

She was on the upper boat deck, on the same level with the
Captain's quarters. In order to reach her own cabin she'd
have to go to the next deck below. Only a short distance away
from her towards the right, was a stairway which must lead
downward to that deck. She glanced again at the man in
the red bathrobe, and, as she did so, he turned a little and
she could see the glimmer of white bandages about his head.
She did not wish to meet his look ; she did not wish to pass
him. It was an obscure yet urgent impulse. She turned
abruptly towards the open stairway leading to the deck
below.

The foghorn stopped and all its clashing echoes died away.
The small thud of her heels seemed very loud in the sudden
silence. She felt that the man at the railing was watching her.
Without definable reason, she hastened her steps so as to pass
quickly out of his range of vision.

The deck below seemed deserted, too. She reached the
last wet black step and turned sharply around the stairway.

But the deck was not deserted ; it was, instead, horribly
inhabited.

Marcia stopped, holding the railing. The foghorn began

again, so waves of sound broke over the deck, shaking the ship and all the impenetrable grey world about her with dreadful tumult. It kept on sounding while Marcia stood, looking down at the dark, swarthy little man who lay with his eyes no longer suspicious and wary but blankly open, staring upward. He was Manuel Para, and his throat had been cut.

A very long time seemed to have passed when suddenly she knew that someone was coming down the stairway immediately above her, following the steps her feet had taken. She looked up. It was a man in a red bathrobe. She could see him, and he had no face, but only white bandages with holes for eyes.

And it was strange, she thought in some remote level of awareness, that there was something familiar about the way he moved down the steps towards her. It was almost as if she knew him.

XI

THE FOGHORN stopped. The patient in the red bathrobe had, in a swift second or two, come nearer, and Marcia turned and ran.

She screamed, too, without intending to do so, but no one could hear, for the foghorn started again. Waves of sound, lost and despairing and lonely, shook the ship and echoed from the fog drowning her voice, submerging all existence like a nightmare in its own confusion.

But it was not really a nightmare. She reached a companion-way and whirled into the lighted ship. Two nurses in smart little caps seemed to float out of the lights. They said things to her, and instantly there were people and voices everywhere.

The scene dissolved and shifted again, like a dream. She was in a small office. She was in an arm-chair with chintz cushions. A metal filing cabinet stood in a corner. A nurse with a captain's bars on her collar was beside her, saying: " Now, now, it's all right. Now, now . . ."

But it wasn't all right, because someone came to the door and opened it a few inches and whispered to the nurse. Marcia watched her pretty young face lose its colour, turn pinched

and white. She cried: " Who was it ? It can't be ! *Murder*
. . ."

The pale-grey walls had photographs upon them. Between the curtained ports on a bracket was a small green pot of ivy. Beyond the open door was the nurse's stateroom, its high bunk neat and flat under a blue cover. The whispers at the door stopped. The young nurse closed the door and went to sit at the desk, as if the position reinforced her. She said stiffly : " It's true. He was one of the seamen, Manuel Para. He was in the lifeboat with you."

She looked at Marcia, and, after a moment, said : " You are cold. I'll get you something hot."

But instead she went to the telephone on the wall above the desk. Again Marcia's whole consciousness seemed to reach out for physical details, small and reassuring. She watched the nurse set an arrow at a number on the face of the telephone as gratefully as if the nurse's action, as if the cheerful neat little office had the power to deny the dreadful disorder on the deck outside, amid the wet veils of fog, with the desolate, lost sound of the foghorn drowing all creation in its own despair.

The nurse turned from the telephone. " He already knew. He says to check the wards. I have to go. I'll send someone to you." Suddenly she was gone.

Why was Manuel Para murdered ?

Marcia closed her eyes, and immediately it was as if she were pitching in the little lifeboat again, going down, down, down into darkness and destruction, with a dead man in the boat, with Manuel Para and the other seaman in the boat, with herself and Daisy Belle, Gili and Luther and Mickey dim shapes in the night, huddled together. Held inexorably together by the storm as, now, they were held inexorably together by murder.

A long time must have passed when the door opened at last, and it was Josh Morgan. He lifted her up and held her against him. " Marcia, Marcia . . ."

He was real, too, like the neat little office, like the photographs, like the homely pleasant details of living, except this reality was much better. She was alive and warm and safe ; she had emerged from a fantasy of horror. She clung to Josh Morgan and could not talk.

He seemed to know that. He put his cheek down against her face and held her until her breath came evenly, until the warmth of his embrace had shut out the cold of the lifeboat.

"All right now?" he said at last.

"He was there, Josh. Under the stairway. I started down to B deck, and Para was there. . . ."

"I ought not to have left you alone."

He had gone to find Mickey. Suddenly she remembered that, and Gili and everything that had gone before. She could see Gili's slanting, triumphant green eyes and smiling red lips, and the soft golden shimmer of Mickey's cigarette case.

Josh said: "I didn't find André. He wasn't in his cabin. I looked and . . . Marcia, what happened? Was any one with you when you found him?"

She wouldn't think of Gili now. She replied: "No. Except the patient. He was there by the railing. He followed me down the stairs."

He put her away from him sharply, his hand gripping her shoulder. "*Who* followed you down the stairs? Tell me everything."

But there was not much, really, to tell. A patient leaning against a railing; a man dead on the deck below; the patient descending the steps above her. She hesitated, and added: "I thought for a moment that I knew him. But I couldn't have known him. And I screamed and ran. . . ."

He held her suddenly tighter. "That was what I told you to do; run and yell like hell and . . . Listen, Marcia, what was there about him that you recognised?"

"Not anything, really. There couldn't have been! His face and head were bandaged. It was all so quick and confused. I can't be sure of anything."

"But it was a man? You are sure it wasn't—well, Gili? Or Daisy Belle Cates?"

She hadn't thought of that.

And had the patient with the bandages over his face actually been one of the *Lerida* survivors? Had he murdered Manuel Para? The red-clothed, faceless figure had had for her a curious sense of horror. Actually, though, had a primitive sense of danger outside herself intervened to warn her?

Josh Morgan was so white that he looked grey.

He said: "We'll go to the Captain."

Again the scene suddenly dissolved into another. They left the little office and were in the narrow passageway, climbing stairs, hurrying through the ship.

A ship that was subtley different.

Only the wards were guarded and unchanged, protected by all the minute, invulnerable mechanism of care from even the knowledge of murder. Brightly lighted, cheerful, invincibly protected, it was as if the wards were sanctuary. They had an entity apart from the rest of the ship; the fact of murder was outside and could not touch them.

But the news of the murder had gone like wildfire over the rest of the ship, and there was already a hubbub of swift and controlled activity. Groups of men, transportation officers and staff, accompanied by seamen who were not then on duty, searched the ship, leaving no inch of hiding place unexplored.

The *Lerida* survivors had been brought aboard, and murder and suspicion had been brought aboard with them. It was almost as if the ship herself was aware of it, as if every shadow might harbour murder, as if every creak might betray that stealthy presence. The men searching went armed.

Twice on the stairway to the upper deck Marcia and Josh passed such groups, hurrying and intent, with revolvers in holsters strapped around their waists.

They reached the door of the Captain's quarters. It opened, and Mickey started out, saw them and stopped.

"Marcia!" He was pale and excited; he took her hand and drew her towards him. "Marcia, where have you been? Are you all right? I tried to find you. . . ."

Behind him, Captain Svendsen said: "Come in, Colonel Morgan. You too, Miss Colfax."

Colonel Wells, the medical officer in command, was there, too. The room was shadowy, except for a light on the desk which threw the Captain's weathered face and the weary dark pockets around his eyes into sharp relief. "I was about to send for you, Miss Colfax," he said. "Tell me exactly what happened."

So again she told her story. When she had finished, the Captain and Colonel Wells exchanged a long look.

"There is a patient with a bandaged face on this trip, isn't there, Colonel?"

Colonel Wells cleared his throat. " Right ! He's navy, an enlisted man. If I remember the case correctly his face is burned. He was on a destroyer which was torpedoed. He got the burns—bad facial burns and paralysed throat muscles—swimming through oil that was on fire."

" I think I've seen him on deck."

" He's ambulatory ; nothing the matter with him except his face and throat. He'll eventually get a plastic and skin grafting job. However, he ought not to have been on deck to-day. No deck privileges were granted owing to the fog. And "—Colonel Wells cleared his throat again—" and besides, it may not have been he. There are hundreds of red bathrobes. And I suppose if any one wished he could get hold of some gauze and wrap up his face. It would be an excellent disguise for a man or for a woman."

The Captain's eyes were like pins of light, impaling Marcia. " Was it a man or was it a woman ? "

" I thought then that it was a man. I suppose it could have been a woman."

" You didn't recognise him ? Or her ? "

" N-no."

" You are not sure. Was there anything familiar about him ? His height ? The way he walked ? The way he carried his arms ? There are a hundred ways in which you recognise people besides seeing their faces. What was it ? "

" I don't know. I don't know anything about him. Except that he was there."

" Have you seen the patient Colonel Wells mentioned ? "

She had seen hundreds of patients. She could not have identified one of them in any way, but she could not remember any whose face was bandaged except the figure on the stairway. She said so quickly. Captain Svendsen made a brusque move of impatience and Colonel Wells moved to the telephone. " I'll check on this man," he said. They listened to his terse questions. He said finally, " Tell him to report to the Captain's quarters at once. Send his field jacket along with him. Right, Lieutenant." He hung up the receiver and turned towards them. " His name is Jacob Heinzer. He's not in a ward, he's in one of the cabins. Ambulatory, as I say, and perfectly able to take care of himself. Matter of fact, I've never even seen his face. The present bandages won't be removed until he gets to the surgeon. But aside from that he's all right. However "—Colonel Wells looked out into the fog again for a moment and said—" if he was there on the stairway, why didn't he report the murder ? He must have seen Para ; he must have seen Miss Colfax. And what happened to him ? I got there as soon as it was reported to me ; it couldn't have been over five minutes. He wasn't there then ; I'm sure of that. Of course in five minutes on a ship anybody can get anywhere almost. But, still, I cannot help thinking of the ease of assuming that particular disguise—a red bathrobe, gauze. Every patient on board has a red bathrobe. They were issued to the *Lerida* survivors also, men and women alike. As to the gauze . . ." The Colonel shrugged. " That should not be difficult either."

The Captain's bleached eyebrows were drawn sombrely together.

" What about the knife ? No weapon was found ; it could have been thrown in the sea. It doubtless was."

" From the wound I'd say it was a sizable knife. Not a pocket-knife. But that could not have been taken from any of the surgeries or dispensaries," said Colonel Wells flatly. " That is impossible. The cases are locked."

The Captain sat down. He looked thoughtfully at his red, strong hands. " We'll have to try to establish the approximate time of the murder ; try to investigate from that basis. You examined the body, Colonel ? "

" Right. But I can't say to the minute when he was murdered, Captain. I'd say he'd been dead not much over an hour, certainly more than half an hour, at the time I looked at the body. That was immediately after the murder was reported. But that is only approximate as to time. There were no other wounds, no marks of struggle. I'd say the murderer took him by surprise."

" That's over an hour's leeway," said the Captain. " It's a wide margin of time on a ship, with people coming and going constantly." He turned again to Marcia. " How long were you on the boat deck before you found Para ? "

" I don't know exactly. I went there directly from here."

He glanced at a watch strapped on his thick red wrist. " That must have been about two hours ago. It has been nearly an hour since the murder was reported. According to

Colonel Wells, then Para might have been murdered during the time you were on the boat deck."

Colonel Wells interceded hurriedly. "I can't be sure of that, Captain. There's an inevitable margin of a few minutes more or less either way . . ."

The Captain went on: "Surely Para could call for help; surely he would struggle. It seems incredible, Miss Colfax, that you, sitting on the deck directly above, heard nothing."

"There was the foghorn," said Josh suddenly. "It drowned every other sound. I was on the boat deck, too, talking to Miss Colfax . . ."

"When?" said the Captain.

Josh told him quickly. He wasn't sure about the time. But he had met Miss Colfax and Miss Duvrey. Miss Duvrey had gone inside. He and Miss Colfax had strolled aft, he had got out a steamer chair for her and they had talked awhile.

"Where did you go then?"

"Inside. I was, in fact, in the officers' lounge when I heard of the murder."

"Did you see or hear anything while on deck that can now be construed as evidence?"

"Nothing."

The Captain eyed him thoughtfully for a moment and then turned back to Marcia. "You talked to Miss Duvrey while on deck and to Colonel Morgan. Any one else?"

"No. That is . . ." She'd forgotten Luther; she amended it. "Luther came along. . . ."

The Captain seized upon it instantly. "Luther Cates? Where had he come from? The deck below?"

"He was walking around the boat deck. I saw him come towards me."

"From what direction?"

"Forward."

"How long did he talk to you?"

"A few minutes—five or ten."

"Where did he go?"

"Along the deck aft."

"How long was this before you discovered Para?"

"Perhaps twenty minutes. I wasn't thinking of the time. It may have been longer."

The Captain surged impatiently upward to the telephone.

" I want Mr. Luther Cates. Announce it over the P.A. Right. Yes, here in my quarters." He sat down again heavily.

Colonel Wells said : " We'll have to investigate everybody's movements for at least an hour, Captain, if we hope to establish any alibis. Frankly, it seems to me an impossible undertaking. The murder was a perfectly simple and quick affair. Anybody could have done it and escaped notice. The decks were deserted on account of the fog. The foghorn covered any sounds of struggle or calls for help. The time limit is elastic. To attempt to establish alibis for nearly a thousand people seems to me "—he shrugged—" a monumental task."

"Six," said the Captain bluntly, " would satisfy me. Six . . ."

Again Marcia's thought touched them all, listing them: herself and Mickey, Gili, Luther and Daisy Belle Cates. And now the remaining Portuguese, Urdiola. Perhaps everyone in the room counted with her, but only the Colonel spoke. " That's right," he said, avoiding Marcia's eyes, avoiding Mickey's, looking only at the Captain. " Six . . ."

Someone knocked on the door, and it was a patient in a red bathrobe, with bandages over his face and head concealing it entirely. A nurse was with him.

There was another moment of silence in the cabin. Then the Captain said:

"Come in, Heinzer. Come in. Now, then, Miss Colfax, can you identify this man ? "

The nurse, her young face puzzled, gave the patient a little push forward, and he walked slowly into the middle of the cabin and stood there, seeming puzzled and uncertain himself, apparently surveying them all with that hidden, shadowed gaze. Marcia, her heart hammering, watched him. What had the Captain said—his height, the way he walked, the way he carried his arms ? A hundred ways to identify a man.

And here there was nothing. He could have been the figure on the stairway ; he could have been anybody and anything. He was completely anonymous.

She was aware that everyone in the room, even the nurse, was watching her. She met the Captain's waiting eyes and shook her head. " I can't tell. There's nothing . . ."

The Captain leaned back in his chair, his mouth grim. " All

right," he said. "Take him away. Will you question him outside, Colonel?"

The Colonel moved forward and held out his hand for the field jacket, the thick envelope which contained the patient's record, which the nurse gave him. She put her hand again on the arm of the tall figure in red; again it seemed to move slowly and uncertainly, still puzzled, still mute. They reached the door, the little procession of nurse, patient, doctor, and suddenly the patient seemed to try to speak and question. There was a hoarse rasping whisper of sound, his hands moved. The nurse urged him into the passage. The door closed behind the Colonel's erect, uniformed shoulders. And Marcia thought sickly, I can't tell; I don't know. And if it wasn't this man, then it was one of us.

Her heart was still pounding. Again everyone in the cabin looked at her.

"It could be this man?" said the Captain.

"Y-yes. I suppose so. Yes."

"Or it could have been someone else?"

"Yes."

Again he waited for a moment, hunched forward, staring thoughtfully at his hands. Then he reached for the telephone again.

"There's only one course for me to follow," he said. "This is my ship. I cannot take chances with lives under my protection. But as much for the safety of the *Lerida* survivors as for other reasons, I'm putting every person who was on the *Lerida* lifeboat under guard."

He took down the telephone. But Marcia did not hear his orders, for she was thinking again of the inexorable link of circumstance that seemed to hold the survivors of the ill-fated and ill-found little Portuguese ship together. It was like a chain, it was like a rope, from which one of them might hang.

Josh moved to light another cigarette. Mickey stared down at the rug. Colonel Wells returned as the Captain put down the receiver.

He closed the door and advanced briskly into the cabin. "His name is Jacob Heinzer. He's a naturalised American citizen, thirty years old, born in Argentina of French parents, living in New York since he was twenty." He put the field jacket down on the table near the Captain. " He says he knew nobody from the *Lerida*. He only knew that some survivors had been picked up. He says he was not on deck at any time during the day. He says he was alone in his cabin and knew nothing of the murder until I told him. Here's his record if you want to look at it."

The Captain glanced at the envelope and then up at the Colonel. " Do you believe him ? "

The Colonel shrugged. " I don't know. I have no reason not to believe him."

" That is not an alibi," said Mickey suddenly.

He had been silent so long that everyone turned quickly towards him.

" No," said the Captain. " No. That's not an alibi. Do you know anybody by that name ? "

Mickey shook his head. " Not to my knowledge. Certainly he would have had no motive in attacking me and Marcia, unless it's a case of war nerves, a brainstorm, something like that."

" Is that possible, Colonel ? " asked the Captain.

Again Colonel Wells shrugged. " Anything's possible. He seems all right to me, however, except for his wounds."

Again the Captain pinioned Marcia with his sharp, shrewd eyes. " How about you, Miss Colfax ? Ever heard that name before ? "

She replied much as Mickey had done. " Not so far as I know. Certainly I cannot think of any motive that anybody might have for trying to murder me."

Josh stirred suddenly. " Captain," he said, " if I may interrupt . . ."

" Yes, Colonel Morgan ? "

" Obviously the person on the stairway either wished to be seen and thus reported by Miss Colfax, or intended to murder her. If the former, it was obviously a disguise. If the latter, she is in very definite danger."

XII

DANGER? Marcia thought again, incredulously, Murder? Why should a man by the name of Jacob Heinzer wish to murder her? Why should any of the *Lerida* survivors wish to murder her? Yet the hands on her throat that first night on the *Magnolia* were fact.

The Colonel said slowly: " So she would report it. So that a man in a red bathrobe and bandages would be suspected, you mean, Colonel Morgan, instead of the real murderer."

Josh nodded. The Captain said shortly: " We'd better put Jacob Heinzer under guard, too, Colonel. And now then . . ."

There was a knock at the door, and he said impatiently: " Come in, come in."

It was Luther, his faded eyes anxious. " Somebody said you wanted to see me, Captain."

" Close the door. Now, then, one of the *Lerida* seamen, Manuel Para, has been murdered."

" Yes, I know." Luther glanced at Marcia and smoothed his scant hair nervously. " It must have happened about the time we were talking. Do you know who did it, Captain? "

" That," said the Captain bluntly, " is why I sent for you. You were on deck about that time. Did you see Para? "

" Either alive or dead? " An obscure twinkle came into Luther's faded eyes for an instant and vanished. " No," he said soberly. " After I spoke to Miss Colfax I walked on around the deck and then inside the ship. I was lounging around the lobby of the upper deck—the deck which, I suppose you call the boat deck; at any rate, where the life-rafts and lifeboats are mainly located—when I heard of the murder." He hesitated, and then lifted his stooped yet somehow elegant shoulders in a brief shrug. " I have no alibi, Captain, if that is what you want."

" It would help," said Captain Svendsen dourly. " I'll have to have statements from each of you." And again there was a knock on the door. This time, however, it was Major Williams, followed by three officers.

The Captain, with Colonel Wells' assistance, gave them

quick directions. The *Lerida* passengers were to be placed under guard. The decks were to be searched again, the patients carefully checked. Inquiries were to be made about a patient with a bandaged face having been seen about the ship. Inquiries were to be made about Manuel Para—who had seen him, where, when.

Marcia turned to speak to Mickey, but Josh Morgan stood beside her instead. Mickey, though, met her look and smiled.

Ordinarily, Mickey's almost classically proportioned features wore not so much a sombre expression as one of immobility; so the sudden warmth of his smile and the light it gave his clear grey eyes were like a flash of sunlight through a flat, grey sky. How many times in the past had she remembered that smile and clung to the memory as if it had been a lifeline thrown to her through the storm! Even then it was warm and candid and reassuring. Gili's claims were—must be— as fantastic as they sounded. And the fact of murder could not really catch Mickey and herself in its suffocating web.

She told herself that defiantly, but there was no chance to talk to Mickey. There was no chance to talk to anybody, for the group around the Captain suddenly broke apart. An officer went to Mickey and Luther and all three moved towards the door. The Captain went quickly away, too, adjusting his oilskins with impatient, angry-looking red hands. Josh Morgan started to speak to her, but a young lieutenant intervened curtly: "Will you come with me, Miss Colfax?"

So she went along the narrow grey passageways again, with the motion of the ship pressing up against her feet and the lieutenant at her elbow. They went along the stairway, and at the lobby around what had been the purser's desk knots of nurses turned pretty young faces and perky little caps to give them curious, suddenly silent, glances.

They reached the cabin on B deck, and already a seaman, with a revolver strapped on a belt around his waist stood in the passageway. "I've searched the cabin, sir," he said quickly to the lieutenant. "I did not find any sort of knife. No gauze, either. But there are three red bathrobes . . ."

"Thank you. I'll report it."

The young lieutenant opened the door, motioned her to enter, and closed the door firmly behind her. Daisy Belle Cates was already in the cabin, pacing up and down its narrow length, smoking nervously, pausing abruptly with a sharp look of question on her long, fine face.

"Marcia!" She came quickly and put her brown hand with its broken fingernails on Marcia's shoulder. Her voice was sharp and thin as a knife. "Is it true? Did you find him? They made me come here. I was in the nurses' lounge and they sent a seaman to find me. He searched the cabin." She caught her breath. "Who did it? Who killed him? What did you see?"

Daisy Belle had courage. Daisy Belle had faced the storm on the *Lerida* with the horror of the night in the lifeboat without flinching, with coolness, making sure Luther had a warm coat, taking a turn at the oars along with the men, passing brandy from hand to hand, never showing in any way the fear that, as a sensible woman, she must have felt. Daisy Belle could look at death and say, "My face is not much loss, but I've always rather liked my legs." It was strange to see terror peer openly from Daisy Belle's eyes.

The next moment, though, it was veiled. She had taken Marcia to the bunk, drawn up blankets around her, called the guard and asked for hot coffee, anything hot, and got it very quickly. Marcia, staring at the grey underside of the bunk close above her head, and seeing on its clean and shining blankness the face of Manuel Para, told again that short and ugly story, with its even shorter and uglier footnote.

"*Was* it the patient?" asked Daisy Belle.

"I don't know. I couldn't possibly say."

"Heinzer," said Daisy Belle blankly. "Heinzer—I never knew anybody by that name."

And Gili flounced into the cabin, her eyes glittering and narrow, her face both angry and frightened. She flung herself into a chair with a furious and baffled look at a young officer who had escorted her there, and who now settled his blouse around his shoulders with a suggestion of relief and left hurriedly. And then Gili saw the coffee, helped herself largely and hungrily to it, looked at Daisy Belle and at Marcia over the edge of the cup, and said unexpectedly: "They said he was murdered. That's two."

Daisy Belle was bringing another cup of coffee to Marcia. She stopped so abruptly that the coffee splashed into the saucer.

"What do you mean—two?"

Gili eyed her. "Things go in threes—always." She said it coolly. But when she lowered the cup there was a greyish line around her scarlet mouth. Daisy Belle said violently: "What utter drivel!" And, as coolly as Gili, poured the spilled coffee from the saucer back into the cup. Her hand was shaking nevertheless.

And Marcia thought queerly, if Gili is frightened—and she looks frightened—then she didn't do it. And Daisy Belle was frightened, too.

The fact was, of course, that suspicion had already added itself to the cabin, as inevitably and almost as horribly as murder had added itself to the lifeboat. "There's a dreadful contagion about murder," Josh Morgan had said. "Perhaps it's fear, perhaps it's something else."

So began actually a period of waiting which held Marcia and Daisy Belle—and Gili, perhaps, too, although Marcia never knew what Gili was thinking and planning behind those slanting, green eyes—in a kind of spell of inactivity. They could only wait—wait and listen for any hint as to the investigation which was going on in the rest of the ship.

The rest of that day passed like that, except that Daisy Belle, first, and then Gili were questioned by the Captain.

He came with Major Williams to their cabin in order to do so; and he was unexpectedly, indeed brutally, frank. He had questioned the others who were on the *Lerida* lifeboat. He enumerated them, checking each off on his fingers, his oilskins and his solid figure and red face seeming to fill the cabin. "André Messac, Luther Cates, the seaman, Urdiola, Miss Colfax." He paused, looking at Gili, who avoided his gaze sullenly, and then at Daisy Belle, who rallied to the attack promptly.

"What do you wish to know?"

He told her bluntly. "Anything you know about the murder of Para; or Castiogne."

"But I've already told you I know nothing about Castiogne . . ." began Daisy Belle, but he cut in.

"Tell me, please, exactly what you did to-day—where you were, who talked to you, everything."

"I see," said Daisy Belle after a moment. "We are all suspect. Very well, I'll try to remember." She lighted a cigarette deliberately, put back her head with its thin, reddish-grey curls, and faced him coolly. She had had breakfast early. She had gone on deck for a cigarette or two, found it cold and dismal, drifted back through the ship and eventually to the nurses' lounge, where she had found some magazines and read. She had gone to lunch, had looked for Marcia there and didn't find her.

Neither the Captain nor Daisy Belle glanced at Marcia, yet somehow, irresistibly, she had to explain. "I was on deck," she said. "I'd had breakfast late. I did not go to lunch."

Daisy Belle took a breath of smoke and went on. She had returned immediately to the lounge, and read again until a young officer came to find her. He told her of the murder and the Captain's orders for her to return to the cabin. She paused again, imperceptibly, and then added: "Any number of them must have seen me. Some of them must remember seeing me."

Gili's green eyes flashed. She cried: "Oh, you are afraid! That is a—what do you call it . . . ? It is legal. A legal word . . ."

Daisy Belle gave Gili a fraction of a glance and said coolly: "Never mind. You know what it means all right," and put out her cigarette.

The Captain's blond head jerked around toward Gili. "What about you? What's your story?"

Mickey and Luther, more sophisticated, treated Gili as if she might have been a duchess. To the Captain, black was black and white was white. There were no shades between, and simply and cruelly his manner put Gili on the black side. Unexpectedly, and somehow rather pathetically, she accepted it, and replied with unaccustomed meekness: "I didn't do anything really all day. I went on deck and walked and then I had breakfast. A nurse took me down to the saloon. And then I—oh, I went around over the ship, looking at things, talking to "—she lifted one shoulder in a ghost of a shrug— "talking to this one or that one. Nothing much. They all seemed very "—a shade of discomfiture crossed her face— " very busy," said Gili, somewhat regretfully. "So many handsome men, too."

Daisy Belle's mouth twitched. The Captain said: "Continue, please. Where were you when the murder occurred ? "

" I don't know when that was. I know nothing. . . ."

" When you heard of it, then ? "

" Oh, well. That "—Gili glanced at Marcia—" I had met you on the deck. You remember ? "

" I remember," said Marcia.

Gili went on rather hurriedly : " And then—you remember —the handsome officer, the Colonel, came. And I—oh, I thought you might wish to be together, you and he. So I—I went into the ship. And in a few minutes I . . ." she hesitated. Her eyes slid to Marcia and then away. She caught her lower lip in her teeth for a second and suddenly said : " I met André and we went on deck—that is, on the other side, the—the left . . ."

" Port," said the Captain automatically. And Marcia thought swiftly, so Gili went straight to Mickey after making the claims she had made.

" We were there smoking and talking for—oh, it must have been for an hour or longer. A long time. Then, well . . ." she shrugged. " People were running. We heard about the murder."

Daisy Belle said dryly : " The word is alibi, Gili. I felt sure you understood it."

Major Williams said : " That agrees with André Messac's statement, sir."

" I know." The Captain turned to Marcia. " Does that square with your opinion about the length of time that passed while you were on deck and after you spoke to Miss Duvrey ? "

" Yes. That is, I wasn't thinking of time. It seems about right."

The Captain looked at Gili again. " You were on B deck ? "

Gili bit her lip. " Yes, but we knew nothing of the murder. Nothing. It is a big ship. How could we know anything of what happened on the other side of it ? "

The Captain for a moment looked rather hopeless, as if, in spite of himself, he agreed. And certainly owing to the fact that the exact time when Para was murdered was not known, owing to the layout of the ship and the accessibility of the deck to any portion of it, any attempt to rule out any of the *Lerida* survivors by means of proven alibis was a forlorn hope at best. Probably it seemed so to the Captain, for he gave a sort of angry sigh, stared bleakly at the grey port opposite for a moment, and finally said: " Two men from the *Lerida* lifeboat have been murdered. It stands to reason that one of the others in that boat did it. I've questioned all of you. I've got all your statements. So far, I'm bound to admit, I've found no discrepancy."

He paused briefly. Marcia thought, then Mickey *was* with Gili, for his statement obviously had agreed with Gili's. What had they talked of, there in the fog, for an hour or more?

The Captain went on: " Since it is not likely that two murderers are on this ship, I have to conclude that the person who tried to kill you, Miss Colfax, and who attacked Monsieur Messac a few minutes earlier that same night, is the person who succeeded in killing Castiogne, and, to-day, Para. So far I can find no motive linking you together. If you know of anything of the kind you'd better tell me now." He looked at her sharply, and must have seen in her face a complete denial, for he did not even pause. " If any of you knows of any suspicious circumstance, or anything at all which is an inaccuracy, a discrepancy, as you see it, any time or anywhere, it is your duty to tell me. Now . . ." He paused then. So long, indeed, that the waiting silence in the little cabin seemed freighted with things untold.

Yet there was nothing more that Marcia could tell him, except, of course, Mickey's real name and identity, and that had nothing to do with two murders or with the attack upon Mickey and herself. She looked at Daisy Belle, whose fine-drawn face was lifted frankly and openly, but who also did not speak. She looked at Gili, who was equally still, but whose look suddenly to Marcia seemed secretive and listening. It was so strong an impression that she thought swiftly, why is she listening; what does she expect me or Daisy Belle to say? And then she knew.

Gili had accused Daisy Belle and Luther Cates of being Nazis. To Marcia, at least, it was an impossible story to accept. She thought that Mickey and Josh Morgan found it equally difficult to credit. Certainly all three of them had tried to persuade Gili to tell no one else; certainly, so far, Gili had let herself be persuaded.

But suddenly that very acquiescence seemed somehow

wrong. It was not like Gili. It did not fit what Marcia knew
of her. It was as if something in a familiar picture had swung
suddenly awry. And that thought brought her to another.
Some time, not long ago (just before she'd walked down the
stairs, wasn't it, and found Para?) something else had suddenly and obscurely seemed wrong. For a moment there had
been that same curious and troubling sensation of something,
some very small thing that was askew, that was again wrong.
Whatever it was it had eluded her. She could not pin it
down and identify it.

She could, however, with Gili now. It would have fitted
the picture of Gili if, under pressure of the investigation into
murder, she had blurted out her accusation of the Cates'
again. She did not do it, and that was wrong. It was not so
easy, though, to understand why.

The pause had lengthened. Captain Svendsen's bleached
eyebrows were drawn heavily together. Major Williams was
fidgeting nervously. Still no one spoke. Suddenly the Captain
opened his straight-lipped mouth, closed it again with a snap,
whirled around and walked out of the cabin without another
word. Major Williams gave them a worried glanced, mumbled
something, and disappeared behind the Captain. The door
closed.

Daisy Belle reached for a cigarette. Gili stared at the floor.
Marcia sat down slowly. She must be cool and calm, like
Daisy Belle. But Daisy Belle hadn't seen what she had seen
there in the fog under the stairs.

Well, she wouldn't think of that.

She wouldn't think of Gili.

But she must find a way to see Mickey.

After a long time Marcia decided also that she would not
think of Josh Morgan and the way he had held her and
suddenly, unexpectedly, kissed her. So, for a queer short space
in time, everything but his nearness, his mouth upon her own,
was blotted out. She got up restlessly, walked to the port,
stared into the fog, came back.

Daisy Belle put out one cigarette and lighted another. Gili
went to the mirror, combed out her hair, went to sprawl on
her stomach in her bunk, her long hair over her face.

Dinner came eventually on trays, passed in to them by the
seamen then on guard.

Gili, tossing back her long locks of hair, questioned him. " Is there any news ? What are they doing ? Have they found who murdered him ? "

But he mumbled something and went away. They heard the click of the lock, and after that no one came near them. Lights were on in the cabin by that time and the ports were dark grey.

Night came early, due to the fog. There were eventually no sounds at all from the rest of the ship. They felt isolated and alone, as if they were travelling towards an unknown destiny in a ghost ship. It was curious, thought Marcia once, to realise that all around them the busy life of the hospital ship went on. In the cabin there was only the far-away throb of the ship's engines and the feeling of motion and the occasional distant sound of the ship's bell. And the three women, shut up together, each thinking her own thoughts.

Eventually, too, speaking only at intervals and then saying nothing, they got into the three narrow bunks. Daisy Belle turned out the light, and there was only the soft shaft of faintly crimson light coming from the port opposite the door. Probably none of them slept. Certainly for Marcia the darkness, the occasional wail of the foghorn, the lap and rush of water outside, all merely served to heighten and sharpen the questions that seemed to fill the cabins as if they had substance.

If Castiogne had been murdered in the lifeboat, who among them had done it and why ? Why, then, was Para murdered ? Was the figure in the red bathrobe with the bandaged, eyeless face that of Jacob Heinzer, the patient—and if so, why did he deny it ? And if it was not, then who had assumed that disguise, and again, why ?

Josh had answered that ; but if Marcia were actually in danger (and those hands on her throat had been real ; there was no question of that), what possible link was there between her and two Portuguese seamen whom she scarcely knew by name ?

Again she could not extricate herself from endless circles of conjecture, which went around and around on themselves and arrived nowhere. Mickey and herself, Daisy Belle and Luther Cates, Gili, and the other seaman, Urdiola. Suddenly in the night, her eyes wide open, staring at that soft band of crimson striking into the cabin from the port, it seemed to her that no one perhaps had paid enough attention to Urdiola, the small, swarthy seaman with the shifting dark eyes and the wizened monkey-like face. Certainly he must have known more of Para and of Castiogne than any one else.

But the Captain had questioned him. He had questioned everybody from the *Lerida*. If he had extracted any information at all from Urdiola, he would have acted upon it.

Sometime, still looking at the round, dimly lighted port, Marcia's eyes closed and blocked it out.

It was a long and weary night, with heavy fog, and the U.S.A.H.S. *Magnolia* pushing her sturdy way through it, with the Captain on the bridge all night. Although none of the patients and none of the survivors of the *Lerida* knew it, the night watch everywhere on the ship had been doubled.

Morning dawned grey and chilly, with the fog, if anything, heavier, and the foghorn sounding at three-minute intervals.

It was that morning early that Urdiola was charged with murder and the other *Lerida* survivors were released.

Mickey came to the cabin on B deck. The foghorn was sounding again when he knocked, so Marcia did not know he was there until he opened the door. His eyes were bright and eager, going from one to the other of the three women in the cabin. He said, "Urdiola killed them both. He's arrested and "—his clear, light-grey eyes fastened on Daisy Belle—" he's got your diamond, Daisy Belle."

They were having breakfast. Daisy Belle, staring at Mickey, forgetting her tray, jumped up. The tray clattered to the floor, and Daisy Belle cried above the clash of china : " But Castiogne had my diamond ! "

Marcia put down her own tray and reached to set upright the small pot which was pouring a stream of coffee on the floor. Mickey came quickly to kneel at Daisy Belle's feet and help pick up the spilled dishes. Gili did not move but sat rigid, exactly like a cat which is crouching, not moving a hair, until danger is past.

XIII

EVEN THEN Marcia noted that—probably first because Gili was nearest Daisy Belle, and it would have been natural for her to move first to Daisy Belle's assistance—and then she looked again because of that extraordinary stillness, and because of the pasty, glistening look of fear which sprang instantly into Gili's face. She had seen that look in her face before. What, then, did it mean? And what did Daisy Belle mean? And, for that matter, Mickey?

He was speaking to Daisy Belle: "I'm sorry I startled you. Here, do sit down and I'll get you more coffee, more everything. I'm afraid this is pretty well gone."

Daisy Belle sat down on the bunk very stiffly. Her fine, long face was grey, her eyes were topaz-bright and blank. She said: "I gave it to Castiogne. That is, Luther gave it to him. It was to pay for our passage. It was a bribe. . . ."

Mickey, bending over the spilled dishes, scooping up egg and a sliced orange, said: "Yes, of course. That's what Luther told them. He recognised it at once." He rose, opened the door and spoke to the seaman who was still on guard. "Can you get another breakfast tray in here? That's right. Thank you." He turned back into the cabin. "Furthermore," he said, "and after due consideration, we are all released. They just haven't got around to informing you three yet."

Daisy Belle said: "Tell me what happened. Tell me . . ."

Gili still did not move, but it was as if everything about her listened. Mickey sat down on Marcia's bunk, directly opposite Daisy Belle, and reached up to draw Marcia down beside him. "Well, it's a short story," he said, "but a convincing one. Naturally, it looked from the first as if Castiogne's death and then Para's were actually the result of some sort of private feud among the three *Lerida* seamen. I mean—well . . ." he shrugged. "None of us had anything to do with them, and they might have had any number of grudges and fights and God knows what. I can't see why one of them would take a punch at me, or, for that matter, hurt Marcia, unless, of course, whoever did it had some reason to think one

or both of us had witnessed the murder of Castiogne ; as I
certainly didn't and neither did Marcia."

Daisy Belle's brown, battered hands made a quickly
controlled gesture of impatience. Mickey saw it and went on :
" Well, everybody else thought so, too. It's an obvious
conclusion. They questioned Urdiola at length yesterday. He
wouldn't admit anything, said he hadn't even seen Para since
early yesterday morning. They weren't satisfied. They
searched his bunk yesterday and Para's bunk, next to him,
and found only Para's seaman's papers, no money, tucked
under the blanket. Well, they thought it was odd that there
was no money at all with the papers. So they gave Urdiola
a real search, and found some money and the diamond."

" Did Luther "—Daisy Belle was gripping her hands hard—
" did Luther identify it ? "

" Of course, right away. As to that, Urdiola broke down
immediately and said he'd got it from Para, or, rather, that
Para had given it to him."

" Para gave it to him ! " cried Daisy Belle. " But it was
Castiogne . . ."

" He said that Para, yesterday morning early, had given
him a little packet and told him to hold it for him, and, if
anything should happen, to send it to Para's wife. The
Captain asked why Para did that, why did he think he was in
danger, and Urdiola said he didn't know. Oh, his story is very
thin, very specious. At any rate he said then that he didn't see
Para again, but he heard of the murder a few minutes before
they sent for him to question him. So he scurried back to
their bunks. Nobody was around. He unwrapped the packet,
found Para's papers, a little money, and the diamond. He
slipped Para's papers under the blanket of Para's bunk,
put the money with his own, and hid the diamond in his
shoe."

" Do you mean "—Daisy Belle was leaning forward, her face
an anxious, lined mask—" do you mean that the Captain
believes he murdered both Castiogne and Para for the diamond
—my diamond," she said in a tone of horror.

" There's nothing else to think," said Mickey. " He's a
stupid fellow. Only a stupid fellow would try to get away
with a story like that. And only a greedy and stupid fellow
would murder like that for a jewel. Probably he thinks it's

much more valuable than it is. Although," said Mickey, looking rather searchingly at Daisy Belle, " it is a very large and very fine gem. I had a look at it. The Captain sent for me and Luther immediately to ask us if we knew anything of it, or, rather, to ask Luther. He'd know I'd never have money enough to own a jewel like that. So Urdiola wasn't so far wrong if he got the idea that he'd never in his dull life have a chance to get hold of that much wealth again. Everything," said Mickey rather slowly, " is relative. What's only a trinket to you, Daisy Belle, is a lifetime of ease to a man like Urdiola. It's a sound motive for murder all right."

She moved her lips but did not speak. Mickey went on : " Naturally, they believe either that Para murdered Castiogne for the diamond and that Urdiola knew it and in his turn murdered Para for the same reason. Probably, in that case, it was actually suggested to him by Para's killing of Castiogne. Urdiola's got about the intelligence of an ape, and I, personally, doubt whether he'd think up anything very enterprising on his own initiative. Either that or Urdiola murdered Castiogne for the stone, and Para knew it and wanted to split with him—threatened him, maybe, with disclosure, unless Urdiola came across with part or all of the proceeds. Of course Urdiola insists that all three of them were the best of friends. Particularly Castiogne and Para. He says they were boyhood pals, inseparable. Told each other everything. That's Urdiola's story ! " Again Mickey shrugged. " It's hard to say. Probably we'll never know. But the motive's there all right, and the murderer."

" Has he "—Daisy Belle wet her lips—" has he confessed ? "

" Oh, no. He has barely the wit to stick to his story and deny murder. He'll keep on denying it, I suppose. He just stands there and shakes his head."

" Where is Luther ? " said Daisy Belle.

" Still with the Captain, I imagine."

Daisy Belle got up. " Where is my coat, Marcia ? What did I do with it ? I've got to see Luther. . . ."

" But Daisy Belle, your breakfast. Wait . . ."

" Here it is." She found the nurse's coat and flung it around her shoulders and turned intently to Mickey. " Are we really free ? Can I go ? Will the guard stop me ? "

" I don't think so. . . ."

The guard didn't stop her. Perhaps he had, as they talked, received orders to let them go. Daisy Belle's coat flashed through the door and she was gone.

Then Gili, who had not moved ; Gili, who had not spoken ; Gili, who had waited and listened and all but held her breath, got up, too, in one sudden, lithe motion, reached for her coat, hung it around her shoulders, and gave Mickey a swift green glance. " I'm going, too," she said. " I've been shut up in this hole too long. I'm going to get some fresh air." She reached the door and put her strong white hand upon it and paused, as if she were waiting, invitingly, her green eyes holding Mickey's.

But Mickey leaned back against the bulkhead and shoved his hands in his pockets. " It's foggy out," he said.

Still for an instant Gili waited. Then, as Mickey did not move, she bit her lip, opened the door, said : " I'll be on the boat deck . . ." and left the cabin, closing the door hard behind her.

Marcia said : " But she—Mickey, she wanted you to go with her ! "

" Nonsense," said Mickey, lounging back and staring absently at the bulkhead.

" But she—she almost demanded it. As if . . ." she was about to say puzzled, and quickly, " as if she had a right to demand it." She stopped the words on her lips. And Mickey said, still staring at the bulkhead, in an absent, careless tone : " Oh, Gili's always that way."

Something was in Marcia's throat, swelling and beating. She waited for a moment, looking at Mickey, who still stared absently at the bulkhead.

"*Always*. . . ." said Marcia finally.

And Mickey said : " Always quick tempered. Always going off on tangents. Hard to manage. . . ." He stopped abruptly and his clear grey eyes focused and sharpened. He turned to Marcia quickly. " That is," he said, " she seems to me. . . ." He stopped.

Marcia said : " How long have you known her, Mickey ? "

His grey eyes, almost as grey as the fog but very clear around the sharp, black pupils, opened wider. " Gili ? "

" Yes. Tell me, Mickey—exactly."

" But you know. She was in Lisbon. What do you mean ? "

She swallowed hard. " Tell me the truth, Mickey. She has your cigarette case. She called you Mickey."

" I don't know what you mean ! Don't be a fool ! I don't know Gili at all, except on that damned little ship, and before that I saw her around the bars in Lisbon. If she's got my cigarette case she . . ." he shrugged. He got up and stood above her, his hands thrust in his pockets, his eyes angry now, bright and wide in his thin face. " She may have taken it, borrowed it ; I don't know. I don't remember. If she knows my name, you told her."

" No, no, Mickey, I didn't. . . ."

" What did she say ? Did she call me Mickey ? Then she's heard you call me Mickey. I've begged you not to."

" She said. . . ." Her voice sounded tight and harsh ; she made herself go on. " She said that you came back to me because I had some money, enough for you and her."

His eyes were suddenly bright and fixed with anger. He did not speak for a moment, only stood there looking down with that angry brightness. Then he cried : " You believed her ! Marcia, how could you ? Have you questioned her ? "

" Questioned Gili ? "

" You've been shut up here all night together. You've had time and opportunity to talk."

" This is between you and me, not Gili. . . ."

His face cleared. He cried : " You were right, darling ! You are always right. Gili doesn't matter."

She said slowly : " Mickey, you spoke as if you knew her well. As if you'd known her a long time. As if the things she said could have been true."

" Marcia, listen to me. Answer me. Do you believe me or Gili ? "

She did not reply. He added suddenly, watching her : " You've known me for five years—Gili about five days. And you'd take her word against mine ? "

She put back her head and met his eyes. She said directly : " Are you in love with her ? "

" In love with Gili ! " cried Mickey, and laughed. He took her hands and kissed them lightly. " You're jealous. You're a silly child. You know that I love you. I came back to you. Nothing—nobody else means anything to me. I love you."

He straightened up and looked straight down into her eyes with his own clear, grey gaze and said: "You do believe me, don't you? Never mind, my darling. I'll get Gili. I'll make her take back whatever silly things she has told you."

"No, no...."

"Yes, yes, I will. I'm not going to have her upsetting you with any such nonsense."

"Mickey, why would she say anything like that?"

He stared at her for an instant and then shrugged and smiled. "Gili doesn't need a motive. Surely you can see what kind of a woman she is. She did it out of—I don't know what—mischief, malice. Because she likes men, and at the risk of sounding as if I like myself, perhaps she settled on me!" He laughed and said: "After all, you like me. Perhaps she thinks she might, if she could get me detached from you. Not that she'd have a chance . . . Oh, Marcia, darling, don't look so serious. I'm only joking. A bad joke," said Mickey, sobering swiftly. "But she isn't worth a serious thought. Believe me, my darling. I'll go and get her. . . ."

"No." Marcia got up and faced him directly and angrily. "No. If I believe you, Mickey, I believe you. I don't want to talk to her."

"But, Marcia . . ." He looked bewildered and then smiled again. "Darling, you're very sweet when you are angry. Although I don't know what I've done...."

"Forget it," said Marcia, so briefly it sounded curt. She caught her breath and made herself speak more coolly and naturally. "If we've been released, Mickey, let's get out on deck. I feel as if I'd been in this cabin for a month."

"Right," he said. "It's a relief to have the thing settled. I mean Urdiola."

She found her coat, and he took it from her hands. "Suppose he didn't do it," she said unexpectedly.

Mickey frowned. "Don't suppose any such thing. Besides, there's no doubt of his guilt. That diamond is a huge and, I should say, a very valuable stone. Shall we go?"

He held open the door. The seaman on guard had gone. It seemed suddenly extraordinarily pleasant to be walking along, free to come and go, without restraint. They reached the lobby, with its glimpses of the busy life of the ship: nurses, doctors, little clusters of lounging patients. They emerged on deck, and it was still foggy and cold and the foghorn smote raucously upon their ears. It stopped, and Mickey said suddenly: " Of course, I can't help remembering that other nonsensical story Gili told us. You know, about the Cates' being Nazis. But undoubtedly that was just another of her notions, Marcia. Must have been. You . . ." He reached for cigarettes, and held the package towards her, and did not finish until he had held a match, too, for her light. Then he said: " You didn't tell any one about it, did you? "

" No. I didn't believe it."

He smiled and gave her a glance of reproach. " Yet you believed Gili when she told you all that stuff about me! Marcia, Marcia! " He shook his head gaily. " Nevertheless it flatters me. But you were right about the Cates'. An accusation like that is a very unpleasant one; it sticks. Denial never catches up with accusation; it's one of the laws of life. I never knew them, but I knew *of* them. Everybody knows of them. I don't believe that they were Nazis. I think," said Mickey earnestly, " that we should just forget Gili's little story. Never tell anybody." He took a long breath of smoke and added: " And, darling, remember, too, will you, *not* to call me Mickey."

She turned to him swiftly: " Mickey, we've got to tell the truth about that. We're going home. We can't enter America with a false name and false passport. We've got to tell them and explain and. . . ."

Unconsciously she had placed her hands on his arm. With a brusque motion he shook them off. His eyes were blazing suddenly, his face white. " *No*," he cried. " *No*. . . ."

" Mickey. . . ."

" I said not to call me that."

" But you. . . ."

" Marcia, you've got to promise me never to tell any one that I'm Michel Banet. Promise me now."

" No. . . ."

" You must. . . ."

" Mickey, I can't."

He waited a moment while the foghorn sounded again, its desolate, dreary wail coming back at them in echoes from the surrounding fog. She looked up, bewildered, half-frightened, into his white and angry face. Naturally he felt bitter.

Naturally he was nervous and taut and quick to anger. Yet something inside her insisted stubbornly that she was right; that he must be made somehow to see that rightness for himself and her. She tried to speak, and the foghorn blared again, and suddenly Mickey took her hands and held them quickly to his lips, and then whirled around and left her standing there at the railing. She cried: " Mickey," and the foghorn drowned the sound of her voice and he disappeared quickly into the ship.

She started after him, to reason with him, to do anything that would make peace again between them. But after the first step or two she stopped. He'd get over his anger; he'd come back; he'd talk to her, reasonably and quietly.

She told herself that and did not quite believe it. She glanced along the deck—B deck on the same level with her cabin. Aft, under the stairway the previous day, she had found the body of Manuel Para.

Nothing was there now, and again, as on the previous day, the deck was deserted by patients and nurses and doctors. She did not wish, however, to pass the place where Para had sprawled so horribly, looking up at nothing with those blank dark eyes, so she turned in the opposite direction towards the bow. And then she saw Josh Morgan.

He was ahead, leaning against the railing. His coat was slung over his shoulder and his cap pulled low, yet immediately she recognised the set of his shoulders silhouetted against the pearly-grey fog, the line of his head, the tilt of his cap. She wondered how much of the scene between herself and Mickey he had seen or guessed at.

As she thought that he turned abruptly and called, " Hallo! " and came towards her.

For a moment or two as they approached each other the foghorn was silent, and there was only the wash of water along the sides of the ship and the quiet sound of their footsteps.

Then they met. It was actually at a sheltered turn of the deck. Only the blank, glistening white bulkheads could overhear anything that was said.

But neither of them spoke. Josh's face looked rather white in the fog, his eyes very grave and dark. He carried a lighted cigarette, which he tossed over the railing. Then without a word he put his arms around her and held her close against him. And Marcia, as if another woman had got into her body, as if she could not have helped it, moved closer within his embrace, and still blindly, still without willing it, turned her face upward so his mouth met her own.

XIV

SHE DID NOT intend to move as she had done ; she must draw away.

This was a man she scarcely knew ; a man she did not love ; a man who was nothing to her.

Except that his mouth was so hard and warm and strong upon her own that she could not move, she could not think. She was not herself, she was nothing that she had ever known or understood, and all her body was charged with that newness and strangeness—too new, too strange, too bewildering just then to conquer.

Josh actually drew away first. He lifted his head, looked down at her, and laughed a little, then said : " I love you, Marcia. And I remember now where I saw you. For I did see you, you know. So I've loved you really for five years. Only I didn't know it was you."

Still the woman who was not Marcia, who had no right to be in his arms, nevertheless possessed her body. She leaned against him and looked up into his eyes without reservation, and said, half whispering, utterly candid as if there were no barriers between them : " I never saw you before. I'd have remembered you."

" We didn't meet. But I remember now. It was at a concert in Paris—during the entr'acte. You were with some people— Americans. I saw you and I watched you. It was in October. It had been a warm sunny day. That night was starlit and cold. I know, because I walked home and I kept thinking about you, and I sat on the little balcony outside my room and looked at the stars and smoked and kept on thinking about you. So whenever I see you now you're against the stars. One of them," he said, and laughed again rather unevenly.

"There, in the Captain's cabin, you didn't know me. You didn't recognise me...."

"No, I didn't. Except—well, I told you that yesterday. I said I wanted to kiss you the first instant I saw you, and I did. And I felt as if we ought to know each other; but a lot of things have happened to me, and to everybody since that October night. I never knew your name. I never saw you again. I never knew anything about you. And about that time I got involved in—well, never mind that. Do you want to know what you wore that night? I'll tell you. You had your dark hair done up high with a pompadour; you wore a white dress, sort of thin and long. And it fitted so well I was afraid you were very rich! Are you, darling?"

"*No!*"

"Good! And you had some red stuff around your waist that went down in a sort of fold all the way to your feet, and your mouth was very beautiful and red, just the colour of the sash-thing, and your eyes very blue, and I loved you." He held her again so her head came against his shoulder. "My star, all done up in red, white, and blue, very fancy, very dignified, very beautiful. How was I to recognise you in a nurse's uniform, in the middle of the Atlantic, with your hair in a little wad on your neck, after a night spent in a lifeboat? Nuts! Petrarch wouldn't have recognised Laura in a Mother Hubbard."

"This is not a Mother Hubbard!"

"Then you see, last night, I realised it was you. The girl I'd been in love with all that time."

"You can't have been! You..."

"Well, I wanted to be in love with you! I think I was, really. At least, I was exposed to it, so it only took a second look five years later to make it come alive. My figures of speech are mixed, but I'm not. Look, Marcia, I'm talking a lot of nonsense. But "—he held her so he could look deeply into her eyes—" but I do love you. It—well, it just happened. Like that. That meeting that wasn't a meeting five years ago doesn't really have much to do with it except that I liked you right away, the first instant I saw you, standing there at the concert. That's been a long time, and a lot of things have happened, and in some ways, I suppose, we are different people. But that doesn't matter. The only thing that matters is you and me and the people we are now."

That sunny long-ago October in Paris, concerts on chill fall nights—and Mickey.

Mickey, the one she was going to marry, the man she'd waited for and loved. Loved? she thought suddenly. But that had nothing to do with love! That was—well, what? And it didn't matter; she couldn't analyse it, for now she knew all in a minute about love and the quality of love. The new Marcia had informed her; every drop of blood in her body, hammering in her pulses had informed her.

And she was to marry Mickey.

He saw the change in her face.

"What is it? What's wrong? Tell me..." And then he guessed. "You've remembered André."

She must have made some gesture of assent, for his face changed subtly; it became older, harder, uncommunicative. He took his arm away and got out cigarettes. "I see. André... Help me light this blasted thing, will you? I can manage, but..."

She took the lighter and held it for him until the cigarette between his lips showed red. He did not meet her eyes, though, when she looked up. "Thanks," he said, and took the lighter and dropped it in his pocket. "This crazy arm of mine."

She glanced at the white sling supporting his right arm. "You were in combat?"

"Yes." His face had no youth or gaiety or tenderness; even his voice was remote and impersonal. "I stayed around Paris that first winter. It was a "—he paused and smoked and said, looking out over her shoulder into the fog—" it was a busy winter. One way and another. Then in the spring, when the Germans came..." Again he paused; there was also a hiatus in his story, for he said finally: "I eventually got home by way of England and into uniform. I was sent back to England and then to Brittany. From there my story is just the same as everybody's, except I didn't get a scratch until just before the war was over. Then I got a piece of shrapnel in my shoulder. They dug it out and it is healing. Well, the story of my life again." Without a change in face or voice he said: "What are you going to do about this—André?"

Mickey, not André. Mickey, who needed her, who had come back to her.

She moved away from Josh, not realising she had moved. The deck under her feet was real. The railing, wet and cold under her fingers, was real, too. Not this world she had so lately and bewilderingly discovered in the embrace of the man who walked across, following her, and leaned against the railing.

Josh said again, but as if a long time had elapsed, as if something had changed since he had spoken: " What are you going to do about André ? "

She would not look at him. " I'm going to marry André."

" Why ? " said Josh quietly.

" Because . . ." She stopped. It was as if the memory of Josh's kiss had the power to press upon her lips, silencing them. Josh said evenly : " You were going to say because you love him. Do you ? "

She had to break through the strange and lovely spell upon her lips.

She said, unsteadily, staring down at the black water rushing away from the ship : " I've told you. We were to be married. He was sent to a German concentration camp. I stayed there, in France, waiting, hoping . . . Then finally he came back. As you see him. His hands . . . You heard what he said. . . ."

" I've heard," said Josh Morgan rather grimly, " what a lot of men have said and experienced. Is that why you are marrying him ? From pity, I mean ? "

Pity ? She said, after a moment, stiffly : " He came back to me. I'm the only thing he has left from a life of . . ." She checked herself, on the verge of telling Josh of Mickey, and of all the glow and triumph that life had given him and promised him before the Nazis took it away.

And Josh said coolly : " What about Gili ? "

Gili ?

" That was nothing."

" Don't try to lie to me, Marcia. You can't get by with it. What exactly did she do to you yesterday ? It was something about André, wasn't it ? Had she staked out a claim upon him ? "

" No. That is, it was not true. She happened to be at the

same hotel in Lisbon while we were waiting for a passage on the *Lerida*. He never saw her before that."

"I see." His profile was clear and brown against the thick, pearly curtains of fog. "I gather that Gili claimed to have come to Lisbon in order to join André."

"Yes, but . . ."

"How did she happen to tell you? Exactly what brought it on? Do you know?"

"She had borrowed his cigarette case. I saw it and recognised it. It was, oh, very silly, really."

"Go on," said Josh inexorably. "What did she say about André."

She did not want to tell him and she had to. "She said that he had come back to me because I had money—some money, enough—and that he needed money for himself, and, she said, for her. It was stupid of me to listen to her."

"Well," said Josh reflectively, "Gili is a predatory and unscrupulous little . . . Well, never mind that. She could be serious, or she could be simply malicious and stupid, trying to make trouble between you. That's true. The point is, do you believe André?"

"Yes. He loves me; he needs me. It sounds trite. . . ."

"Very," said Josh, suddenly irritable. "You're being childish. You're seeing yourself as the heroine of some play. Either you love him or you don't."

She thought of Mickey, and the way he had looked when he came to her in Marseilles, and said quickly: "I love him."

Then she felt the almost sickening shock of irrevocability. Words once said cannot be unsaid, no matter how swift, how defiant, or how false they may be.

But she was to marry Mickey, she told herself bleakly. Even if she had tried to take back the words she had spoken, those hasty words, too final, she could not, for Josh, sealing that finality, said abruptly: "All right. That's that. We'll get on to another subject. And God knows there are several other subjects at hand. You've heard about Urdiola? What do you think of it? Seems reasonable, doesn't it, that he did it?"

She nodded, and Josh smoked and looked with narrowed eyes out into the fog and said suddenly: "Too damned reasonable. A quarrel among the three Portuguese over a diamond, two murders because of it. Oh, yes, it's reasonable.

I was there when Luther identified the diamond. He did so right away, took one look at it, and got very red and told the Captain he'd got it from his wife to give to Castiogne for arranging their passage. Did you bribe Castiogne for a passage?"

"No. That is, if André had done so he'd have told me. He arranged everything."

"You supplied the money?"

"Yes, but no more than enough for our passage and a— a loan to André. Naturally, he hadn't a cent. He was lucky to be alive."

"You called it a loan, I suppose, to save his feelings."

"Why not?" Again for an instant anger caught at her, but it subsided almost at once. She said wearily: "It wasn't much; only a little over our passage money, which wasn't much either. Oh, that isn't important."

"Are you sure," said Josh, "that you aren't rich?"

"I'm sure. My father died while I was in France. After the war was over his lawyer got in touch with me and sent me some cash. He told me that I'd have enough money if I left the investments he had made as they are; but I'm not rich."

"Not like the Cates?"

"Heavens, no! Theirs is one of the big American fortunes. Everybody knows that."

He said reflectively: "Luther said they had nothing with them now but Daisy Belle's jewellery. They've been selling it, he said, piece by piece. He said he'd wondered why the diamond was not found on Castiogne, but supposed he had sold it and banked the money in Lisbon or something of the kind. Naturally, he wasn't anxious to tell it, so he didn't volunteer the information. But then, when he saw the diamond there on the table in the Captain's cabin, he didn't hesitate. I'll say that for him. And the fact of its turning up in Urdiola's possession right after Para's murder does sound bad. I've been thinking—suppose Para murdered Castiogne in the lifeboat. Would that have been possible?"

She thought back again, as she had so irresistibly, so many times, to the black, nightmare hours on the *Lerida* lifeboat. 'Yes. Yes, I remember that he bent over Castiogne. I thought he was trying to revive him."

Josh was looking at her quietly and thoughtfully. " Para, then, could have killed him and removed the diamond if he knew that Castiogne had it. Or he could merely have removed the diamond after somebody else murdered him. Is that right ? "

She shivered and pulled her coat more closely about her throat. " Anything could have happened that night in that boat—anything."

" I believe you," said Josh. " And I think that was when either Para or Urdiola took the diamond. Urdiola's story could be perfectly true or it could be the unimaginative lie of a very stupid man." He paused and smoked and said suddenly : " Marcia, was it Urdiola that night ? Who tried to murder you, I mean ? "

" I don't know. It was dark and so sudden and dreadful. I don't know."

" I've got to ask you this, Marcia. Please answer me quite honestly. Have there been any other attempts—besides the man in the red bathrobe yesterday ? "

She hesitated, not wanting to acknowledge it, and thus somehow mark its authenticity. But she told him : " Someone tried the handle of the cabin door the same night, perhaps fifteen minutes before I went to André's cabin, and met you on the way, and he and Gili were there. That was all that happened," she added quickly. " I opened the door to the corridor as soon as I could make myself do it. Nobody was there. It probably was nothing."

He thought for a moment, turning again, so she could see only his straight, uncommunicative profile. " Yes," he said finally, " probably it was nothing. And probably whoever was on the stairway yesterday merely wanted to be seen in that disguise. They've questioned the real patient, Jacob Heinzer, as exhaustively as they can. It's very hard for him to speak. But they've inquired, and they've examined his records, and so far there isn't a thing to link him up with anybody on the lifeboat. Colonel Wells says that aside from his wounds, he's all right. I mean, no question of nerve strain and battle fatigue or anything of the kind." He paused for an instant, and continued in a rather odd and tight voice : " Does your— André believe that it was Urdiola who attacked him ? "

" He said he didn't know why Urdiola would attack him

or me, unless because he thought we knew something of Castiogne's murder."

"What do you think about it?"

"It's the only motive he could possibly have had; but I don't know what he thought I had seen. And in any case we are safe now, all of us."

"Yes," said Josh. "Well, I shouldn't count too much on that."

"*What do you mean?*"

He would not meet her eyes. "I don't know. Anything, nothing. Only—listen, Marcia, once before, twice before, I've said you were in danger. Well, I still think so."

"But Urdiola is locked up!"

"In spite of that. In spite of everything. I think," said Josh Morgan, his voice suddenly rough, "that you have been in danger ever since an American ship came into view from the lifeboat."

"Josh. . . ." But the foghorn began again, suddenly and harshly checking her question. She waited, and Josh still would not look at her, still stood with his arm against the railing, looking into the fog, looking into nothing as if he were seeing there something clear and definite, something frightening, something that had power, something she could not see. The foghorn stopped and he turned to her. "Now, then, we'd better go inside. You're getting cold." He put up his hand and touched her hair, very gently, very lightly, with a deeply thoughtful look in his dark eyes. "Your hair's all misted," he said.

"You must explain. There's something you know or guess."

"Marcia," he said abruptly, "is there anything *you* guess or know that you've not told me?"

His tone was so direct and so grave that she answered almost without knowing she was replying: "There's nothing I know. But I . . ." She hesitated, trying to put a very nebulous impression into words.

"What, Marcia? Tell me."

"Twice—I'm not sure I can make you understand—but twice I've had an odd sort of feeling that something was wrong somehow. I mean, not what I'd have expected it to be. So it didn't fit."

"Such as what?"

"Well, one time it was with Gili—when she was talking to the Captain. Somehow I'd have expected her to tell the Captain the same story about the Cates being Nazis that she told us."

" And didn't she ? "

" No. She looked very quiet and secretive somehow, and didn't mention it."

He thought for a long moment, watching her, and finally said : " It's just as well. I didn't believe it. It sounded too— I don't know—too much as if she enjoyed the interest she was creating by the story. Too much Gili," he said dryly. " But what else was it, Marcia ? "

" It happened just after you had talked to me on deck and then gone inside. I remember that. I was lying back in the chair, thinking about the whole thing, really ; about nothing in particular, except perhaps Gili and the things she had said to me about André. But I can't think of any special thing ; it was only that all at once I felt as if I—well, as if I'd missed some turning in a road that I ought to have recognised. As if "—she used the simile that had entered her own thoughts— " as if I knew a picture, but that something in the picture was suddenly crooked and wrong. Oh, I know that makes no sense." She broke off, annoyed at her own clumsiness and ineptness. But Josh's face was very thoughtful. He repeated : " Something wrong in the picture. Something . . ." he stopped.

For a long time—minutes it seemed to her—he just stood there motionless, as if he'd forgotten her existence. And then quite suddenly he moved and looked at her with bright, intent eyes that still did not seem to see her, and took her arm. " I think I see what you mean," he said, and whirled her around. " You'll have to go inside. You're cold. Your hair's all wet. Now . . ." They reached the lobby, and everywhere was warmth and cheer and people, and he said, quite cheerfully himself : " Now mind what I told you, Marcia. I'll see you later. . . ."

He vanished abruptly towards the stairway, so abruptly that she stared after him, puzzled. Then she turned again towards the cabin, slowly, thinking over the long conversation she'd had with him ; the long and somehow very final conversation. For he had accepted her decision about Mickey

completely; there was no doubt of that. It was in his manner,
in his impersonally friendly tone, in everything about him.

So that was in the past.

She reached the little cabin, which was empty, the bunks
neatly made up. She went to the port and gazed out for a
long time into the fleecy grey; it was as if the ship made no
progress, as if life itself had stopped.

Only it hadn't, she thought after a long time. It would go
on and on and on. But for ever without Josh. For ever without
another moment of the real kind of life she had touched for
an instant, there on the deserted deck in Josh's embrace, and
had failed to grasp. The rest of it would be for ever unreal,
a sequence of shadows.

She did not know exactly when she realised that some one
had entered the shadowy cabin behind her. Quite gradually,
however, the fact telegraphed itself to her senses. Someone
was in the cabin; someone stood between her and the door;
someone who had entered very softly, very stealthily, without her knowledge.

XV

THE HARD, terrible hands that had gripped her there at the railing on the dark deck seemed to reach out again towards her.

She did not move. She could not move, she could not turn, she could not speak. Even if she could have forced her stiffened throat to scream wildly for help, it would not have mattered, for the foghorn began again, roaring over the ship, hurling itself back from the fog, effectually drowning any sound, any cry for help she might have made.

Somehow, though, the sound itself set her free from that first moment of paralysed recognition. Her mind was racing. It seemed important, first, not to let whoever stood behind her know that she was aware of that furtive presence. Only thus could she hope to avoid a physical struggle which could have only one conclusion ; she knew that instinctively. And next she must think of some expedient, some way to escape. The foghorn stopped.

Actually the thing she did she had not planned to do. It was a quick, instinctive impulse. She spoke. She called out clearly and evenly: " Daisy Belle, did I leave my toothbrush in the bathroom ? Look, will you ? "

Daisy Belle, of course, was not in the bathroom. Nobody was there. The door was slightly ajar. But if whoever stood in that cabin with her could not see quite into the bathroom, if whoever was there believed her, believed that someone else was near, believed that she was not alone. . . .

Her heart, her breath, everything about her seemed to have stopped. There was no sound—only the dying echoes of the foghorn filling the cabin, pressing against her ears, shutting out other sounds.

And then nothing. No rustle, no sound, no door closing, no motion of any kind.

Somehow, when that silence and feeling of emptiness persisted long enough, she turned.

No one was there.

The cabin was empty, and, as she had thought, the bathroom door only slightly ajar. Any one standing about in the centre of the cabin could not have seen that no one was in the small room.

Certainly no one was there now or anywhere.

Her heart was beating again hard, her breath coming painfully in hard gasps as if she'd been running.

A small hump of something white lay on the floor. She walked towards it and stared down.

It was a bandage, made of gauze, twisted and turned so it made a rather crude sort of helmet.

Such as the patient in the red bathrobe, with the bandaged face and holes for eyes, might have worn.

Only it was not a real bandage. It had not been a patient.

And Josh had been right.

Without rhyme or reason, without any basis of motive or cause, he was right.

She must tell Josh. She must tell the Captain. Yes, that was it. Report it to him.

Urdiola was locked up and charged with murder.

Who, then, had come like that into her cabin? Who had made and worn and, in escaping, dropped that disguising helmet, which lay now so limp and so horribly convincing?

Josh had been right.

But she did not go at once to the Captain. Instead she locked the cabin door. She sat down in the chair under the port and looked at the twisted tangle of white gauze. Who could have worn that, and why?

She was still there when much later Daisy Belle and Gili returned to the cabin. They returned together, and she heard their voices as one of them tried the door and then knocked. Otherwise, she thought, in a kind of spell of horror, she could not have moved to open the door. But Daisy Belle's crisp sensible voice was incredibly comforting and reassuring. She got up, and on her way to the door picked up the gauze helmet.

The touch of the thin material in her fingers was convincing, too. She hated to touch it. She rolled it up tightly, put it in the pocket of her coat, which still hung over her shoulders, and opened the door.

"Why did you lock the door?" said Daisy Belle, more as an exclamation than a question. She snapped on lights abruptly, and the cabin leaped from its dim grey shadow to light, under which Daisy Belle looked tired and old and with sharp lines on her thin brown face. Gili crossed to the bunk, and stretched out with the lazy indolence of a cat upon it and said nothing, but only gazed at the bunk above her with enigmatic, narrowed green eyes. She said nothing, in fact, until Daisy Belle said briskly that it was time for lunch, and she'd wash up first, and disappeared into the bathroom. Then Gili instantly roused. She swung her long handsome legs around and sat up.

Gili said: " You talked to him ! You talked to Mickey ! " She shook back the long blonde lock of hair that hung over her face and cried: " You with your fine lady ways. And your money. Don't answer. I don't care. Why do you suppose Mickey wanted you if it wasn't for the money he could get out of you ! Listen . . ." Her hands curled hard around the mattress, and she leaned forward, her eyes narrow and furious. " Listen. I could tell you that I heard you call him Mickey ; that that's how I knew his real name. I could tell you that I—borrowed his cigarette case, that I saw it and picked it up and used it. I could tell you that I said everything I said just to tease you. Or to make you angry with Mickey so you'd give him up. I could tell you anything like that. And you'd believe me."

" Gili, be quiet. Gili . . ." It was as if those clawing strong hands were tearing down a wall, shredding a hard woven fabric.

Gili cried, drawing her mouth back from her teeth as if she were at bay herself, not Marcia. " But I'm not going to. Do you understand ? I'm not going to give him up to you. He doesn't need you now. He's got everything he wants from you. He's through with you. He belongs to me. You with your smugness and your money—that doesn't matter. You can't have him."

Mickey had said: " Do you believe me or Gili ? " Marcia remembered that as clearly as if again he had spoken the words in her ears. She said: " I don't believe you."

" You think I'm lying ! " Gili put back her head so the blonde ends of her hair flung outward savagely and laughed and cried: " Lying ! About Mickey and me ! Lying . . ." She stopped laughing. She sprang to her feet and across the

room, and her hands were reaching out like strong white
claws towards Marcia, and Marcia slapped her face—hard,
along one cheek.

Gili stopped. Marcia's hand tingled. Daisy Belle was in the
bathroom doorway, staring.

Gili's hand went slowly to her jaw. She said: " I didn't
think you had it in you."

Marcia hadn't thought so either. She looked at Gili's
reddened cheek with dismay and a certain sense of shock,
but without even a twinge of apology. Daisy Belle said
briskly: " Best thing in the world for hysterics! Now, then,
let's go to lunch." She put her hand on Marcia's shoulder
and turned her towards the door. She said to Gili: " You'd
better come, too. Pin up your hair. We'll wait. Hurry."

It was like a schoolmistress making quick order of childish
chaos. And, like a child, Gili sulkily obeyed. She combed
her long hair. Jerking it savagely, she pinned it up, and gave
Marcia and Daisy Belle a sullen, brooding look, and, as Daisy
Belle motioned towards the corridor, again obeyed.

It was difficult, though, to sit over a long lunch, listening
to the pleasant, animated talk of the nurses at the same table,
knowing that Gili sat on the other side of Daisy Belle, eating
steadily, saying nothing, but with a look in her green eyes
that bided its time.

Do you believe me, Mickey had said, or Gili?

Her fingers still tingled. Gili's face still showed a reddish
mark. Marcia had never slapped anybody in her life before
and she thought gratefully of Daisy Belle, who had put the
whole absurd scene on its proper level. It was typical of
Daisy Belle to see, to understand, and kindly, promptly, and
loyally to act.

But she thought also that lunch would never end. It was
the second sitting; they had been late. The officers' tables at
the other end of the room were vacant long since. She did not
see Mickey, she did not see Josh Morgan, she did not see
Luther, she did not see any one she knew. And when the mess
boy finally served them coffee and the remaining little group
of nurses trickled out of the room, going back to the wards,
she still had no chance to talk to Mickey or to Josh Morgan.

The three women started back to the cabin together, Gili
swishing along ahead, still angry, still with that look of latent

biding fury in every motion she made. Daisy Belle, her fine long face very troubled and tired looking, stopped for a moment in the nurses' lounge as they passed it, and came out with an armful of magazines.

"There's nothing else to do," she said, answering Marcia's glance. "And, my dear, don't talk to Gili now. Don't, just yet, talk to André. Wait. Time," said Daisy Belle Cates, with a queer note in her voice—like sorrow, like regret—" time is a gentleman."

Daisy Belle, of course, had heard everything Gili had said. But Daisy Belle did not know of the crumpled roll of gauze in her pocket.

So she left Daisy Belle at the door of the cabin. She said something, anything about going on deck, about exercise. Daisy Belle put one hand upon her arm and then quietly relinquished her hold. "Very well," she said, "you know best."

Marcia, walking slowly along the warm, brighly lighted passageways, reminded her self that she must be very careful. She must stay where there were people. She must not be alone, not for a moment. But she would find Josh Morgan.

She didn't. He was not in the lobby on B deck, nor in the busier lobby on A deck; he was not in his cabin, for she inquired of an obliging young sergeant who took her there and knocked on the door and opened it, showing an empty cabin, with Josh's cap and coat slung on the bed. She could not find him, and, not wanting to see Gili again, not wanting to talk to Daisy Belle and see the knowledge in her eyes, no matter how understanding that knowledge was, she went to the nurses' lounge and sat there pretending to read. Actually she was aware only of that limp roll of gauze in her pocket and of Gili.

Do you believe me, Mickey had said, or Gili?

It was like a merciless, nagging refrain.

And then gauze, of course, was evidence. Since she could not find Josh, as she wished to do, the obvious course was to give it to Captain Svendsen.

It was later than she had realised. The lights were on now everywhere, and the fog was creeping again into the ship, as it did somehow at night.

She'd not wait longer for Josh. She looked for him, nevertheless, as again she went through the lobby and up the stairs.

And when she knocked on the door with its gold-lettered sign—" Captain Lars Svendsen "—and opened it, Josh was there.

He sprang up when he saw her and came towards her. The Captain, sitting at his desk, put down his pipe and rose. Colonel Wells was there, too, and turned to watch.

Josh said " Hallo " in a matter-of-fact tone. The Captain said courteously : " Come in, come in . . ." Colonel Wells smiled impersonally and politely.

The Captain went on : " I'm glad you came, Miss Colfax. Colonel Morgan has been trying to make me believe that you are in danger. I don't mean that I have ever doubted your belief that you were half-strangled the first night you were on my ship, but I did think it might have been due to your overwrought nerves. Now then, as you know, the thing is over ; thank God, we've got Urdiola and a sound case against him. You know all about that ? "

She moved her head in acknowledgment. Something about her look, her silence, suddenly seemed to strike Josh as wrong. She was aware of his sharpened attention and the little frown that suddenly came between his eyes. The Captain said : " But I don't mind telling you, Miss Colfax, that it would help if you can identify Urdiola as your assailant. Can you do that ? "

She shook her head. She started to speak and stopped and took the gauze helmet from her pocket.

Josh understood first, and sprang forward to her side and took the roll of gauze from her hand. He swore and held it so they could see it, and then put it on the Captain's desk. " See that . . . See that. . . ." he cried almost incoherently, and was back at Marcia's side, his right hand on her shoulder, compelling her to look at him, compelling her to speak. " Tell us what happened. Tell us—hurry. . . ."

But she had not realised how unsubstantial a story it was until she told it and saw the Captain's face, fixed and hard as granite. Colonel Wells coughed and lighted a cigarette and said nothing. The Captain waited for a moment, tapping his pipe absently on the arm of his chair, eyeing her with those bright, shrewd, hard eyes. Finally he said in a dry voice :

"Very interesting, Miss Colfax. Exactly when did this occur?"
She told him.

"And you actually saw no one?"

"No. But that was on the floor."

He glanced at the gauze-heap impatiently. Colonel Wells came over to the desk, picked up the gauze, looked at it, said: "Inexpertly made. No nurse or doctor made that," and put it down again.

The Captain said: "Urdiola is locked up. The patient, Jacob Heinzer, is naturally not under guard, but I expect we can check on his whereabouts. I'll try. In the meantime, though, are you perfectly sure any one was really there?"

Before she could reply, Josh Morgan said suddenly: "Captain, I'm afraid I'm guilty of withholding some evidence."

"What's that, Colonel?" The Captain's bleached eyebrows were suddenly heavy and threatening.

"The fact is, sir, the Cates' couple have been accused of collaboration with the Nazis. And, if the story is right, Castiogne knew it."

"Castiogne! You mean that you think he tried to blackmail Cates? But Cates said he gave him the diamond for passage bribe. Cates said . . ."

"Right, sir."

"Wait." The Captain touched a bell and gave quick orders to the boy who appeared. "Get hold of Mr. Cates and his wife. Get them both here. Now then, Colonel Morgan, exactly what *do* you mean?"

As if he knew that she was willing him not to tell it, Josh would not look at Marcia. He stared instead very intently at the end of his cigarette while he told Gili's story, almost word for word, exactly as she had told it.

The Captain listened, and, as Josh finished, began to pace the cabin angrily. "Why didn't you tell me before now?"

"Because I didn't believe it."

The Captain paused briefly to shoot him an angry—and troubled—look. "And do you believe it now?"

"I believe that Marcia is in grave danger," said Josh obliquely.

As he spoke, the boy returned, and ushered Daisy Belle and Luther together into the room. And immediately Marcia thought they guessed; and that, therefore, incredible though it was, it was true.

Daisy Belle did not look at Marcia. Marcia was thankful for that. The Captain cleared his throat. "Close the door," he snapped, and the boy who had brought them ducked out into the passage and closed the door firmly.

Daisy Belle said quite clearly to Luther, looking up into his tired, pale face: "I was right, Luther—I was right." She took his hand in her own, and suddenly, like a child, her face crumpled and she began soundlessly to cry.

Josh brought a chair and she sat down in it automatically. The Captain said: "What's this story? What's this . . .? Look here, Cates, why did you give that damned diamond to Castiogne?"

Luther took a long, unsteady breath. Then he moved to stand beside Daisy Belle. He looked down and said: "You were right, dear. I ought to have told them before. All right. . . ."

He put his hand upon her shoulder, lifted his worn, lined face, and said steadily: "I gave the diamond to Castiogne to pay him for securing our passage, as I told you. That was true. But there is something else—something my wife and I ought to have told you, perhaps. But we had hoped to forget it eventually. It is not pleasant."

His voice stopped. Daisy Belle patted the hand on her shoulder and ignored the streaming tears on her cheeks. Luther went on: "You see, my wife and I, during the years when France was occupied, were "—he swallowed hard, so his corded, thin throat worked but his faded blue eyes did not waver—" we were what you could call Nazis; what everybody will call Nazis. We had to live in the home of someone who proved to be a Nazi. An old acquaintance, who offered us a refuge. We did not then know what he was; we had already taken food and shelter. But circumstances were such that, even after we suspected, we continued to take what we thought we had to have. There is no excuse for us. We realise that."

Daisy Belle cried suddenly: "It was not your fault, Luther. It was mine. You had to have drugs; you had to have digitalis. I thought you were dying."

"Don't, my dear." His thin hand pressed down upon her

shoulder. "Since Castiogne's death we began to think that, in some possible way, the fact could have a connection with the murders. So we had talked of telling you the truth. And it does not matter, you see, because," said Luther with sudden dignity, " in any case we can never forgive ourselves and our own weakness. We can never really forget that we've taken food and coal and medicine from bloody and shameful hands."

There was again a long silence in the cabin. Colonel Wells turned abruptly and stared out over the fo'c'sle. The Captain drummed on the table with his pipe. Josh Morgan did not move. Finally the Captain said gruffly : " Why do you think it had a connection with the murder ? "

" I don't know," said Luther simply.

" According to the story I've heard, Castiogne knew that you had done this. Did he try to blackmail you ? " asked the Captain bluntly.

" No. As we told you, the diamond was—well, a bribe. We saw him in Lisbon. He said he could arrange it for money. We had no money, so we gave him the diamond. And he got our passage."

There was another silence ; then the Captain said suddenly : " Thank you ; you may go."

With unbroken dignity they left. Daisy Belle, passing Marcia, stopped for an instant beside her chair and touched her lightly with her hand. " My dear," she said, " don't look like that. It's all right."

The door closed upon them. Colonel Wells unexpectedly and loudly blew his nose and the Captain looked at him angrily.

And Josh said suddenly : " All right. But I tell you Marcia's in danger. And I don't see..." He stopped, stared at the floor, suddenly seemed to take a resolution, and strode over to the Captain. " There's one more thing, sir. The man travelling with Miss Colfax is not André Messac. I knew André Messac. He was my close friend. This man is a former concert pianist. I have seen him and heard him play many times. His name is Michel Banet, and "—Josh's voice went on as hard and harsh as iron—" his hands show marks of torture which he says he received in a German prison. In fact, however, I believe him to be a fleeing Nazi war criminal."

The cabin seemed to Marcia to darken and tilt. The Captain's face, purple and swollen looking, seemed to tilt with it. She heard him shout : " Why haven't you told me this before ? Why . . . ? "

She heard Josh's answer, too, quite steady and firm : " For a good reason, sir. A good reason. . . ."

Even in the crazy tilting room she heard them giving orders, demanding André Messac. But they meant Mickey Banet—Mickey Banet—Mickey Banet. . . .

The name droned through her senses like a hammer, over and over and over.

It was, however, for ever too late to ask questions of Mickey Banet.

He was found on deck. He was unconscious. He had been shot apparently with a service revolver, and died shortly after, although everything possible was done to save him.

Before he died he rallied briefly and made a curious and terrible statement. A woman, he said, had shot him.

In the same full, deceptively strong voice he told them that he would explain it all later.

It was, however, the last thing he said.

It was about that time that a young second lieutenant who had been a member of one of the armed searching parties reported to his immediate superior the loss of the revolver which had been issued to him.

XVI

ANY ONE could have taken the revolver.

The young lieutenant had been assigned night duty. The revolver had been taken some time during the afternoon while he slept. Any number of people had gone along the passageway outside the quarters he shared with six others ; naturally the door had not been locked. He had placed it beside his bunk ; he admitted he was a sound sleeper. Although his superior officer had some words to say on the subject, it was not really a censurable act, and in any case it was spilled milk.

Unless by mere chance some witness came forward, it was almost hopeless to try to discover who had taken it. It could have been, as they knew from the beginning, any one on the ship.

Except the Portuguese seaman, Urdiola. He was still locked up. Obviously he could not have shot Mickey Banet either. He was not, however, absolved, for there still remained the diamond, and the extremely sound case against him in the matter of the murder of the other two Portuguese.

While it was difficult to believe that the murder of Mickey Banet had no connection with that of the two Portuguese seamen from the *Lerida*, there was at the same time no way of dismissing the diamond in Urdiola's possession, except to accept the story he told as a true one, which on the face of it did not seem likely.

At the same time it seemed most unlikely that there were two murderers on the ship.

Also, in the case of Mickey Banet's death, there was not even an attempt on the part of Colonel Wells and Captain Svendsen to establish alibis on the part of the other *Lerida* passengers ; that, too, was obviously a hopeless undertaking. The time of the shooting was uncertain, limited only by the time when the young second lieutenant had gone to sleep, which was immediately after his lunch, and the time when Mickey was found, which was about dusk.

The doctors believed it had occurred at least an hour before he was found ; they could say little more than that. No one apparently had happened to visit the particular section of the deck where he was found (towards the stern, in the shadow of the rank of lifeboats, as a matter of fact, very near where he had first been attacked) during the afternoon. Again, because of the fog the decks had been forbidden ; they were cold, wet and slippery.

From that portion of the deck the sound of the shot might not have been heard in any case. There were ventilators near and the sound of the motors which drove fresh air through the ship would have muffled it. Probably, however, he had been shot during one of the intervals while the foghorn was sounding. At any rate, no one had heard the sound, or at least had reported it.

The revolver which the young lieutenant had lost was not found. The other revolvers which had been issued to those small searching parties were immediately collected and examined. There were not many of them and none had recently been fired. They were reissued, and again the watch was doubled.

A search was made for the missing revolver, but it, too, was a hopeless inquiry. If one of the *Lerida* passengers had it, naturally it would not be hidden in the cabins they occupied, and there was all the rest of the ship and hundreds of hiding places for so small an object. Nobody, however, really believed that it was still on the ship ; not with the grey, deep Atlantic to hide it for ever from mortal eyes—as the ocean had already hidden, every one felt sure, the knife that had stabbed Castiogne, the knife that had slashed Para.

It was, of course, a different pattern of murder, and that again suggested that Urdiola might have killed the two Portuguese, but that someone else had killed Mickey Banet. It also suggested that that person could have been, as Mickey Banet had said, a woman.

It was hard to believe that a woman could have had the strength and the terrible courage to stab the burly, strong young third officer, Castiogne. It was almost impossible to believe that a woman could have walked up behind Manuel Para and quietly and deftly slashed his throat.

But a woman could have held and aimed that revolver and pulled the trigger, leaving Mickey presumably dead.

It must have been, they reasoned, a shock to the murderer to hear that he was not dead, that he had even briefly revived. If so, however, that person did not betray the frightful suspense by any word or look. It would have been instantly observed, for the *Lerida* passengers at the Captain's orders waited together in the officers' lounge.

It was a long and horrible wait. The red-covered chairs were damp and chill to the touch. No one read the magazines on the long table. It was like waiting in a hospital reception-room to hear the news from a sick bed. Eventually, while they waited, Josh and Colonel Wells came to tell them briefly that he had died.

Neither of them, however, told them then what Mickey's last statement had been. They stayed only a moment and went away again.

Among the four people in the lounge there was very little expression, either of relief or regret, at the expected news. Gili sat huddled on a sofa, her long, streaked hair shading her face, and neither moved nor spoke. Luther looking ill and tired to death himself, put his drawn face in his hands and kept it there so long that Daisy Belle went to him with an anxious inquiry in her eyes.

" Are you all right ? "

" Oh, yes." He lifted his face reassuringly, but she put her fingers on his wrist for a moment nevertheless. He gave her a faint, patient smile, and, apparently satisfied, she walked to the black glittering port and stared out into nothing. Marcia thought, this is not possible ; Mickey cannot have died like this ; but she knew it was true.

There was after that another long wait ; a corpsman came about midnight with sandwiches and hot cocoa in thick cups on a tray. Luther questioned him, and he told them that the ship was being searched. They had not found the murderer. When Luther asked about Urdiola, he said he was still under arrest.

" Then Urdiola couldn't have done it," said Daisy Belle. Her face was parchment grey ; she was cold, and kept her nurse's coat tight around her tall, spare body. Luther, his face pale, too, and his lips blue, handed around the cups of hot cocoa.

Marcia drank slowly, holding it in both her cold hands.

There is a state of shock that is almost like an anaesthetic; fortunately under an anæsthetic one has no feeling. Marcia thought that once, staring into the brown cocoa, remembering as if from a time long past Mickey's candid, clear grey eyes, his smile, the things he had said. Also she recalled the thing that Josh Morgan had said which precipitated the search for Mickey. A Nazi war criminal, trying to escape a Europe which was too dangerous for him now that the Americans had come.

Mickey, with his hands tragic and maimed by those same Nazis.

She was strongly aware all the time of Gili's presence across from her, and perhaps Gili was as strongly aware of her. Their eyes did not meet until Josh returned.

He came into the room quickly, and every one looked up with a jerk. His face was very white. The ship had been by that time thoroughly searched, and no revolver was found, and nothing leading to evidence concerning Mickey Banet's murder had been discovered, he told them tersely.

"What are they going to do?" asked Luther, his face ashen under the brilliant light and the pouches heavy below his tired eyes.

"Investigate as best they can. Hope, I suppose, that somebody saw something and will come forward to say so. They are making an urgent appeal. Anybody who knows of anything at all suspicious is asked to go to the Captain at once."

"Do you think that will come to anything?" asked Luther after a pause.

"I don't know. The Captain is coming here. He said he'd be along in a few minutes."

There was a sharp silence, and then Daisy Belle said abruptly: "To ask us if one of us murdered him!"

"Yes," said Josh quietly. "I suppose they'll ask that. And they'll ask you to volunteer any evidence, or even, I imagine, any opinions, that you may have."

It was then that Marcia became aware of Gili's eyes, bright and green and fixed, staring at her thoughtfully. She did not speak, however, but only sat there, her long blonde hair hanging lankly about her face, her eyes fastened upon Marcia in that thoughtful way. Before any one else spoke the Captain and Colonel Wells came into the room.

Mainly they looked terribly tired. It had been Colonel Wells, a surgeon before he became commanding officer of the medical unit for the *Magnolia*, who had operated on Mickey. He came to Marcia directly. " I'm sorry," he said, and with a kindliness which reached through the stiff self-control that had erected itself around her like a shell. " I did what I could. Whatever he was, or wasn't, I'm sorry." But there was also a sharp and cold question in his eyes.

Captain Svendsen, however, swiftly took matters into his own hands. They all knew, he said, what had happened. If any of them knew anything of the murder or suspected anything they must understand how urgently important it was to tell them. He did not wait for any one to speak, but went on : " Shortly before he was found injured a question of his identity arose." He turned directly to Marcia : " You were engaged to marry him. You must have known the truth. Colonel Morgan says that he was really a man by the name of Banet, a concert pianist. Is that right ? "

" Yes."

" Why was he using a false passport and a false name ? "

She told him. It had seemed best to leave Europe as quickly as possible. He had decided to use a passport which had belonged to a friend, André Messac. He had his own photograph substituted.

" Why did he not use his own ? "

" He said he had none. He had nothing, no personal possessions. It would take time to secure a passport of his own."

" If he had turned Nazi he would not have dared to apply for one. He would have been afraid to let his identity be known anywhere in France, wouldn't he ? "

" I suppose so. Yes."

" And you subscribed to his plan to use a false passport. Why ? You must have known that that is a criminal offence."

At the time it had seemed the only course which might help, quickly, to restore Mickey to himself. Now it seemed futile to try to explain it. She replied : " It seemed right then. We intended to do something about it in Buenos Aires, go to the American Consul and tell him the whole story. But then . . ."

" But then . . ." prompted Captain Svendsen.

"Then he determined to keep the name of André Messac."

"Why?"

She told him that, too. Mickey had been on the threshold of a great career. It had been taken from him. He had wished, he said, to save his pride and never again to be known as Michel Banet, who had promised so much and done so little.

There was a short silence, so they could hear the throb of the ship's engines driving the ship on and on through the fog.

"When did he tell you that?" asked the Captain suddenly. "On the *Lerida*? On the *Magnolia*?"

"The night after we were taken aboard the *Magnolia*."

"And you agreed to keep his real identity a secret?"

She had neither the wish nor the strength to defend herself. "For the time being—yes."

"What were you going to do when you arrived in America? Go through life as Mr. and Mrs. André Messac? A false name, a life of lies?"

It was, of course, what she had asked herself almost in so many words. She said: "I thought that he would agree to tell the truth."

Captain Svendsen turned to Josh. "Will you tell Miss Colfax exactly what you told me while Colonel Wells was operating."

Josh had been leaning against the table, the white sling for his wounded arm looming up brightly. His face looked almost as white. He looked at Marcia, and crossed to pull up a small chair near her. He sat down and leaned forward to take her hand. "Marcia, I knew André Messac—that is, I knew an André Messac in Paris. As you told me when I questioned you about him, it is not an uncommon name. Still, it was not exactly a common name either. André was murdered by the Nazis." He looked down at her hand for an instant, his face set and grave.

The Captain showed anger and impatience—a deep-lying anger because of the things the Nazis had done, things he had seen, things he had heard, which could never be undone; another and almost as biting an anger because he could not yet lay hold of the horrible thing he had brought aboard his ship with the passengers he had rescued from the *Lerida* lifeboat, because his strong red hands longed to do so, because he had to get back to the bridge, because he did not know what to do, because the very complexity of his emotions angered him. Captain Svendsen said: " Colonel Morgan, during the first fall of the war, joined a group of French resistance men. André Messac was one of them. So was Michel Banet. André Messac was arrested suddenly by the Germans and shot. Colonel Morgan was always of the opinion that he was betrayed by one of his own men. He thinks that man was the man who came on this ship using André Messac's name. He thinks it was Michel Banet. What do you know about it ? "

" He could not have been a Nazi. Mickey was arrested by the Nazis. He was tortured by the Nazis. . . ."

Josh looked up into her eyes. " Everybody who was tortured," said Josh, with a queer sad note in his voice, " was not a hero. One stands torture, another does not. The Germans knew that ; that was why they tortured. They wanted information about other people. They wanted to break and twist and turn. They had a double lever with Michel Banet : pain and the maiming of his fingers, which meant his whole life. I think he gave in. I think he turned Nazi at once, within a day or two of his imprisonment and torture. Unfortunately for him, it was already too late to save his hands, but he could save his life, and did, by telling everything he knew. I've always thought that André Messac was betrayed by one of a very small group because André was so "—he hesitated—" so very intelligent. So cool, so rigid about plans and strict discipline. He foresaw the day that was to come. He knew that first winter how important to France the French Resistance Movement would become. He was a genius for organisation. Even then he realised how unsafe it would be for men to know too much of each other in that organisation. Even then, in the beginning, he arranged it so you knew the fewest possible names, the fewest possible men who were allied to you. Michel Banet was one of the few who knew André Messac was our leader. I knew it. Perhaps a few others. But Michel Banet was arrested, and almost immediately André was arrested and shot. I did not know that Michel Banet had betrayed. I only knew that André must have been betrayed. Banet had disappeared. The rumour was that he was killed, too. The Germans were in Paris. War between the United States and Germany seemed inevitable. I got back home, as I told you, and into the Army. But you don't forget people like André. Well, when I knew that a man had turned up on this ship using that name, when I saw that man and knew it was not his name but a man I had known to be taken by the Germans only a day or so before André was murdered, I "—he stared down again at his hand still holding hers—" I had to find out the truth."

The Captain said: " Why didn't you tell me? Why didn't you warn me . . . ? "

Josh lifted his head. His face was very white and he looked as if he did not see Marcia, did not see anything but a sombre and terrible picture that hovered in his thoughts. " Because I had to kill him with my own hands," said Josh.

There was a long silence in the lounge, with its blank and glistening ports and its red cushions. Then the Captain cried: " But he said a woman did it ! " He looked at Marcia. Every one looked at Marcia except Josh, who, with his dark head bent, stared down at her hand and his own, locked together.

XVII

Colonel Wells cleared his throat and stepped forward. " We might question Miss Colfax," he said.

" All right," said the Captain, " question her. If she murdered him, will she admit it ? If she took that revolver, will she say so ? If she knew he was a Nazi . . ."

Suddenly Marcia took in the sense of the Captain's words. " Mickey said a woman shot him ? " she cried.

And Josh told her.

" Before Banet died he made a—a sort of statement. He was conscious for a minute or two ; he was under drugs ; he seemed fairly strong and as if he might make it, really. He said that a woman had killed him, and he said that he'd explain or something like that later."

He paused, and the silence in the lounge was so sharp it was as if somebody had screamed. Josh went on : " But he died before he spoke again."

And that sharp and terrible moment of listening, of heightened terrible silence, passed.

But to somebody in that room, Marcia thought suddenly, there had been a second of terror while Josh quoted Mickey's words and then paused before he added that Mickey had said no more. Somebody had waited for a name.

Somebody ? All of them. She glanced swiftly around the room and everybody else was doing the same thing. Covertly, swiftly, eyes searching and speculative, suspicion unveiled and bright.

Then the Captain said heavily and point-blank : " If you killed him, Miss Colfax, it would be better for you to say so now."

" No—no, I didn't. . . ."

" Did you know he was a Nazi ? "

" No."

" But you admit that you knew he was travelling under a false name and that you connived in his deception ? "

" Not connive . . ."

" You knew it ? "

"Yes."

Colonel Wells said slowly: "Whoever killed him must have made two attempts: the first one, that night on the deck when Banet was knocked out. Miss Colfax couldn't have done that, for she was attacked the same night, about the same time as Banet. Certainly by the same person who attacked Banet, so . . ."

"Oh, no!" cried Josh. He put down Marcia's hand and got up. "Oh, no! I did that. I hit Banet."

"You . . ." began the Captain, his great fist doubling up. "That was you. . . ."

"I told you that I wanted to kill him with my own hands."

"You didn't tell me that you had tried," said the Captain grimly. "Did you shoot him?"

"No, I didn't," said Josh. "But I wanted to. I've been wanting to for five years. . . . That is, I'd been wanting to kill whoever it was that betrayed André Messac. I heard there was an André Messac on board, among the *Lerida* survivors. . . ."

"I told you," snapped Captain Svendsen.

"Yes. I thought, but André Messac is dead; he was reported dead. Then I thought, perhaps he's alive. Yet I—I realised that he couldn't be alive; so it couldn't be the same man. In that case, you see, it would have to be another André Messac, or somebody using his name. If it was somebody using his name, I had to find out why."

Captain Svendsen's face was red with anger. Colonel Wells said pacifically: "It was your duty to report the thing to the Captain."

"Yes, I suppose it was. But I simply never thought of that. I only wanted to see the man using that name. So I looked for him on deck that night. The instant he came along under the light I recognised him. I'd heard him play many times. And I saw red. There isn't any other way to explain it," said Josh simply. "I saw him, and it was like a flash of —of electricity or something. There was Michel Banet, using André's name and passport, the same man I'd thought might have betrayed André. So I hit him. I didn't say anything, I didn't question, I didn't—well, I suppose I didn't know what I was doing, except," said Josh very clearly, "that it was what I'd wanted to do for five years. . . ."

The Captain broke in harshly: " You wanted to kill Michel Banet ? "

" I wanted to kill whoever it was who'd betrayed André Messac to the Germans."

" Then you killed him to-night ? "

" No," said Josh soberly, " I didn't."

" But you . . ." The Captain's face was swelling with rage again, and again Colonel Wells stepped in peaceably. " What did you do ? " he asked Josh. " Why didn't you report it ? "

Josh paused for a moment, thinking. He said finally : " The thing I had to do seemed perfectly clear to me. I'll try to tell you. After I hit him I—well, came to. I realised how stupid it was. I leaned over him, and he seemed to be knocked out but not really hurt. I knew he'd pick himself up again in a minute or two and be none the worse for it. I didn't think he'd seen me. And he'd never known me in the Paris days. I was only one of the audience. I didn't think that he knew that I had had anything to do with the French underground. I was more in André's confidence than anybody. I knew a few of the other names. At any rate, it was dark there on the deck, and I—well, naturally, I hadn't stopped to say, ' Look out, I'm going to hit you,' or anything of the kind. I just slammed out at him when he came from under the light past me, and I saw his face, and knew it, and the whole thing seemed to check. It wasn't even a case of a fight. I just wanted to kill him. Only," said Josh, " as it happened, I didn't."

" Go on," said Colonel Wells.

" Well, as I say, it was dark where I stood on deck. He passed under a light and then came towards me. I was pretty sure that he didn't even see me. Later that night I went to his cabin, and then I was sure that he didn't recognise me, and I think he was honestly puzzled as to just what had happened. He must have known that somebody hit him, yet he pretended not to know that or anything about it. I've wondered why," said Josh.

Again for a moment no one spoke or moved. Then Josh went on : " At any rate, I left him there and tried to get myself together. The thing to do, I decided, was to keep quiet and find out everything I could about him. If he was guilty

I'd prove it. But I "—he looked again at the Captain and said stubbornly—" I had to do it myself. André was my friend. It was . . . I had to."

The Captain glowered at the floor. " Well—well, go on."

" What did you do then ? " asked Colonel Wells.

" I walked on around the deck, thinking. He was a fake. But why ? Then I met Marcia and talked to her for a little. I questioned her about him. I didn't get very far. I went to my quarters, had another smoke, or started to, and suddenly thought I'd better get back and see if I'd hit him "—Josh paused and said rather grimly—" half as hard as I'd intended to. After I'd had time to think, I didn't want to kill him till I'd found out the whole truth. I wanted to keep him alive. So I went out on deck again, on the port side. I walked around the stern, intending, as I say, to see if I'd really killed Banet, and found Marcia. I didn't see anybody get away. I hadn't heard anything ; but there she was, and I at least was entirely convinced that someone had tried to murder her. You didn't quite believe it, Captain—neither did you, Colonel Wells, in spite of the mark on her throat. But I had found her and I believed it."

Had the hands, thought Marcia, that had reached towards her so mercilessly from the shadows of the deck held that equally merciless revolver that had killed Mickey ?

The Captain's bright, angry blue eyes searched her face. He demanded : " Why should any one try to murder you and succeed in killing Banet ? And the two Portuguese ! There must be a link. What is it ? "

Josh said quickly : " Whoever tried to kill her then tried at least twice again."

The Captain turned again to Josh, his eyes blazing. " You ought to have told me about Banet ! " he cried, and Josh replied obstinately : " I did not believe that Michel Banet had anything to do with the murder of the two Portuguese."

" You still required a private revenge ? " asked Colonel Wells.

" In a sense, yes. But there were other reasons. For one thing, Marcia—that is, Miss Colfax," he amended, as if for for the first time he realised that he had been calling her Marcia—" was engaged to be married to him ; consequently she had to know that he was using another man's name and she had to know the reason for it. So that was an argument in favour of Banet. I had a certain "—he hesitated and said—" faith in Miss Colfax's own faith in him. And I had faith in her," said Josh very quietly.

And you knew, thought Marcia, that I had said I loved him and was to marry him. You could not strike me like that, through Mickey.

He would not look at her. He continued quickly, as if to cover any possibility of question on the part of the others: " Besides, it was a very serious charge I had to make. It was based on nothing but my own imaginings really, and it was a charge that would stick to him all the rest of his life, and to his wife. So . . ." he shrugged and finished in a very impersonal and quiet tone. " So naturally I had to be sure that my suspicions had more than a grain of fact before I reported them."

" You said you believed him to be a Nazi war criminal. Why ? " asked the Captain.

Gili had not moved or spoken ; neither had Daisy Belle and Luther. Yet it seemed to Marcia that, almost perceptibly, their tense stillness sharpened.

Josh said : " I think he was a war criminal because he was so frantically determined to escape Europe. I think he may have been used, possibly in some minor way by the Nazis. I think he was afraid of revenge—perhaps by someone in Germany whose relative he had injured ; certainly he was afraid of being caught by the Americans."

" But would the Germans have trusted him ? " asked Luther suddenly. " Did you get any proof ? "

Josh looked at Marcia. " I'm afraid I've hurt you very much, Marcia. I'm afraid I've got to hurt you more," he said, and turned to Gili. " Where is the cigarette case ? "

She wasn't going to answer. For a moment the decision, sullen and unmistakable, was in her face. Josh said : " We know you have it. It was Banet's. Where is it ? "

She still hesitated for a moment. Then, with a sulky gesture, she pulled the case from the pocket of her uniform. She said, half-muttering, eyeing Josh : " I borrowed it. I—borrowed it. . . ."

He took the thin gold case which flashed in the light. Again Marcia had a swift and fleeting memory of that case and dappled sunlight on a table, and Mickey's smiling, candid and terribly blank grey eyes.

Josh said to the Captain: " This case belonged to Michel Banet. How could an expensive trinket like this have been permitted to remain in the possession of a prisoner in a German concentration camp for five years ? "

The Captain took the case in his hand and looked at it, and said judicially : " Well, it couldn't." He looked at Marcia: " Did Banet own this before the war ? "

" Yes." Her voice was almost a whisper, as light as the soft autumn breeze in those bronzed chestnut trees in Paris. The Captain weighed the case in his hand. " No," he said thoughtfully, " they wouldn't have let a prisoner keep a trinket like this. But it's not proof, you know," he looked at Josh ; " it's not proof."

Josh turned to Gili. " You knew him in Germany," he said. " You came to Lisbon to wait for him. You were both getting out of Germany as fast as you could. But you couldn't use German money. So you had to get money. You planned the whole deception with him. . . ."

Gili had leapt to her feet, and stood there, trembling and white, and cried at the top of her voice, shrieking : " You are lying. That's not true. They said a woman killed him. It was Marcia. She did it because she thought he loved me. We quarrelled and she struck me. She was beside herself. And you "—she whirled around to Daisy Belle—" you saw it. You heard it. You know I'm telling the truth. She murdered him. Marcia murdered him ! Mickey said it was a woman. Why don't you arrest her ? "

XVIII

CURIOUSLY, it was almost in the very moment that Gili spoke—so wildly, and yet with at least one ingredient of truth—that Marcia perceived a change which had taken place in the relationship between Josh and the two ship's officers. Up to then there had been a definite feeling of confidence between them that, in some intangible yet perfectly marked way, was now gone.

But Josh was now on the other side of the fence. He was one of the suspects, she realised suddenly. He had wanted to kill Mickey. He had admitted that; he had admitted attacking him. So he was now suspect.

But then she was suspect, too. It was not credible. There is an innate faith in the power alone of truth to reveal itself which is like a protective shield.

It is also, however, a deceptive faith. She was not really frightened by Gili's words or by that fact—again incomprehensible—that Mickey had said a woman shot him. But when she saw the long look that the Captain and Colonel Wells exchanged—and pointedly excluded Josh Morgan—she felt something very like fright.

If Mickey had spoken the truth, *if* a woman had shot him, then there were only herself and Gili and Daisy Belle who could conceivably have had a motive for doing so.

And immediately Daisy Belle came to Marcia's defence. In doing so she naturally confirmed the portion of Gili's accusation which was true, but it was her obvious design to defend Marcia. Without waiting for that long look between the two ship's officers to turn into questions, she leaned forward, her hands linked tightly together. " Captain," she said, " there was nothing about that so-called quarrel that was serious or that would give rise to murder. It was like a hysterical explosion between two schoolgirls and it stopped as quickly and easily as it arose. Nerves are unpredictable. It was . . ." She drew herself up. She was a dignified, poised and experienced woman disposing of a childish storm of temper. " It was nothing," said Daisy Belle, calmly and impressively.

"She slapped me," said Gili vindictively. "She attacked me. You saw her."

Daisy Belle's eyebrows lifted slightly. "You needed it," she said to Gili.

The Captain looked at Marcia. "But you did quarrel? You did strike her? What did you quarrel about?"

Josh said suddenly: "I expect Mrs. Cates knows."

Daisy Belle gave him a flicker of approval and said quickly: "I do indeed." Gili started to get up, angrily, and settled back again, eyes lambent and shining, face sullen. Daisy Belle continued: "I'll tell you exactly. Gili said that this Banet person had only wanted money from Marcia and that "—her eyebrows lifted again—" and that Gili wouldn't give him up. That, I believe, was the main theme of her declaration."

"Did she say," asked Captain Svendsen, sticking heavily to the point, "that she had known him anywhere else?"

Daisy Belle thought for an instant: "I'm not sure she said exactly that. It was a very strong implication. I mean the few days on the *Lerida* and the *Magnolia* could scarcely have given her the—well, proprietary rights she seemed to feel that she had."

"But she didn't definitely say how long or where she had known him?"

Gili relaxed a little. The sullenness in her eyes was giving way to a gleam of triumph. Daisy Belle said: "I'll try to tell you exactly. I may not be able to remember the words precisely. But she seemed very angry about something. She told Marcia that she could tell her anything she chose to tell to account for having a cigarette case, that one, I suppose, and to account for having spoken to Mickey by name like that; calling him Mickey, I mean. I did not see the significance of that then and paid no attention to it. I couldn't help, however, hearing the whole thing. She said she could tell Marcia anything she chose to tell her and that Marcia would believe it, owing, I suppose, to Marcia's faith in André —that is, Banet. But that she—Gili—didn't intend to, that he had only wanted money from Marcia and that now he was through with her. Or words to that effect." She paused. "As I say the implication is inescapable. There was no question in my mind but that Gili had known him for a long time, and that she was accompanying him on this trip and making her position with regard to him known to Marcia."

"What did you think of it?"

"What did I . . ." Daisy Belle gave him an astonished look. "I thought what was undoubtedly the truth. This Banet person had deceived Marcia. He had pretended not to know Gili beyond the casual acquaintance all of us had there in Lisbon and on the *Lerida*. He was using Marcia; and Gili through jealousy or bad temper, told Marcia the truth. Perhaps she hoped to separate Marcia and Banet. Perhaps"—Daisy Belle shrugged and said, with a fine edge to her charming voice—"perhaps Gili was afraid of losing him. Certainly she could only have embarked upon that fervent little flirtation with Castiogne on the *Lerida* in the hope of arousing Banet's possibly flagging interest in her."

She paused very briefly, and Gili started forward with a defiant and angry motion, and then, as if she saw the bait barely in time, drew back with a sort of gasp and shut her lips tightly together. Daisy Belle said: "In any case, I felt perfectly certain that what Gili said was the truth. She knew all about him. Ask her . . ."

"I didn't," said Gili suddenly. "That is not true. I knew nothing of him. I—I said all that because I—I liked him. And I hate Marcia. She thought she owned him. Well, I—I said all that to tease her. To—yes, I liked him and I thought she might leave him alone. He didn't love her. I could see that. I thought I might make a quarrel between them." She looked around with short, sharp glances at every one as if to test their credence and said: "That's it exactly. Why not? A girl has to get along. I've nobody. . . ."

"Why were you on the *Lerida*?" asked Josh.

"Why . . . ?" She caught her breath, eyed him smoulderingly for an instant, and said: "Because I wanted to go to Buenos Aires, of course."

"Why?"

"Because . . ." She bit her lip. Then with a flash of those shining green eyes she turned to the Captain. "I've done nothing. Marcia killed him. She was furious. She struck me. She went straight and stole the revolver and shot him. Mickey said it was a woman. And she had a motive. It was a . . ." She seemed to hunt in her mind and then flashed out triumphantly: "It was a crime of passion. That's what. A crime of passion." She gave a vigorous nod, so her long, streaked blonde hair fell over her face.

And Josh gave a short, hard laugh. "You really are a fool, Gili," he said. "You know the truth about Banet. Tell it, for God's sake, and save yourself."

"I didn't kill him. She did. And I have nothing more to say."

Josh turned to Captain Svendsen. "This was not the first time she told Marcia all this. The first time, though, she was more specific. Marcia, tell them what she said to you."

She thought it would be difficult to tell. It was not. She told the ugly little story quickly and as impersonally as if it had happened to someone else. Gili had said about the same thing that Daisy Belle Cates had heard her say on the later occasion, except that she was more specific. Marcia remembered the words too well: "She said that they wanted to leave Europe, that they had no money. That he came back to me in order to get money for both of them."

"When was that?" asked Colonel Wells.

She told him, the first day they had been on the *Magnolia*. About noon. "And you believed her?"

"For a moment. Then I didn't."

"Did you question Banet about it?"

"After I'd thought about it, I could not believe it. Then I asked him about it—yes. He said it was not true."

"And you believed him?"

She nodded. Suddenly she was drugged with weariness and shock. The motion of the ship, the lights, the white faces around her, beyond everything the knowledge of Mickey's murder and of the things that Josh suspected of him, seemed all of it to weigh together too heavily to be supported.

Perhaps every one felt something like that. It was late and growing later. The Captain, however, gave it words.

He questioned Gili bluntly. It was a curious, dogged struggle between them, and for the moment Gili won. "I've told you everything I know. Everything . . ."

"Was Banet a Nazi?"

"I don't know."

"Where did you know him?"

"In Lisbon; and on the *Lerida*. That's all."

"Why did you say he belonged to you?"

"I told you that."

"But he was a Nazi?"

"I don't know." And then she added: "Ask her. Ask Marcia. She killed him."

Colonel Wells said: "As Colonel Morgan points out, to-day is not the first time Miss Duvrey made her claims about Banet to Miss Colfax."

Josh picked it up quickly. "So if Marcia had been going to shoot him, she'd have done it then. Not now." He said it as if it were obvious, but he watched the Captain with, it seemed to Marcia, a too-well concealed anxiety. And the Captain said doubtfully: "Perhaps only to-day she was convinced." He looked at his watch. "I've got to get back to the bridge. The ship is as safe with my first officer as with me, but I've never left the bridge in a fog in my life before!" Anger crossed his face again. He looked at them and said shortly: "Well, on land there are police, and fingerprints and laboratories and all that. I'm no detective and no psychiatrist. I don't know about clues. But . . ." he paused for an instant. His sheer physical strength and solidity were as impressive just then as the deep anger that was in his eyes. "But," he added, "I am master of this ship. And I'll see that, whoever did this, hangs. Whether Banet deserved it or not, it was murder; those two Portuguese were murdered. Urdiola is still locked up. I do not believe that there was any way for him to have escaped and murdered Banet."

Colonel Wells interrupted: "I beg your pardon, Captain. The patient with the bandaged face. I inquired about him. He has an incontrovertible alibi for the whole day. Usually he's a little hard to check on—that is, it seems that he has rather a habit of taking advantage of the sympathy everybody feels for him and wandering about the ship when and as he pleases. But except for his meals he spent the entire day in one of the wards playing bridge with three other boys. He went to mess with two of them who are also ambulatory. They'll all swear to it. So he could not have gone to Miss Colfax's cabin just before lunch and he could not have murdered Messac—that is, Banet. He is out as a suspect."

"He was never in," said the Captain bluntly again. "Now

then, there's something that you people may not know about
a ship. I said I am no detective. I wouldn't know what to do
with a fingerprint if I had one. But on a ship, no matter what
happens or when, sometime, somewhere, an eye-witness turns
up. I have a long experience at sea. You can count on that
as being true. So any information that any of you have
intentionally or unintentionally concealed might just as well
be given to me now. It will come sooner or later, some way."

Oddly, he actually seemed to feel the confidence that was
in his words. It radiated strongly and rather terrifyingly from
that solid, thick blue figure. He turned to leave the lounge
and then turned back : " And I might add," he said briefly,
" that I have wirelessed home a full report, together with an
urgent request for all available information about every
Lerida passenger I picked up. I did this the day we rescued
you. I have already reported Banet's real name and murder.
I should very soon begin to receive any facts which the State
department or the F.B.I., or any other source, is able to
secure."

He moved towards the door.

And Gili said : " Stop."

She got out of the corner of the sofa in one motion, it
seemed, and across the lounge to the Captain. " Will you
promise me protection ? "

" So you're going to confess," said the Captain.

" No, no ! " she cried. " I have nothing to confess. I don't
know who murdered Castiogne or Para. I didn't kill Mickey.
But if you've wirelessed for information . . ." She stopped
and sucked in her lower lip and, her eyes sullen but frightened,
cried : " I didn't mean to be a Nazi. I couldn't help it. I
had to be a Nazi to—to live ! "

" That is what they all say," said the Captain. " What about
Banet ? Hurry up. Tell me anything you know."

Suddenly she was willing ; too willing, now that Mickey was
dead, now that she believed they would know anyway as soon
as the replies to the inquiries the Captain had sent out were
received ; now that she had decided to throw herself on his
mercy.

Mickey as André Messac probably would have been
reasonably safe, at least for some time, from those inquiries ;
he would not have been safe as Michel Banet.

This emerged at once. She talked rapidly, loudly, repeating herself, diclaiming responsibility—a torrent of words so frankly designed to ingratiate herself by accusing Mickey that even Daisy Belle with her civilised tolerance for human fraility looked rather sickened. Gili told everything she knew, apparently, not once but many times.

Mickey had been a Nazi. He had turned Nazi immediately, and to convince his torturers of his sincerity had betrayed André Messac and others. Gili knew that. He had boasted of it in the early, egotistically triumphant days of the Nazis. Gradually he had worked into a position of some small eminence among them—in a branch of the Gestapo as a matter of fact. His business was that of informer. Gradually the Nazis began to trust him. He was bitter about his hands, but apparently had no thought of revenge. Instead, he seized every opportunity to solidify his standing with the Nazis— probably he believed that if he had a future it lay now with them.

He was by no means a major war criminal. Still, he had achieved enough importance in a small way, so, when the war was over, somebody was sure to inform the Americans, or at least so he feared, which amounted to the same thing. And his real name was known in America, perhaps not as well and familiarly as Mickey, with his artist's naïve egotism believed, but well enough to offer danger.

So he had to escape. He had to hide his identity. It was an added touch of cold cruelty that he really had got André's passport from his mother, who believed Mickey, as Marcia had believed him. And he had to have money.

"He made me come, too. He loved me," said Gili, with even then a sidelong glance of triumph at Marcia.

The trouble was that while she fully confirmed Josh's surmise about Michel Banet, she denied any knowledge of murder or a motive for murder.

Again, doggedly, she resisted their questions.

And rather curiously but obtrusively she reiterated her previous statement, that she and Mickey had been together at the time following the murder of Para when the pseudo-patient in a red robe with his face bandaged and concealed had come down the stairway towards Marcia. Curiously, except it gave Gili an alibi, too.

The Captain, however, accused her flatly. " You murdered Banet," he said. " You were jealous, you were afraid he'd leave you. . . ."

Gili then laughed harshly and with frank scorn. " Murder the man who was going to provide me with—with food and a home and clothes ? What can *I* do in America ? I worked in a barber's shop in Berlin. That's where I met him. I didn't love him, but he loved me. He would have taken care of me. Murder *him !* " said Gili and laughed again.

It was then that the Captain gave up. He turned to Colonel Wells. " Colonel, will you see to the disposition of these people that we discussed ? Thank you. Colonel Morgan, I have to tell you that your movements about the ship are now restricted."

" You mean I'm suspect ? "

The Captain said with a troubled, almost solemn gravity : " You had a strong motive—a comprehensible motive. By your own admission you tried once to kill Banet. But I do not believe that a dying man would attempt to deceive. I believe that a woman killed him."

Daisy Belle got up and stood with dignity under the harsh light. " You mean, obviously one of us."

" I don't know who else," said the Captain plainly, and went away, tired and angry, hurrying back to the bridge.

The fog, as always at night, was deeper. It clung to the ports, it crept into the passageways, it misted the brass and the leather.

Colonel Wells said wearily : " He'll question you further to-morrow. I do beg you to consider what he says. If anybody knows anything at all, it would be better in the long run to let us know it."

Luther got up wearily, too. He looked grey with fatigue. " Maybe the eye-witnesses will turn up. Somebody must have seen something. Banet couldn't just have lain there on the deck for hours without anybody happening along."

" Apparently," said Colonel Wells, " that is exactly what he did. Now then . . ."

He went on briefly and quickly to explain. Their cabins were to be changed. The ship was full but it was not crowded ; somehow they had shifted people about. The *Lerida* survivors were to be separated. He would show them.

Josh, Marcia knew, wished to speak to her. He came close to her, touched her arm and started to speak, and Colonel Wells said : " Will you come now, please ? "

Josh's lips said mutely : " Later . . ."

Marcia, probably by mere chance, was allotted the cabin on B deck, which formerly the three women had shared. Already Gili's and Daisy Belle's few clothes and cosmetics, all loaned or donated by the nurses, had been removed. She did not see to what cabins Gili and Daisy Belle were taken. She had an impression that Luther remained alone in the cabin he and Mickey had shared.

The ship seemed to stand still. It had, in fact, slowed almost to a stop, owing to the extraordinary thickness of the fog, and the foghorn had resumed its monotonous, constant wail. Like a city, the U.S.A.H.S. *Magnolia* was in a state resembling that of seige.

Yet murder still apparently walked these slippery decks amid the crimson haloes of shifting fog-wreaths.

It was along towards morning that the ship slowed suddenly and hove-to. Marcia did not hear the cries of " Man overboard ! " and she knew nothing of the launching of the boats and the flashlights which strove vainly to pierce the fog.

A wakeful patient had seen an object resembling that of a man go past the port near him. He had heard, so still was the ship, the heavy splash in the water far below. He had given the alarm.

XIX

THERE IS ONLY one way a man can disappear from shipboard, and that is into the sea.

There are, however, three causes for such a disappearance ; it could be a matter of accident, suicide, or murder. Neither accident or suicide seemed as reasonable a hypothesis as the fairly unreasonable theory of murder.

And yet with the murder of Mickey Banet, there had been a curious tacit conclusion that the ugly cycle of murder had now run its course.

No one had said so. The ship was, as Marcia had thought, like a city in a state of seige—guarded and alert. The troublesome and trouble-making passengers from the *Lerida* were separated. Each of them was under so heavy a burden of suspicion by the very fact of his presence in that doomed little lifeboat, that surely, one would have thought, and obviously the ship's officers did think, that no one of them would dare to add further to the burden of suspicion against himself. Certainly no one of them now would commit a further murder.

Yet it had happened. No one had heard any commotion or altercation on the foggy, hazy deck. No one had seen anything except the ward patient. The corpsman on duty had given a quick alarm. The ship was stopped and the crew got out boats. A quick check of wards and passengers was made and Luther Cates was missing.

The probability was that even if he were still alive he would not be found. True, the ship have been travelling at a very low speed and the alarm had been given instantly. Even so, the *Magnolia* moved some distance before she could stop and before the small boats could be launched.

The fog, too, seriously hindered the search. The occasional glitter of waves below shifting grey wreaths reflected the lights from the ship in confusing glimpses of red and gold. The fog was the more impenetrable because of the rosy reflected glow near the ship.

It was still dark, in spite of approaching dawn, when Josh came to Marcia. She was awake and knew that the ship had stopped. She had heard the subdued echoes of commotion, but did not know the reason for it, or for the brief visit of Major Williams, who, checking the whereabouts of the *Lerida* passengers, knocked on the door and called to her. When she replied he hurried away again.

She was wrapped in a red bathrobe, standing at the port listening and watching the misty flares in the fog. The searchlights were gleaming this way and that from small boats when Josh knocked. " It's me," he called. " Josh . . ."

She went then and opened the door, which she had bolted.

He stood white-faced in the passageway, fully clothed, except that his collar wasn't fastened. His head was bare and his dark hair shone with moisture. His overcoat shoulders were damp. He came in quickly. " It's a man overboard. Luther. So far they've not found him."

" Luther ! What happened . . . ? "

" Nobody knows." From the open port, in the distance, a voice floated dismally over the water, eerily muffled by fog. Josh went to the port, looked out at the shifting wreaths of fog, the flares from the boats. " They'll never find anybody in a fog like this," he said. " But the chances are, of course, that he was dead before he struck the water."

" Luther . . ." she said at his shoulder, whispering. " Why ? "

Josh turned to face her. " I wanted to talk to you last night. I couldn't. Marcia . . ." he said very gravely, " I'm sorry."

" You mean about Mickey."

" Even to you, Marcia, the cigarette case roused a sort of question. Do you remember telling me that you had been thinking of Mickey and Gili and the things that she had said, and that something seemed somehow wrong to you—out of the picture ? Wasn't that it ? Subconsciously, it seemed wrong to you as it did to me. Yet something happened just then, and you really didn't pin the thing down."

There were other things, she thought suddenly, too ; excuses she had made in her mind for Mickey, things he had said and done, the way, even with the war over, he had seemed nervous and too wary ; his insistence on taking passage on the *Lerida* to Buenos Aires, not home ; his determination to use a false name.

She said slowly, staring out into the drifting fog : " There were always explanations—always reasons . . ."

A voice called again, eeerily across the water. Josh said:
" Marcia, I believe it would have made no difference in Banet's death if I had told the Captain earlier that I knew who he was and what I suspected."

The air from the port was raw and cold. She pulled the over-size bathrobe close around her throat.

" And I had to tell them about Mickey Banet to save your life, Marcia, it was Banet who tried to murder you."

" *Mickey!* " She stared at him in bewildered disbelief. " *Mickey* tried to murder me ? "

" Yes."

" But . . . Oh, no, Josh! Why would he do that? There's no reason, no motive . . ."

" Oh, my dear, my dear! Don't you see that there was a very real motive, a very strong one. Mickey was not really an important war criminal, but *he thought* he was. He thought that at any moment his name would be known everywhere—his name and what he had done. Probably it would have been known eventually. That's true. He had a sort of fame before the war. Mainly, though, it was a case of the wicked fleeing where no man pursues. He was afraid of his own guilt ; he was afraid. He intended never to let any one know that he was Michel Banet the traitor, the Nazi. But you knew his real name."

" So did Gili ! So did Gili ! . . ."

" But you insisted on telling the truth. He knew that you would continue to insist upon telling the truth about it."

" Josh, he couldn't have tried to kill me that first night on the *Magnolia*. He was unconscious. You saw him. . . ."

" Wait, Marcia. This is what I think happened. I thought so," said Josh soberly, " that first night on deck. I could see how he might have done it, but I couldn't be sure. Let me tell you. I told the Captain, but I didn't put it as fully or as truly, Marcia, as I'm going to now to you. The fact is, you see, that I couldn't reconcile you and your love for him with what I thought I knew of him. You being you, I didn't see how you could love him if he was the heel that I thought he was. That "—he shrugged and watched her gravely and said—" that restrained my hand, there at first. I didn't know what to do. And then I realised that I was in love with you. It happened just like that. One minute I just liked you. The next minute I knew that I . . ." He turned, and seemed to look all around the cabin for a cigarette, found a package in his own pocket, drew it out and said: " The next minute I loved you. And you told me and you convinced me, Marcia, that you loved him, no matter what he was, and that you intended to marry him. So then I had to be so sure, you see, that he *was* a heel before I hurt you. And then . . ." He would not look at her now. His face was stern and white and tired. He said: " Then I knew beyond any doubt that he was trying to kill you. It was Michel Banet," he said, " who accidentally dropped the gauze bandages here in your cabin."

" But Josh, it couldn't have been Mickey then either. Gili and he were together the first time I saw the patient, or whoever it was. . . ."

" Marcia, Marcia! " He threw away the cigarette he had barely lighted. " Listen to me. Go back to that first night on deck. Go back to the moment when you sighted an American ship from the lifeboat and knew she was American. Don't you see that you were Banet's danger? You knew who he actually was. He could never hide his identity so long as you were with him. And you were going straight to the United States, where he was known. Castiogne's murder suggested the whole thing, perhaps. That with the fact that Banet knew that in the end you would insist upon telling the truth. Did you insist? "

" Yes, yes . . ." she whispered.

" I don't think," said Josh, " that in the beginning he even thought of trying kill you; but I do think that he intended, when you got to South America, simply to stay there. Certainly he never intended to come to the United States. And then, after all his careful plans—and it must have been rather a chore, as a matter of fact, to keep Gili quiet—but anyway, after all his careful planning, think how he must have felt when he was suddenly hauled aboard an American ship due for the United States. And then you would not be persuaded. You said he had to tell them who he really was. You insisted. And Castiogne had been murdered. Banet reasoned that if you were murdered, too, they would only hunt the harder for whoever killed Castiogne. Yes, I think that put it into his mind."

"But it couldn't have been Mickey that first night on deck," she repeated. "He was unconscious. . . ."

"Oh, was he?" said Josh, and shook his head. "I don't think so. I didn't think so then; I didn't think I'd hit him hard enough. This is what I think happened. Perhaps we'll never know, but "—he took her hand and rolled up the sleeve which was too long for her, in neat, tidy folds as he talked— " I think that I did knock him out. Just for a minute or two. I think he came to, just about as you found him. He didn't know what had happened. He must have been genuinely puzzled. That, or there's somebody else on board he expected to try to injure him. And in that case . . ." He paused for a moment, as if to explore some new but very tenuous and perplexing idea. Finally, working away at the neat little roll of cuff he finished it, and reached for her other hand, and went on : " At any rate, he must have thought, here's an alibi. Unconsciousness. And there were you. I think he planned quickly to follow you, to get rid of you—over the railing, quickly—bruise on his face which would tend to prove his alibi. You would have disappeared, and both of these things would appear to be linked up with Castiogne's murder. And he would go free. I think he was always an opportunist, perhaps very luckily, and that's the reason why his attempts to murder you failed."

She must have made some motion to speak, for he went on quickly : " Let me finish. He picked himself up, if I'm right, as soon as you'd gone inside. Probably he thought of his little plan the minute you left him and regretted he hadn't thought of it sooner. He knew that you'd come back with people, and that that chance, which had seemed in a flash so good, was gone. But there was still a bare chance of getting you alone. I think he must have thought of the whole thing very quickly. You went inside the ship. Could he have followed you ? "

She thought back to the confusion of grey passage ways, and her sense of bewildering strangeness to the ship. " I think I'd have known he was there. I think I'd have seen him."

" Are you sure? Couldn't he have entered the ship without your knowing it ? Watched you from some passageway or corner, so he saw it when you went to the deck again, but on the port side ? Are you sure he couldn't have done that ? "

She thought back again to those swift and confused moments and said slowly: "He could have done that, I suppose. Yes."

"He must have done it. He could have watched even from the starboard door directly opposite, keeping himself out of sight. Then, when he saw you go out on the port side of the deck, he ran quickly around the stern. And you came that way as he hoped, and in the shadow it was easy. He had a sort of an alibi; you were alone. So there was his chance again, and he tried to kill you and heard me coming."

"I can't believe it was Mickey," she whispered. But she did believe it.

Josh said: "Then he ran back to the starboard side to the spot where you'd left him—there to be found later, still apparently unconscious. It wasn't actually an alibi for the time of the attack upon you, but it had all the effect of one. Both of you presumably were attacked at almost the same part of the ship and almost the same time. Anybody would conclude that it was the same person who did it, and certainly it would be linked with the murder of Castiogne. At least "—he tucked the sleeve up carefully and released her hand and said, looking now into her eyes—" at least I can't figure it any other way. I think, too, that on his way back to his cabin from the dispensary he tried the door to your cabin, just tried it, just on the chance of your being alone, just on the chance of finding you there. I don't know. But he need not have returned to his cabin where Gili was waiting for him more than a minute or two before you and I reached it."

"Proof. . . ."

"Your faith was very stubborn, darling, and very blind. The proof is that, since Banet died, the attempts to murder you seem to have stopped. Whatever other link was between Castiogne and Para—whoever murdered Mickey and Luther— you are now safe."

The air from the port was cold and misty on her face. Again the distant voices of men searching through fog and darkness for the body of a man overboard drifted eerily to their ears.

The ship was, in fact, in a turmoil. Wards, passageways, decks were, for the moment, unguarded. It was an orderly confusion, concentrated on the search which the Captain

himself was directing, but it was confusion. Any one could
have gone quietly along those warm, grey passageways just
then without being seen. Anything could have been done
just then without being heard. But Mickey was dead.

So she was for ever safe from those tortured and terrible
hands.

Josh lifted his head and listened. " Murder at sea," he said
slowly, " is so horribly simple. A body sliding past a port, and
then nothing. We'll never know how unless Luther's body
is found, but a woman could have done that, too."

A woman could have held the revolver that had been used
to kill Mickey. Conceivably, a woman could have contrived
to silence Luther for ever in the black and foggy sea, but not
Castiogne, not Para. She said : " Josh, do you mean that
Mickey killed Castiogne and Para ? "

Josh's reply was not really a reply. He said : " It's always
possible Urdiola told the plain truth."

" Do you mean that *he* killed Mickey ? But Mickey said it
was a woman. . . ."

Josh, staring out into the greying fog, said slowly : " Certainly somebody killed Mickey. But I do think that it was
Mickey who came to your cabin yesterday in another attempt
to kill you. Those gauze bandages around his face made a
simple and easy disguise. I've inquired about the gauze.
Almost anybody could have managed to snag that from some
supply cupboard or dressing tray. But when you came to the
Captain with that horribly twisted thing, I knew beyond all
doubt that Banet would kill you if he could. Up to then I
hadn't really been convinced. I'd told myself I must be
wrong. My whole theory was based upon the character of a
man you knew and loved so much that you were going to
marry him."

" Who killed him ? "

" I don't know. . . ."

" He said a woman. . . ."

" Yes, I. . . ." Again a new and troublesome thought
seemed to cross his mind. He thought and frowned and shook
his head. " If it was a woman, there's only Gili and Daisy
Belle. I don't think it was Gili, for the exact reason she gave.
She needs food and clothing and shelter, and just at that
moment Mickey was her only hope of getting any of them.

And Daisy Belle would have no motive. Even if Banet were trying to blackmail her on account of the Nazi business that Gili told us about, that threat was spiked when they came across and confessed all that. So Banet couldn't have held that over Daisy Belle's head and thus provide a motive for her to murder him. I simply don't know why he was killed, Marcia, unless somehow it actually is linked up with Castiogne and Para and the diamond. Yet Urdiola is locked up. I suppose he might have got out somehow, but I don't see how, and neither does anybody else. Luther could have had originally the same motive as Daisy Belle, but he would have, since they've come out with the truth, the same lack of motive. And nothing accounts for Luther's murder. Nothing links up the two Portuguese and Banet and Luther."

He paused, and said suddenly: "Except, of course, the theory that Luther knew something damning to the murderer. And there's no getting around the fact that Svendsen and Colonel Wells have got exactly four suspects, if Urdiola's out: you and me, and Daisy Belle and Gili. I didn't murder Banet or anybody; you didn't. There is only Daisy Belle and Gili, and I simply don't think either of them did it!"

He looked out of the port, staring into the queerly variegated fog, black and grey, spotted with dim flares of orange and red light. He said slowly: "Gili wouldn't murder her only source of supply—Banet. Daisy Belle's whole life is bound up in Luther—she wouldn't murder him. I don't see how the killing of the two Portuguese comes into it and both of them were killed. And, to tell the truth, Marcia, while I am as sure as I'll ever be of anything that Michel tried to kill you, and I think he did it for fear you would tell his real identity, nevertheless, I still can't see why he'd get rid of you before he got more money out of you. Darling, darling, that's brutal. But it's true." Again he stopped, and thought this time for moments while she stood at his side, the cold damp air in her face, and then said: "It's queer. Just as you decide there's no way out, all at once you think you see it."

He turned from the port, put his hand thoughtfully under her chin, and said: "My darling, my darling, no matter what happens, you are safe. Nothing now can hurt you ... Do you want to go to Daisy Belle? She's in the Captain's cabin. I think she needs you."

She didn't want him to leave. There was so much she had to say, and yet had no words. He said, matter-of-factly: " Wrap yourself up if you go on deck. It's damned cold," and touched her cheek lightly, and walked out of the cabin and closed the door.

For a long time Marcia did not move.

The cabin was cold. She stood huddled in the long red bathrobe, gradually aware of the chill and stealthy fingers of fog. Presently she moved across the cabin, intending to dress, intending to wrap up in a coat, intending to go to Daisy Belle, and then sat down on the edge of the bunk, staring at nothing.

She roused herself finally with a sharp realisation that some time had passed since Josh had gone, while she thought of Mickey, and of the past, which was wrong ; things that had happened could never be reconciled. Their only virtue was that they were gone.

Josh had said that Daisy Belle would need her. She'd better go.

She had on grey pyjamas, men's pyjamas, too big for her, like the bathrobe. She'd not wait, though, to dress. She'd wrap herself in the thick nurse's coat that lay over a chair under the port. She went to get it, and, as she reached for it, Josh returned.

She heard the door open and heard him enter the cabin quickly, and she turned, saying : " Josh. . . ."

Her voice died in a gasp, as if hands had already caught her throat.

Yet she had really barely a glimpse of the tall figure in the doorway—the figure in a red bathrobe with white bandages over its face—for the electric light switch clicked, and the cabin everywhere was in darkness.

There was a dim rosy twilight which outlined the port.

There was the soft rustle of motion.

And then in the thick silence an unintelligible choking whisper, which said nothing, which merely made sounds.

XX

BUT MICKEY was dead.

He had once come to her cabin, masked and fearfully anonymous, like that, but he was dead.

And the patient—the real patient, what was his name?—what could he want of her?

As if it were the most important thing in life just then, she sought frantically for his name and remembered it. Jacob Heinzer, Jacob Heinzer. What could he want of her?

The whisper had stopped.

There was a listening quality in the silence. And then she was listening, too, every nerve in her body strained to hear, for there were shouts from the fog, shouts from the darkness and the black sea, shouts of men who had found something.

It sounded as if they said: "Found—found..." So it rang and echoed bewilderingly. Perhaps actually it was what they shouted from boat to boat. At any rate, from that, from a sudden commotion on the decks, from the play of lights and the chug of a small boat coming hurriedly back to the ship, she knew that something—a man, Luther, alive or dead?—had been found.

Yet it seemed unimportant; it was part of another world. It had nothing to do with the small, horribly limited, black world around her just then. And clearly in the silence she thought, Mickey said it was a woman. Gili—or Daisy Belle?

If it was Gili, she would fight. If it was Daisy Belle, she would reason with her. If it was the patient, Jacob Heinzer, there was nothing she could do. There was no recourse and no appeal against a terrible, formless anonymity, against as formless and masked a purpose.

She cried, summoning strength and voice and will from desperation: "*Daisy Belle, you must listen to me. Daisy Belle....*" Her voice was unexpectedly loud, strained, and harsh and clear in the small space around her.

Daisy Belle did not answer.

If it was the patient, the mysterious Jacob Heinzer, then he did not move.

If it was Gili. . . .

Suddenly, and as clearly almost as her own voice sounded upon her ears, an intangible but positive emptiness sounded upon her senses.

She had heard no move. If the door had opened upon the lighted corridor outside she had not seen it.

But the sense of emptiness, of being alone in the small space, pressed harder and harder upon her. It was so convincing in a queer and primitive way that her breath of its own accord began to come more freely, her heart seemed to resume beating. She knew that she was alone.

The echoes from the sea were less loud. The small boat had chugged rapidly around, probably to the other side of the ship. Had they found him? Was he still alive?

The question touched her mind, but merely touched it. Mainly she was questioning the statements of her own nerves and awareness. The door had not opened, the patient (who could not be the patient; who could not be Jacob Heinzer) had not opened the door and walked out—or had he?

Perhaps he had gone while she, distracted by the hollow echoing shouts and commotion, had turned instinctively to look at the port. But had she turned?

If it was Daisy Belle, if it was Gili. . . .

But she was perfectly positive and certain nobody was then in the cabin.

And then there was something she'd been about to do. There was something that she must do. She'd been reaching for her coat; she'd been going to Daisy Belle. As she thought that, suddenly the door swung open and Josh's figure was outlined against the light of the corridor. "Marcia . . ." he cried. "Marcia. . . ."

The light streamed into the cabin. Nobody else was there, but she still could not move. She said stiffly: "Turn on the light—beside you—there by the door."

"Marcia, they've found him. He's still alive. They've found him. . . ." He snapped on the light and she blinked and looked. Only she and Josh stood in the lighted small cabin. Josh came quickly to her. "It's all true, Marcia. Don't look so—so white and terrified, my darling. Everything is all right now."

"Everything. . . ."

"My darling . . ." He put his arm around her and made her sit beside him on the edge of the bunk again and said : "The Captain and Colonel Wells talked to Urdiola again. They think he may be telling the truth. And—Marcia, listen, why would Mickey Banet say that it was a woman who killed him ? I mean—if it wasn't a woman, if it really was a man, why would he say it was a woman ? Unless," said Josh, "he wanted to protect that man."

"Josh. . . ."

But he swept on excitedly, talking rapidly. "And why would he protect the man who killed him unless he wanted something from him ? "

This caught her attention. "But Mickey was dying. . . ."

"No, that's it. He was dying, but *he didn't know it ;* he didn't think so ; he was under drugs ; he had a false sense of security ; he thought he was going to live. He tried to protect whoever it was that killed him. Exactly as he did when I hit him, and he didn't know who it was that hit him, but he knew damn well it was somebody. Yet he came out with that vague story about having slipped or fainted. No, we ought to have known then that it was somebody whose life and whose *continued* life was important to Banet. And Gili all but told us . . . Only she didn't know she was telling us. She knew that he had almost in so many words told her to keep quiet. Perhaps she suspected why, but she won't admit it if she did. We ought to have known it all along. There were only you and Gili and Daisy Belle and Luther Cates and the mysterious patient. . . ."

"Josh," she cried, "he was here ! He went away just before you came. . . ."

"Here ! " He jumped up. "Here ! What do you mean ? "

She told him quickly.

He stood, however, for a long moment without speaking. And then suddenly began to speak in a queerly measured and deliberate way.

"Mickey," he said, "hoped to make a living for the rest of his life. Gili, when she told him what she and Castiogne had overheard, showed him the way. That, you see, is why he was through with you. There was a way which he suddenly discovered by which he could get much more money than you could supply. Much more. . . ."

She did not understand him. She did not understand the listening look on his face. It was as if he were talking not to her but to somebody else. Somebody invisible, who was not there, and yet might hear him. He went on: "Castiogne hoped to do that, too, with a diamond and a promise. He was fobbed off. Para was Castiogne's confidant and partner; he was in on the same unhealthy enterprise. He was afraid. He knew what had happened to Castiogne, so he gave Urdiola the diamond to keep for him to send to his wife. He knew he was in danger, but he had by then another partner, and that partner was Mickey Banet, who had invited himself into the game and was going to stay in."

He looked at the door of the little bathroom and said: "Come out. . . ."

There was no one there; the patient had gone—only he hadn't. Unbelievably the narrow grey door swung slowly open.

A red, thin figure, masked in white, stood in the doorway.

Josh said gravely: "It's all over. You haven't got a chance. They found him and got him back; he's still alive. He told them exactly what happened—how he'd slipped out on deck and you came along and offered him a cigarette, and, as he took it, slugged him. The next thing he knew he was in the water—swimming, floating, swimming. It was sheer luck for him that one of the boys in the ward heard the splash and gave the alarm—sheer luck that he was found. But bad luck for you."

The figure did not move. The eyeless face stared inscrutably and blankly at them. Josh said: "Everything is known. You must have heard me. What exactly did you do for the Nazis? Or rather," said Josh, "how much money did you turn over to them? And why? Because you thought they were going to win? Because it was easier? Because you didn't care about anything but your own immediate safety? Why?"

There was a sort of whisper from the tall figure. Then it swayed a little queerly. But everything swayed and vibrated actually. The ship was moving again, gathering speed, steady upon her course.

Josh said: "Take off the bandages."

A hoarse, strained whisper was intelligible: "My face— no, no. . . ." The hands made gestures. Josh said: "You're not Jacob Heinzer. He's still alive. They got him out of the water. He'll testify against you. You're Luther Cates."

The engines were going harder. The familiar motions and creaks of the ship were louder. Josh said: "Why did you come to this cabin? How did you do it? Why?"

Luther's voice from those bandages said wearily: "I came to see Daisy Belle. I did not intend to hurt Marcia. I didn't intend to touch her. I only wanted to talk to Daisy Belle. I thought she'd be here in this cabin. I didn't know that only Marcia was here. I was alone in my cabin. I thought with all the tumult on deck I could get here, without being seen, and I did. I had the gauze hidden under a cushion in the officers' lounge. Nobody thought of looking there. I took it from a dressing tray. I had seen Heinzer. I had to disguise myself like that in order to approach Para, for he knew I'd killed Castiogne and he knew I'd kill him if I could. But I didn't come here to kill Marcia. I thought Daisy Belle was in this cabin and that perhaps I could speak to her alone. I had to tell her my plans. I had to, and then I heard them shout from the boats out there that they'd found him—Heinzer. So I knew then there was no escape for me. I couldn't leave this cabin. I couldn't...."

Josh said: "You'd better get to a doctor..." and suddenly sprang forward as the thin, red figure wavered and crumpled against the door.

"Get the doctor, Marcia—hurry—go on...."

She thought, even then, that Josh wanted to save her the thing that he knew was going to happen.

Luther Cates had a bad heart attack. He lived until the day came fully. He did not make any further statement.

It was not necessary.

A few hours later replies to wirelessed inquiries which the Captain had sent began to clatter into the ship's receiving sets. All the money that Luther Cates with his great wealth had banked in Switzerland before the war was gone. It had gone without any question to the Nazi cause.

Daisy Belle had not known it. She had not dreamed that Luther's own collaboration had been so expensive, so positive, and so appalling.

"My own," she said brokenly to the Captain, "seemed so great. It was as if we shared a dreadful burden of guilt. I never dreamed that there was anything worse; so much worse. I knew that there was a shortage of cash; we used my jewels for everything. I didn't know why. I thought it had something to do with war conditions, with getting funds...." She stopped and, after a moment, continued very slowly: " I think he did it because—well, simply because it was easier. He had the money, so it was available. They wanted it, perhaps they brought pressure." She paused again and said wearily : " I don't think Luther was politically a Nazi, but I—it is very difficult for me to say this, but it must be true—I think he thought they were going to win. I think it was "—her voice choked over the words, but she repeated it —" it was easier. We were among Nazis. They knew about the money. He bought our freedom and comfort."

The Captain said: " The diamond he gave Castiogne was not a passage bribe, then ? "

She had thought the whole thing through. She said steadily : " I think it was the first payment for silence to Castiogne. Luther came to me on the *Lerida*, the day of the storm, and said it was to pay Castiogne for getting us a passage. Actually it must have been shortly after Gili and Castiogne heard us talking. Castiogne must have seen his way to blackmail and undertaken it immediately. He must have come at once to Luther for money. And then—then Mickey Banet heard the tale from Gili. And he thought, as Castiogne did, that here was his chance to bleed Luther. Were they partners, he and Castiogne ? "

Gili had been questioned. Gili still said that she didn't know.

She had admitted, however, that when she had talked of the thing, accusing the Cates, there in Mickey's cabin the first night on the *Magnolia*, she had been afraid of Mickey. " I knew then that he didn't want me to talk of the Cates couple and of what Castiogne and I had heard them say. I knew Mickey was trying to make me stop talking of it. So I stopped. I didn't know why he wanted me to stop talking of the Cates and Castiogne. I never knew why." She had paused there, and presently added sullenly : " I knew Mickey. I knew when not to question him."

He had tried, too, to ensure that Marcia kept the, to him, potentially valuable secret about the Cates by playing on her loyalty to Daisy Belle. "An accusation like that is a very unpleasant one," he had said. "It sticks. Never tell anybody." And Marcia had been only too glad to agree.

Josh said now, thoughtfully: "Gili told him what she'd heard, and what she thought Castiogne would do with the knowledge of the Cates which Castiogne and Gili so unexpectedly shared. To Banet it was like the discovery of a gold mine. Banet did not tell Gili his immediate realisation of that. Instead, knowing that Castiogne already knew, he suggested to Castiogne that they become partners. Castiogne had to agree. But Castiogne must have already confided in Para. Perhaps Para was to be the strong man. At any rate, as Urdiola says, Castiogne and Para were close friends. I think that Castiogne had not told Mickey that Para was already his partner. I don't think Mickey knew or guessed that until the diamond was found; perhaps he never knew it. But Para knew that Mickey was one of them, and told Cates later on the *Magnolia*. So it was three people in a conspiracy against Luther. He did not know that at first. He thought it was only Castiogne, and killed him when he saw that an American ship was about to pick you up. He had to do that, for he realised that if he once let Castiogne leave the lifeboat alive he'd be at his mercy for ever. But Para took the diamond from Castiogne while he pretended to revive him. Then Para came to Luther on the *Magnolia*. Luther was dealing now with a stupider man than Castiogne. He got the fact out of Para that Mickey Banet was in on the thing, too. So Luther killed Para. He admitted that he had seen Heinzer, and snatched upon that disguise. Para knew of his danger. Cates had to disguise himself in order to take Para by surprise. And then Luther saw Miss Colfax was on deck. He talked to her and then hurried inside, assumed that very easy disguise again, and made sure that Miss Colfax would see him. His motive, as we said then, must have been to direct suspicion away from the people from the *Lerida*. Banet thought it a good enough idea, apparently, to try the same disguise himself later. He could secure gauze as easily as Luther, and he had a red bathrobe also. The conditioning factor all along was the fact that there were so many red bathrobes, so many patients wearing them, that it was an accepted, usual pattern of the crowded life on the ship; but

Banet was clumsy and frightened. He had cruelty but not the cold courage necessary. He ran and dropped the gauze. Naturally Banet had to be murdered. Probably up to then Cates had had a difficulty about weapons—the knife from the locker in the lifeboat ? A knife stolen from the galley ? We'll never know about that. But this time he had a revolver. He killed Banet. There wasn't anything else to do."

Colonel Wells said : " He might have succeeded in passing himself off as Jacob Heinzer, at least until they got him to the hospital and got the bandages off, and if he were very lucky."

"You can't escape on a ship," said Captain Svendsen. " You can on dry land—once he got ashore and at a hospital he must have thought he could contrive some way of escape. Yes. . . ."

" If he had sat tight and said nothing . . ." began Colonel Wells reflectively, and the Captain interrupted : " If he'd sat tight and said nothing he'd never have got away. He knew it. So the chance he took in trying to take Heinzer's place was, at least, a chance. Otherwise, as Luther Cates, he had no chance. We'd have kept after them, all of them, until the truth came out about the money. Cates was vulnerable and knew it. And he was on deck, and Heinzer came along and suddenly there was a chance. And he seized it. He would do away with Heinzer, assume his place, stay in the patient's cabin, perhaps, make himself as inconspicuous as possible for the rest of the voyage, and try to leave the ship as Heinzer and eventually to escape the hospital. Luther Cates had to be dead. There," said the Captain heavily, " was his one small chance and he took it. Otherwise he had none. And it might have worked if he were adroit enough, careful enough. Heinzer's face was hidden ; his voice was a broken, gasping whisper ; he was ambulatory, and thus had no special care, and Cates, in assuming the patient's identity, would not have been under the close observation by nurses and doctors that a stretcher case, say, would have been under. Once on land, once at the hospital, he must have hoped for a chance to escape. Well," he took up a thick sheaf of papers from his table and said : " here is my report to my superiors. I wish you to listen, and, in so far as you can do so, verify the details."

He read in a precise, deliberate way. The succinct phrases took on a quality of fate and of irrevocability: "... and on perceiving a distress signal we changed our course ... Eight passengers in a lifeboat from the S.S. *Lerida* out of Lisbon; one of these passengers was dead...."

The grim and twisted strands of the story picked themselves out, stripped of anything but fact. " Luther Cates having been secretly a Nazi collaborator in a very important way, killed Alfred Castiogne because the latter had accidentally discovered Cates' collaboration and attempted to blackmail him. Cates did this while in the lifeboat, and, we believe, after he saw that the rescue ship was American and bound for the United States. Unknown at the time to Cates was the fact that Castiogne had already in his scheme two partners. One was Luis Para, and the other was Michel Banet (see next paragraph for further reference to Michel Banet). Once on board the *Magnolia*, Para appears to have secretly approached Cates with a view to blackmail. We have no witness for this interview, but we believe Cates promised to pay, and extracted the information from Para that Banet also knew of his collaboration. Later, Cates, by assuming the disguise of a patient, succeeded in getting close enough to Para to take him by surprise and murder him. Later Cates murdered Banet for the same reason. Luther Cates tried in various ways to throw suspicion upon other people and to clear himself, and finally made an unsuccessful attempt to drown the bona-fide patient, Jacob Heinzer (later rescued from the sea; please see page 3). Cates' intention apparently was to take the patient's place in the hope of later making an escape. Cates died of a heart attack after making a partial confession, which follows...."

It followed, and then patiently yet tersely all the details, with the Captain pausing between sentences as if to permit a dissenting or correcting voice. Then he went on: " Also in the lifeboat was Michel Banet, a former pianist and a member of the Nazi party, who, wishing to escape possible punishment as a war criminal (we believe him to have been only a minor official, but that fright and guilt strongly influenced his actions) assumed a false name, and identity. Having no money, he induced his former fiancée, who knew nothing of his Nazi activities, to accompany him "—The Captain paused here, coughed and continued elliptically—" also Miss Gili Duvrey—let me see, now; oh, yes." He resumed: " Miss Duvrey informed Banet of Luther Cates' collaboration with the Nazis and of Castiogne's knowledge of it and possible intention; apparently Banet forced himself upon Castiogne as a partner. He, too, however, was in grave danger when the rescue ship proved to be American, as his former fiancée would (and later did; see below) insist upon revealing his true identity. Also he no longer needed money from her as he proposed to get much larger sums of money from Luther Cates. He attempted to murder Miss Colfax on at least two occasions as follows . . ." He coughed again here, but continued doggedly, recounting the ugly details. He resumed at last: " Banet, however, was murdered by Cates."

He stopped there as if struck by a thought. He looked hard at the paper. Finally he took up a pencil and wrote, slowly, reading the interpolation as he wrote it: " They were Nazis. They destroyed each other. This was their destiny."

" Why, yes," said Daisy Belle suddenly. " Their destiny—our destiny on this ship, our meeting with fate. Our rendezvous. . . ."

The ship ran out of the fog the next day.

And, finally, steadily, came into Charleston Harbour.

That was very early one morning. The sea was grey, the sky was grey and tranquil. The ship glided evenly along, with the rosy radiance of the Red Crosses around her like a gentle blessing. The decks were lined with soldiers who could walk, leaning out to get their first view of home, shouting through the ports to others who were in their bunks. " I see land . . . I see lights . . . There's a tender. . . ."

It was a tender, streaking busily out to meet them, bringing the boarding party. The public-address system carried welcoming words from the port transportation officer—straightforward, sincere, deeply moving. It was to be the *Magnolia's* last trip from Europe. She was to go now to the Pacific and there continue her high and faithful task of mercy.

Josh and Marcia stood at the railing and listened.

The U.S.A.H.S. *Magnolia* went on slowly along the broad and gracious river, past the lovely old city, her graceful houses dimly outlined in the dawning light.

The sun came up and the river turned to gold. They drew slowly and evenly up to a long pier, and the flag waved against the blue sky. The sun glittered upon the shining instruments of the welcoming bands. Long lines of ambulances and buses stood in waiting. Companies of corpsmen, trained and skilled, were at attention. Music burst upon the ship like a warm embrace. The port commander, a general's stars on his shoulders, came himself to meet the ship. A boy, carried from the ship in a stretcher, put both hands flat upon the pavement and smiled as if he said: "This is America."

Watching the swift precision and care with which the whole shipload of patients was unloaded, it seemed to Marcia that the whole kaleidoscope of war—of hatred and suspicion and terror, of pain and fear—could somehow in the end be shaken down into a firm design of love and mercy.

Josh said suddenly: "I'm going to kiss you." That deck, far above the gangway, was deserted. Josh held her for a long moment. "I love you," he said. "I'll always love you."

The band played and the sun shone. A boy on the gangway threw his cap in the air and caught it and gave a loud shout of happiness. "Home!" he yelled above the band, above everything. "Home!"

And Marcia thought, but this is home, close to Josh, like this, for ever.

THE END

Eberhart   C 1
Five passengers from Lisbon